"When writers as sharp as Margaret Maron, Darlene Fowler, and Jerrilyn Farmer all rave about a colleague as convincingly as they have about Denise Swanson . . . take notice." —*Chicago Tribune*

Murder of a Botoxed Blonde

"With its endearing hero, terrific cast of realistically quirky secondary characters, and generous soupçon of humor, *Murder of a Botoxed Blonde* . . . is a delight."—*Chicago Tribune*

"Tight plotting and plenty of surprises keep this series on my must-read list." —*Crimespree Magazine*

"This fast-paced cozy has it all." —*Romantic Times*

Murder of a Real Bad Boy

"Swanson is a born storyteller." —*Crimespree Magazine*

"Another knee-slapping adventure in Scumble River." —*The Amplifier* (KY)

"Scumble River is a joy to visit." —*Romantic Times*

Murder of a Smart Cookie

"[Swanson] smartly spins on a solid plot and likable characters." —*South Florida Sun-Sentinel*

"[A] hilarious amateur sleuth mystery. . . . [Swanson] has a lot of surprises in store for the reader." —*Midwest Book Review*

"A hoot." —*Romantic Times* (4 stars)

continued . . .

"It's no mystery why the first Scumble River novel was nominated for the prestigious Agatha Award. Denise Swanson knows small-town America, its secrets and its self-delusions, and she writes as if she might have been hiding behind a tree when some of the bodies were being buried. A delightful new series." —Margaret Maron

Murder of a Pink Elephant

"The must-read book of the summer."
—*Butler County Post* (KY)

"One of my favorite series. I look forward to all my visits to Scumble River." —*Crimespree Magazine*

"Current readers will appreciate the trip into Scumble River, while new readers will want to go back."
—The Best Reviews

Murder of a Barbie and Ken

"Swanson continues her lively, light, and quite insightful look at small-town life . . . a solid plot [and] likable characters who never slide into caricature."
—*The Hartford Courant*

"Another sidesplitting visit to Scumble River . . . filled with some of the quirkiest and most eccentric characters we ever have met, with a sharp, witty protagonist."
—*Butler County Post* (KY)

Murder of a Snake in the Grass

"An endearing and realistic character . . . a fast-paced, enjoyable read." —*The Herald News*

"This book is delightful. . . . The characters are human and generous and worth following through the series."
—*Mysterious Women*

Other Scumble River Mysteries

Murder of a Chocolate-Covered Cherry

A Scumble River Mystery

DENISE SWANSON

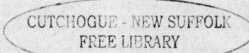

AN OBSIDIAN MYSTERY

OBSIDIAN
Published by New American Library, a division of
Penguin Group (USA) Inc., 375 Hudson Street,
New York, New York 10014, USA
Penguin Group (Canada), 90 Eglinton Avenue East, Suite 700, Toronto,
Ontario M4P 2Y3, Canada (a division of Pearson Penguin Canada Inc.)
Penguin Books Ltd., 80 Strand, London WC2R 0RL, England
Penguin Ireland, 25 St. Stephen's Green, Dublin 2,
Ireland (a division of Penguin Books Ltd.)
Penguin Group (Australia), 250 Camberwell Road, Camberwell, Victoria 3124,
Australia (a division of Pearson Australia Group Pty. Ltd.)
Penguin Books India Pvt. Ltd., 11 Community Centre, Panchsheel Park,
New Delhi - 110 017, India
Penguin Group (NZ), 67 Apollo Drive, Rosedale, North Shore 0632,
New Zealand (a division of Pearson New Zealand Ltd.)
Penguin Books (South Africa) (Pty.) Ltd., 24 Sturdee Avenue,
Rosebank, Johannesburg 2196, South Africa

Penguin Books Ltd., Registered Offices:
80 Strand, London WC2R 0RL, England

First published by Obsidian, an imprint of New American Library,
a division of Penguin Group (USA) Inc.

First Printing, April 2008
10 9 8 7 6 5 4 3 2 1

*To the people of my hometown, Coal City, Illinois,
who have been amazingly supportive*

Author's Note

In July of 2000, when the first book, *Murder of a Small-Town Honey*, was published in my Scumble River series, it was written in "real time." It was the year 2000 in Skye's life as well as mine, but after several books in a series, time becomes a problem. It takes me from seven months to a year to write a book, and then it is usually another year from the time I turn that book in to my editor until the reader sees it on a bookstore shelf. This can make the time line confusing. Different authors handle this matter in different ways. After a great deal of deliberation, I decided that Skye and her friends and family will age more slowly than those of us who don't live in Scumble River. Although I made this decision while writing the fourth book in the series, *Murder of a Snake in the Grass*, I didn't realize until recently that I needed to share this information with my readers. So, to catch everyone up, the following is when the books take place.

Murder of a Small-Town Honey—August 2000
Murder of a Sweet Old Lady—March 2001
Murder of a Sleeping Beauty—April 2002
Murder of a Snake in the Grass—August 2002
Murder of a Barbie and Ken—November 2002
Murder of a Pink Elephant—February 2003
Murder of a Smart Cookie—June 2003
Murder of a Real Bad Boy—September 2003
Murder of a Botoxed Blonde—November 2003
Murder of a Chocolate-Covered Cherry—April 2004

The Scumble River short story and novella take place:

"Not a Monster of a Chance"—June 2001
"Dead Blondes Tell No Tales"—March 2003

CHAPTER 1

Preheat Oven to 350°

School psychologist Skye Denison had endured the situation for as long as she could. Improvements on the outside were well and good, but they didn't make her feel any better about the ugliness on the inside. It was time to put an end to her suffering.

She ignored the ringing telephone. There really wasn't anyone she wanted to talk to bad enough to untie the rope, climb down from the ladder, and find the phone in the mess she had created in her dining room. She sighed with relief when the ringing stopped, but let out a small scream of frustration when it started right up again.

Evidently, whoever was calling knew that her answering machine picked up on the fourth ring and was hanging up after the third. This meant it was someone who called her on a regular basis. Skye paused as she tightened the knot. Who would be so determined to reach her that they would keep punching the redial button again and again?

It wasn't her boyfriend, Wally Boyd, chief of the Scumble River Police Department. He had phoned earlier canceling their date for that night with the lame excuse that "something had come up." His call had been the start of her bad day.

Another possibility was her best friend, Trixie Frayne, school librarian and Skye's cosponsor of the school newspaper, but they had already spoken as well. Trixie had called to tell Skye that a cheerleader's parents were threatening to sue the *Scoop* for slander, and Trixie and Skye were scheduled to meet with the district's lawyer at seven a.m. on Monday. Homer Knapik, the high school principal, would have a cow when he heard the news—then make Skye and Trixie shovel the manure.

A quick glance at her watch and Skye knew it couldn't be her brother, Vince. Saturday morning was the busiest time at his hair salon. Skye's godfather and honorary uncle, Charlie Patukas, the owner of the Up A Lazy River Motor Court, wouldn't bother with repeated calls; he'd just jump into his Caddy and come over. After all, few places in Scumble River, Illinois, were more than a five- or ten-minute drive away.

Shoot! That left only one person, and she would never stop dialing until Skye answered. Moaning in surrender, Skye made sure the rope holding the chandelier up out of the way was tied tightly and reluctantly climbed down the ladder, almost tripping on her black cat, Bingo, as she stepped to the floor. He shot her a nasty glare and darted from the room.

She yelled after him, "You know, you could have answered the phone, buddy. You're not earning your keep around here."

The next group of rings helped her locate the handset, and she lifted the edge of the tarp she had placed on the hardwood floor to protect it. Grabbing the receiver, she pushed the on button and said, "Hello, Mom."

"It's about time you picked up." The voice of May Denison pounded into Skye's ear. "There's a family emergency. Get over here right away."

Skye growled in aggravation as her mother hung up without further explanation. Then her mother's words penetrated the fog of her bad mood. Emergency! Had something happened to Skye's father? Her grandmother? One of her countless aunts, uncles, or cousins?

A busy signal greeted Skye's repeated attempts to call back. No doubt May had taken the phone off the hook to force Skye to come over as ordered, rather than phone and ask questions.

Catching her reflection as she hurried past the foyer mirror, Skye hesitated. Her chestnut curls were scraped back into a bushy ponytail, the only paint on her face was the Tiffany blue she was using on her dining room walls, which did nothing for her green eyes, and the orange sweat suit she had put on to work in made her look like Charlie Brown's Great Pumpkin.

Shaking her head, she decided it would take too much time to transform herself into a presentable human being, and instead grabbed her jacket, purse, and keys from the coat stand. She ran out of the house and leapt into the 1957 Bel Air convertible her father and godfather had restored for her a few years ago, after several unfortunate incidents left her previous cars undrivable.

The Chevy was a boat of a car, which made it hard to lay rubber, but Skye stomped on the accelerator and the Bel Air flew down the blacktop, white vapor pouring from the tailpipe in the below-zero temperature. Seven and a half minutes later, Skye wheeled into her parents' driveway and skidded to a halt on the icy film covering the gravel.

Where were all the vehicles? If there was a family emergency the driveway should be packed with cars and trucks. Did her mom need a ride to the hospital? No, May's white Olds was parked in the garage. What the heck was going on?

Skye flung herself out of the Bel Air and jogged up the sidewalk and across the small patio to the back door. She spared a glance at the concrete goose squatting at the corner. Except for the holidays, when the statue was dressed as anything from a Halloween witch to Uncle Sam, its costume was usually a good barometer of May's mood. Given that it was January 10, too late for New Year's and too early for Valentine's Day, the fact that it was wearing an apron and a tiny chef's hat and had a rolling pin clutched in its wing must mean something, but darned if Skye had a clue as to what.

Shrugging, she continued into the house, calling, "Mom, what's going on? What's the emergency?"

Silence greeted her as she dashed through the utility room's swinging doors and into the kitchen. Still no sign of her mother, but Skye slid to a stop as her gaze swept past the counter peninsula and reached the dinette.

She felt all the blood drain from her head and the room started to sway as she stared at the table. She sank to her knees and closed her eyes, hoping she was dreaming or having a hallucination, but when she opened them again the wedding cake was still there—three layers of pristine white frosting with delicate pink roses and a vine of ivy trailing down its side.

Surely even May, a woman desperate for her daughter to get married and produce grandkids, wouldn't throw an emergency wedding.

Seconds later Skye's mother bustled around the corner from the living room clutching a cordless phone to her right ear. She clicked it off and leaned down. "What are you doing on the floor?" Grabbing Skye's arm, she ordered, "Get up. It's filthy. I haven't had time to mop it yet today."

May was dressed in sharply creased blue jeans, a pale yellow sweatshirt with tiny bluebells embroidered across the chest, and gleaming white Keds. Her short salt-and-pepper hair waved back from her face as if she had just finished combing it, and her mauve lipstick looked freshly applied.

"What's that doing here?" Skye shook off her mother, rose from the light green linoleum, noting that it looked as immaculate as the day it was laid, and pointed a shaking finger at the offending pastry.

May made a dismissive gesture toward the towering wedding cake. "Oh, that. I was bored last night; your father had a meeting at the Moose, so I decided to practice my recipe."

"Okay." Skye hesitated in asking what her mother was practicing for, afraid the answer would involve Skye, a church, and a long white gown. Instead she demanded, "What is the emergency? Is it Dad, Grandma, Vince?"

"Oh, well . . ." May looked everywhere except at Skye. "I suppose I should have made it clear: Everyone is fine. It's not that kind of emergency." May stepped toward Skye and took her hands. "It's a good emergency. The best. You'll never guess what's happened."

"What?" Skye cringed. Her mother's idea of *good* was often not close to Skye's; heck, a lot of times they weren't even in the same universe.

"I'm a finalist in the Grandma Sal's Soup-to-Nuts Cooking Challenge." Grandma Sal's Fine Foods was one of the area's biggest employers. They operated a huge factory located between Scumble River and Brooklyn, Illinois, adjacent to the railroad tracks that ran through both towns.

"Wonderful." Skye hugged her mom, happy for May and relieved for herself. A cooking contest would keep May occupied and out of Skye's affairs. "Congratulations."

"Thank you." May took a step back and wrinkled her nose. "You smell funny."

"I was painting my dining room. Remember? I told you I was taking this weekend to finally get some of the downstairs rooms done," Skye reminded her mother, then added, "If you wanted me all clean and pretty, you shouldn't have said it was an emergency."

"But it is an emergency. I needed to explain something to you before you answered your phone again." May took a knife from the drawer by the stove and sliced into the wedding cake.

Skye flinched, still unconvinced that her mother didn't have a groom waiting in the den and a priest stashed in the linen closet. "Explain what?"

"Sit down and I'll tell you." May handed Skye a piece of cake and a fork. "What do you want to drink with that?"

A double martini straight up? Skye settled for a glass of milk.

May finally pulled a stool up to the counter next to Skye and said, "Now, I want you to promise that you'll let me tell you the whole story before you say anything."

"Okay." Skye frowned; she was a school psychologist, for Pete's sake, a trained counselor. Did her mom really feel it necessary to remind her to be a good listener?

"When I entered Grandma Sal's contest, I couldn't decide which recipe to use. Each entrant was only allowed to send one, but how could I choose between my Two-Hour Decorated Cake and my Chicken Supreme Casserole?"

Skye finished chewing and swallowed. "Well, I think you made the right decision; this cake is scrumptious. I didn't know you knew how to make frosting decorations."

"Maggie taught me the basics."

Maggie was one of May's best friends and the premier fancy-cake baker in Scumble River.

"They're beautiful. You must be a quick learner."

"Thanks." May fiddled with her coffee cup. "Uh, I didn't exactly choose the cake recipe."

"Well, your casserole is great too." Skye forked another bite into her mouth.

"I'm glad you feel that way." May stared out the picture window and kept talking. "Because *you* entered the chicken dish."

"Huh?" Skye choked and had to take a swig of milk in order to speak. "I did what? Why? How?"

"I wasn't sure which recipe would get the judges' attention." May twisted a paper napkin into a raggedy bow. "The cake is more dramatic, but the casserole is more practical, so I wanted to enter both. I just needed another name to use, and I borrowed yours."

"Why me? Why not Aunt Kitty or your friend Hester or Maggie?"

"They were all entering their own recipes. I needed someone who wasn't."

"Then why didn't you tell me?" Skye put down her fork; suddenly the sweet frosting curdled on her tongue.

"Because you would have said no. Then I'd have had to use your father's name, and you know he would have a coronary if I entered him in a cooking contest. He's barely over the fact that I made him wear a pink shirt to the VFW dinner dance."

"Dusty rose," Skye corrected, losing the thread of the argument.

"Pink, red, it doesn't matter what you call it; Jed still finds it hard to accept that dress shirts come in any color but white."

"Uh-huh, let's get back to the contest." Skye tilted her head. There was something her mom was keeping from her. "So you used my name. What does that have to do with me not answering my phone?"

"Because the woman who called to tell me I was a finalist said that they were notifying you next, and I was afraid you'd tell them you hadn't entered and ruin everything."

"I'm a finalist?" Skye took another sip of milk to stop herself from slapping her mother. "Why did she tell you about my entry finaling?"

"While we were chatting she mentioned that more than one entrant with the same last name made the finals. She asked if we were related, and I said yes. I told her that the Chicken Supreme was my daughter."

"Well, they won't let us both compete, so I'll decline when they call." Skye blew out a breath, thankful for her narrow escape.

"No! That's just it. We can both be in the contest. There aren't any rules against it."

"But I don't want to be in it."

"Please. For me?" May's happy expression melted away. "We'll have a great time. We can spend some quality time together."

"I talk to you every day and see you at least twice a week. That's enough quality time for any thirtysomething daughter to spend with her mother." Skye wasn't falling for that old line. The only way May would ever feel she and Skye spent enough time together would be if Skye moved back home. Heck, knowing May, she wouldn't be satisfied unless Skye crawled back into the womb.

"I've been entering this recipe contest for twenty-five years, and I've never made the finals before. I never expected more than one of my recipes to make it this far." May dabbed at a tear with her paper napkin. "This might be my only chance to win. I'm not getting any younger, you know."

"You still have your cake entry." Skye was determined not to let her mother talk her into this. Several of her friends had told her she needed to grow a backbone where her mother was concerned. Of course, they never had to face the heaping helping of guilt May was so good at dishing out to get her own way.

Tears seeped down May's cheeks. "But I want the casserole to have a chance, too. There are four categories: Snacks, Healthy, One-Dish Meals, and Special-Occasion Baking. The winner of each category gets five thousand dollars, and the overall winner gets fifteen thousand. Between us we could win twenty-five thousand dollars. I could finally take your dad on that cruise we've been talking about, and have enough left over to buy him a new used truck. His is running on wire hangers and duct tape."

Skye opened her mouth to say no, but instead asked, "Where and when is this contest? There's no way I can take a lot of time off from work."

"It's at the Grandma Sal's plant, right here in Scumble River." May smiled like a poker player laying down a royal flush. "It starts the first Friday in April and goes through Sunday. Isn't that during your spring break?"

Once again Skye tried to say no, but she couldn't come up with an excuse. Too bad she couldn't claim to be going away for the school vacation, but her mother knew she was spending all her spare cash fixing up the old house she had inherited that past summer.

May was looking at Skye like a puppy asking to be chosen from the animal shelter. How could Skye turn her down? She loved her mother and wanted her to be happy. If that made Skye a weenie, then so be it. There was a difference between having a backbone and being nice to your mom. Heck, there was even a commandment about it.

"I get to keep the cash if I win, right?" Skye teased, knowing her chances of producing a winning dish were slim to none.

"We'll split it," May bargained. "Fifty-fifty—my recipe, your cooking talent."

Skye rolled her eyes. In that case the split should be ninety-ten, in favor of her mother.

After finishing her cake and milk, Skye was on her way out the door when a thought that had been nagging at her subconscious finally surfaced. She stopped and turned to face her mother. "You said there were four categories, right?"

May nodded.

"The cake would be in the Special-Occasion Baking and the casserole in the One-Dish Meals, right?"

May nodded again, this time more slowly.

"So, whose names did you use for the Healthy and Snack divisions?"

"What makes you think I entered those?" May studied her nails intently.

"Let's not do this dance. Just tell me the whole truth. No equivocations."

"What does equivocation mean?" May turned away from Skye and opened the dryer door, taking sheets and towels from its drum.

"Mother!" Skye pulled a towel out of May's hands. "You have three seconds to tell me or I'll drop out of the contest."

May shook out a sheet, remaining silent.

"One."

May picked up two pillowcases and paired them.

"Two."

May closed the dryer door with her knee, her arms full of folded cotton.

"Thr—"

"Uncle Charlie for Snacks and Vince for Healthy."

"Well." Skye had to bite her lip to keep from giggling as she tried to imagine her godfather cooking. "I guess it's a good thing they didn't final."

"Mmm."

"They didn't final, did they?" Skye followed her mother as May walked to the linen closet.

"Yes." May put the clean laundry on the shelf. "Charlie knew I had used his name, and he called just a few minutes ago to say we're in."

"And Vince?" Skye asked. When her brother had become a hairstylist, he'd had a hard time convincing the more narrow-minded townspeople, which included their father, that he was straight. Entering a cooking contest would cause all that talk to flare up again.

"He said it would be a hoot, and he likes the idea of being surrounded by women." May beamed fondly. "He's such a good boy." Vince was thirty-eight, but would forever be a boy to May.

Skye shook her head, hoping neither her mother nor her brother would repeat his statement to Vince's girlfriend, Loretta. Loretta was Skye's sorority sister and sometime attorney. She would not be amused to learn that her boyfriend was one of the only males under seventy among two dozen women.

"It seems wrong for you to have four chances to win, and the others to have only one." Skye wondered how the organizers felt about three finalists coming from the same family— four if you counted Charlie. On the other hand, since the contest had an entry area of only about a forty-five-mile radius, there was bound to be some duplication.

"It's not like I'll be doing the cooking. I just provided the recipes. Sort of like sponsoring a car in a race." May closed the linen closet door. "I checked the rules and there's nothing that says the recipes have to be your own; they just have to be original."

Skye gave up. It wasn't her problem. Her problem was learning how to make Chicken Supreme Casserole without burning down the kitchen. Why did the expanding-bread episode of the old TV show *I Love Lucy* keep running through her mind?

It was the first Thursday in April, April Fools' Day, which was apropos, since Skye had just gotten out of a meeting with the school's attorney regarding the threatened lawsuit against the student newspaper. Due to spring break, there were only one or two people in the school building. Most of the staff was off on vacation, including Trixie, the student newspaper's cosponsor.

The lawyer was confident they'd win the case if it ever went to court, but the stakes were so high Skye was still worried. The superintendent was threatening to do away with the activity if they lost, which would devastate the kids who had worked so hard to make their paper one of the best student-produced newspapers in the state. They had even won a prize for last year's efforts.

Skye cheered herself briefly with the thought that the default mode of school administrators was always no, but they *could* be reprogrammed. Still, why had she ever let Xenia Craughwell write for the *Scoop*?

Granted, Xenia was smart—her IQ was off the charts. She was an excellent writer, and she was seeing an outside therapist, but there was a streak of meanness in the girl that concerned Skye. Xenia just didn't seem to grasp the finer points of right and wrong, which made Skye suspect that it would take more than six months of counseling to make any substantive changes in her.

Xenia had enrolled in Scumble River High in the fall after being kicked out of several other schools, and up until now she had been behaving herself; but Skye should have known from Xenia's record that wherever she went, trouble followed.

Which brought Skye back to the question of why in the world she had allowed Xenia on the newspaper staff to begin with. Skye felt like slapping herself—she had to stop trying to save everyone, and admit that some people were beyond her power to help.

Trying to distract herself from thinking about the lawsuit, she flipped open her appointment book and stared at the pale green index card clipped to Thursday. Her mother's careful printing mocked Skye.

Was she some kind of moron? What in heaven's name was she doing wrong? She'd been practicing the recipe for nearly three months and it still came out a gooey, rubbery mess every time she made it. The only time the dish was edible was when May stood right beside her, guiding her every move.

Poor Wally had dutifully eaten all of Skye's attempts, and gamely lied, claiming to taste improvement each time. Maybe that was why he had broken so many dates lately. At least three or four times since January he had called out of the blue, said something had come up, and had never given her a good explanation for canceling.

He was probably reconsidering his statement that he wasn't looking for a girlfriend who was a good cook. Thank goodness the contest started tomorrow. One more practice casserole and Skye might be minus a boyfriend.

Okay, she didn't want to think about the lawsuit or the recipe. What was more pleasant? *Ah, yes.* She smiled, recalling how excited everyone in town had been about Grandma Sal's Cooking Challenge. In the past, the opening press conference, the welcome luncheon, and the awards ceremony had taken place in Brooklyn, but this year Scumble River's mayor, Dante Leofanti, who was also Skye's uncle, had persuaded the company to move all those events to Scumble River.

Locating accommodations for the three judges, half a dozen contest staff members, and various media personnel covering the three-day extravaganza had been like negotiating a peace treaty, but the mayor had stepped in and gotten everything moving forward.

He had even managed to get the school board to allow him to use the high school gym/auditorium for the contest press conference. As Dante had explained at the town meeting, no way would they let an event that would bring in both positive media coverage and lots of people spending money go back to Brooklyn just to save some scuffing of a hardwood floor.

Skye had watched in awe as her uncle managed to get the townspeople to work together to keep the Challenge in Scumble River. Collaboration was not the strong suit of most of the town's citizens.

Skye tapped the recipe card against her chin, remembering having seen Dante arguing with Uncle Charlie about who got the cottages at his motor court. Charlie would have preferred to give the rooms to the highest bidders, but he and the mayor had agreed to three for the judges, three for out-of-town Grandma Sal's staff, one for Grandma Sal, one for her son and his wife, one for her two grandsons, and two for the media. It was a good thing the cooking challenge was for Stanley County residents only. All the finalists could commute.

Charlie stood firm on the twelfth cabin, explaining that he had a long-term renter and couldn't kick him out. Skye wondered how much the lodger had bribed Uncle Charlie to keep the cabin during the contest.

Overall, the town was ready for the Challenge, even if Skye wasn't. She exhaled noisily. At least, unlike other events Scumble River had hosted, this one was likely to produce nothing worse than burnt chicken. The food might be to die for, but it was unlikely that anyone would be murdered over a recipe.

CHAPTER 2

Assemble the Ingredients

Skye squirmed, trying to find a comfortable position on the wobbly plastic seat. She wasn't sure where the school had found these flimsy folding chairs, but they were not designed for a woman of her generous curves. She felt as if the chair was about to collapse at any minute, landing her on her butt. Skye was okay with her full figure, but situations like this reminded her that society had different expectations.

May and Skye had been the first to arrive. After their names were marked off on the list, they were given red and white checked aprons, a tote bag full of goodies—all products of Grandma Sal's Fine Foods and its subsidiaries—and had their picture taken with Grandma Sal. Then they verified their recipes and were sent to sit backstage to wait for the rest of the finalists to show up. Once all twenty-four contestants arrived they would be brought onstage and introduced to the media, and Grandma Sal would make her welcoming speech.

Skye wished she had brought a book. Her mother was chatting with Uncle Charlie, who had come in a few minutes after Skye and May. The woman sitting on the other side of Skye had been on her cell phone since she arrived—probably because she kept having to repeat herself over and over again, saying, "Can you hear me? Is this better? How about now?"

Skye contemplated telling the signal-impaired woman that Scumble River had more dead zones than a Stephen King novel, but decided against it. Telling her wouldn't do any good. Cell phone coverage was one of those life lessons—like a sign saying WET PAINT—that everyone just seemed to have to test out for themselves.

Skye yawned. She was *so* bored. Maybe she should go talk to her brother. Vince had come in ten minutes ago, causing a stir with his golden blond hair and male-model physique. Vince, May, and Skye all shared the Leofanti emerald green eyes, but Vince used his to better advantage. He had the ability to hypnotize any female between the ages of three and ninety-three.

Shaking her head, Skye decided this wasn't the time to chat with her brother. The smitten women around him would not appreciate his sister diverting any of his attention away from them.

Skye counted the tiles in the ceiling. If something didn't happen soon, she was going to scream. It had been over thirty minutes since the last person arrived, and a quick tally of the people milling around the twelve-by-twelve room made it clear that they were all waiting for one last contestant. They had been instructed to arrive at ten a.m., and it was now closer to eleven.

Skye wrinkled her nose. The room smelled of makeup, sweat, and mold. Up until a few days ago the space had been used as a dressing room for the annual school play, and it housed the drama department's costumes during the rest of the year.

Uncle Dante must have persuaded Homer to have the room straightened up. The principal would never have thought of doing it on his own. Even the uncomfortable chairs, now arranged in four rows of six, would have been too much of a hassle for him. Homer had mentally retired from his job several years ago; he just hadn't bothered to turn in the paperwork.

Clearly everyone was beginning to get impatient. Some wiggled in their seats, others paced, and a few muttered about "talking to someone and finding out what's holding things up."

Skye hoped that one of the more vocal finalists would *do* something. Normally she would be leading the charge, but this was May's moment, and Skye had vowed not to ruin it for her mom, who preferred manipulation to confrontation.

To amuse herself, Skye turned her attention to the other contestants, trying to guess their day jobs. An attractive blonde a few years younger than Skye sat alone, her right leg encased in a Velcro brace and propped up on an empty chair. Small wire-rimmed glasses were perched on her nose, and she was reading the side of a prescription bottle. MONIKA was embroidered on the bib of her official apron.

This reminded Skye that her own name had been misspelled. Scowling, she looked down at the bright red thread reading, SYKE. The staff had promised to provide a corrected apron before the actual contest. If they didn't come through by tomorrow, Skye vowed she would put some sort of pin over the offending error.

Okay, where was she? Right, the blonde. *Mmm.* Either a teacher or a nurse.

Having made her guess, Skye turned her attention to a woman dressed straight out of the 1950s. She wore a wool dress with a full skirt and short matching jacket, high-heeled pumps, and even a little hat perched on her brunette pageboy, its peacock feather dipping over her right eye like an exclamation mark. Her apron sported the name DIANE. She sat erect in her chair, holding her handbag in her lap.

This was a tough one, but Skye guessed that Diane was either an executive secretary or the owner of an antique shop.

Next in Skye's line of vision was a woman built like a linebacker. She had to weigh at least three hundred fifty pounds, and it looked like solid muscle. Nothing jiggled as she paced the length of the small room. Her skin had a blue-black sheen, and her many long braids were pulled back and fastened at the back of her neck. She wore jeans and a T-shirt that said, KISS THE COOK. Her apron read, JANELLE.

Skye was stumped. Janelle could be anything from a professional wrestler to the owner of a construction company.

Before Skye could come up with a firm guess, the last finalist swept into the room, talking a mile a minute to the young man trailing behind her. "Darling, please don't forget to call my editor about the cover of SECRETS OF A HOTEL HEIRESS. Can you believe they thought green was right for my fabulous book? Clearly it should be pink." Without waiting for a reply, she went on, "Oh, and I forgot to pick up my new Vera Wang satin sandals. I'll need them for tomorrow, so call Juanita and have her run into Chicago and get them."

The woman paused to take a breath, and the guy said, "Gotcha, babe. Those shoes are bitchin'."

Skye squinted at the woman's chest and discovered her name was Cherry. Cherry, hmmm . . . well, she did have red hair, but it was chin-length, with ends flipped up and sticking out all over her head. The style reminded Skye more of a cactus than a fruit. The woman's floral wrap dress was unmistakably couture, and the cost of her Fendi tote could have paid Skye's salary for a month. It was hard to tell her age—there were slight creases around her eyes—but such extremely fair skin wrinkled easily. She might be anywhere from her late thirties to early fifties.

What in the world was she doing in a cooking contest, not to mention living in Stanley County? When Skye noticed Cherry staring at her, Skye looked away from the loud couple. It didn't really matter who her competitors were; Skye was pretty sure they could all beat her, even with one spatula tied behind their backs.

Skye was thinking about how awful her last attempt at the chicken casserole had been when the redhead's irritating voice penetrated her thoughts for a second time, and she glanced up. Cherry had sat down and was holding a small leather notebook in her left hand and a tiny gold pen in her right. The man, nodding, stood by her side with his hands in the pockets of a pair of long, baggy shorts. He looked like the quintessential California beach boy—blue eyes, rock-hard body, and deep tan.

Cherry continued, "And, Kyle, do tell Larissa to make sure the baby doesn't nap this afternoon. She claims she doesn't, but I think she lets him sleep as much as he wants when we're gone. I've told her again and again I need him to be tired by the time I get home."

Skye sucked in an audible breath and frowned. She had just read an article in the *School Psychologist Journal* about parents who kept their infants up during the day so they could sleep at night. There was a concern that interrupting the natural sleep patterns of the babies could harm their brain development.

Cherry's gaze fastened on Skye and she glared, then turned back to Kyle and raised her voice. "We seem to have a Nosy Parker eavesdropping on our discussion. Please go over and tell her to mind her own damn business."

"Babe, that's totally bogus." Kyle ran his fingers through his blond curls. "Like, I'm sure no one cares what we're saying."

Cherry ignored him and stalked over to Skye. "You, there, Syke, my husband and I are having a private conversation. Back off."

"Where in this twelve-by-twelve room do you think I could stand and not hear you?" Skye was now completely annoyed. "There are twenty-four of us, which means we are each entitled to about six square feet. Since your *husband* isn't supposed to be here, you'll have to share your six feet with him."

Suddenly Skye felt a tug on her sleeve and looked down into her mother's angry scowl.

"What in the world is going on?" May whispered. "I turn my back on you for two minutes and you're already arguing with someone."

Skye, resuming eye contact with Cherry, said, "Go sit down, Mom. Everything is fine. Cherry and I were just discussing spatial relationships, and the fact that her ego is taking up more than its fair share of the available space."

May tugged Skye back a couple of steps and hissed in her

ear, "I raised you right. You know better than to say things like that to someone's face—you only say them behind their back."

"Don't you think that's a little hypocritical?"

"No, I think it's good manners."

Before Skye could react, the door swung open and one of Grandma Sal's staff walked in. "Okay, now that everyone's here, please follow me onto the stage. Grandma Sal will introduce you; then you can answer some questions for the media."

The contestants hurriedly gathered their belongings and formed a loose line. Skye noticed that Cherry had managed to get into the number one spot.

Skye was surprised to see nearly every chair on the gym floor occupied and several TV camera crews jostling for position just beyond the footlights. Uncle Dante had been right: This was a major event and a good chance for Scumble River to get some positive PR.

A woman in her late seventies stood center stage. Her gray hair was arranged in a soft halo of curls, and her blue eyes twinkled behind wire-rimmed glasses. She wore a pink flowered dress and a matching hat covered in artificial carnations.

Smiling at the contestants, she said, "Ladies and gentlemen, it is my pleasure to welcome you to the thirty-fifth annual Grandma Sal's Soup-to-Nuts Cooking Challenge." She waited for the applause to die down, then continued, "My name is Sally Fine, and I'm CEO of Fine Foods. Helping me with this contest are my son, Jared; his wife, Tammy; my grandson, JJ; and his brother, Brandon."

Skye looked over at the middle-aged couple and their handsome sons. Both young men seemed fairly close in age, somewhere in their twenties. JJ resembled Grandma Sal, a little pudgy, with blue eyes and curly blond hair, while Brandon looked more like his mother, athletic with dark hair and eyes. The couple and their sons waved politely, but none of the four looked pleased to be there. Skye remembered hearing that they lived in Chicago and, unlike Grandma Sal, were rarely seen at the Scumble River factory.

Grandma Sal waited for the clapping to die down, then said, "Our judges are Ramona Epstein, food editor for the *Chicago Post*; Alice Gibson, best-selling cookbook author; and Paul Voss, the restaurant critic for Chicago's leading radio station."

Skye studied the first judge. Even adding the weight of the gold and diamonds she was wearing, Ramona couldn't possibly top the scale at a hundred pounds. Skye wondered if the food editor ever actually ate anything.

Next to the tiny raven-haired judge, Alice looked almost hulking, although she probably was no more than a size twelve or fourteen. Skye nodded to herself in approval. If you were going to write cookbooks, you should at least look as if you tasted your own recipes.

The male judge stood a little apart from the women, his unnaturally blue eyes shooting sparks of disdain. Something about him reminded Skye of an evil Santa. She wasn't sure if it was the red pants, hat, and shoes, the white goatee, or the bowl-full-of-jelly belly.

After the judges came onstage, Grandma Sal turned to the wings and extended her right hand. "Now let's meet the contestants. First, Mrs. Cherry Alexander, a writer from Laurel Lake who is competing in Special-Occasion Baking."

Skye smiled. Good. She could avoid Cherry, since they weren't in the same category. It wasn't as if Skye would take first in her group and go up against the other three winners for the grand prize.

Several other contestants were introduced before Grandma Sal got to the attractive blonde with the injured leg. "Monika Bradley owns her own accounting firm and comes to us from Brooklyn. She is competing in the Healthy Foods division."

Dang, a CPA, not a nurse or teacher. So far Skye was zero for one.

A few more finalists had their fifteen seconds of fame; then the 1950s woman stepped forward, and Grandma Sal said, "Diane White is a cookie blogger from Clay Center, Special-Occasion Baking."

Okay, no one would have guessed cookie blogger for a

profession. Skye's brows met over her nose in an irritated frown. What was a cookie blogger, and was it even a real occupation? Fine, she had one more chance.

The linebacker was the last contestant to be introduced, and before Grandma Sal could speak, a dozen or so men in the audience stood up, stamped their feet, and whistled. Skye couldn't see very well past the footlights, but the guys in the cheering section looked mighty big. Maybe the finalist really was on a football team.

Finally the crowd settled down, and Grandma Sal said, "Last but certainly not least is Janelle Carpenter from Granger. Janelle is a prison cook and will be competing in the One-Dish Meals category."

Yikes! That was Skye's group. Could all those men cheering be ex-cons? If so, it was a good thing Skye didn't have a snowball's chance in hell of winning.

What seemed like hours later, Grandma Sal finally finished her welcoming speech, which had included the history of the company and a loving description of every division and every product sold.

As soon as the older woman relinquished the mike, Mayor Leofanti grabbed it. Skye cringed. Dante was less than five-six, and he carried all of his considerable weight in his chest and stomach. With his thick gray hair slicked back, red nose, and black suit, he looked like a penguin, only not as distinguished.

While Dante started, as expected, by thanking everyone and their dog for helping make this event possible, Skye's stomach growled. She'd had her normal breakfast of an English muffin and tea at eight o'clock, but it was already past noon, and they still had the media questions to face before they would be escorted to the luncheon being held at the Feed Bag, Scumble River's only sit-down restaurant. Wouldn't it be ironic if she starved to death at a cooking contest?

Dante paused, then began his closing remarks. "Grandma Sal's Fine Foods has been a part of Scumble River for close to forty years. Mrs. Fine and her late husband built the factory here in the nineteen sixties, and pretty near saved this town from dying out. They have employed many of you, your parents, and grandparents, and have always been a good neighbor. Scumble Riverites have been able to depend on Grandma Sal's for jobs, charitable contributions, and a future. Because of this, we who have reaped their bounty want to thank them by hosting the best ever Soup-to-Nuts Cooking Challenge."

The crowd clapped and whistled, and Skye smiled at her uncle. He was not a particularly good uncle, and she knew from experience that he was a lousy boss, but he had turned out to be a great mayor. She was truly happy for him and her family that after so many years he had found his niche.

Dante waved, bowed, and then stepped back as Grandma Sal opened the floor to the media. The majority of the questions were addressed to all of the contestants, and anyone could answer. Skye noticed that Cherry usually managed to have the last say on most subjects. Grudgingly Skye acknowledged that the writer had a way with the audience. Her quips generally left them laughing and, more important, scribbling in their notebooks.

They had been standing on the stage for nearly two hours, and Skye was rocking from foot to foot, hungry, bored, and needing to pee, when the owner/reporter of the *Scumble River Star*, Kathryn Steele, asked the group, "What inspired your recipes?"

It took a moment for Skye to realize that her mother had stepped forward and was answering. It took another moment for her to grasp what May was saying.

"My entry was inspired by my daughter's upcoming wedding."

Despite Skye's pleas, the *Star* had run several stories about her crime-solving activities, so she was well-known among the paper's staff, and for some reason she couldn't fathom, they were fascinated with her personal life.

Kathryn's body language resembled that of a golden retriever that had just discovered a flock of ducks hiding among the cattails. "Who's the groom? Has a date been set?"

Skye didn't have time to think or plan what to say, but

she knew she had to answer before her mother did. She leapt forward and, trying to keep the edge out of her voice, said, "Kathryn, you know Mom meant my eventual, some-time-in-the-far-far-future wedding." Skye held up her left hand, naked of any ring. "When I get married you'll see a rock the size of a Christmas-tree ornament on my finger." The audience laughed, and she wrapped it up with, "Who knows how many cooking contests Mom'll win before then?"

Skye shot a sideways look of warning to May, who had her mouth open but slowly closed it without speaking.

The rest of the questions were harmless, and Skye zoned out, concentrating on her increasing need for the ladies' room. Finally the contestants were dismissed. Several raced for the bathroom. Skye had the advantage of knowing the lay of the land and headed for the faculty restroom, located deep within the bowels of the building, which she was sure would be empty.

Whipping inside, she locked the door and was unzipping her pants when she heard loud voices coming from the other side of the wall. Hmm, that would be the teachers' lounge. Skye leaned closer to the wall, curious as to who had ignored the sign on the closed door that said, DO NOT ENTER. TEACHERS ONLY. THIS MEANS YOU.

"Listen up, sweet cheeks. You didn't give me any data on her or her family other than what I already had. You guaranteed me that your information would be up close and personal. I have too much riding on this for your shoddy work to ruin things for me. You have until tomorrow morning to get me the dirt on her and her relatives." The woman's tone was angry.

"I sent you what Grandma Sal sent me. Can I help it if the old broad didn't give me what I asked for? She always does in-depth profiles of the contestants to make sure they're squeaky-clean." This second voice was deeper, but Skye couldn't tell if it belonged to a man or a woman. "I'll reach out to my sources tonight and have the lowdown tomorrow at breakfast."

"You'd better. I doubt you want anyone to know what you're up to."

"Hey, I already got you into the finals. We both have secrets we don't want exposed."

"And I paid you good money for that."

Skye heard the door slam and hurried to finish up. She raced out of the restroom, but it was too late; no one was around. As she went back to wash her hands, she wondered who had bought their way into the finals, and which contestant they were so interested in and why.

CHAPTER 3

Read Through Recipe

Skye and May were caught in the parade of cars driving the three miles between the high school and the Feed Bag. May's white Oldsmobile sparkled as the sun beat down on its hood. It looked as if it had just rolled off the assembly line, but in reality it was over ten years old. That it accrued less than six thousand miles a year and was rarely driven past the county line probably had something to do with the vehicle's pristine condition.

The Olds was sandwiched between Vince's Jeep and Charlie's Cadillac Seville. Looking into the side mirror, Skye could see her godfather scowling and shaking his fist. Scumble River did not usually have gridlock, and Charlie clearly wasn't enjoying the rare experience.

In contrast, Vince was bopping to whatever music was playing on the radio; or, knowing her brother, Skye wouldn't be surprised to learn that the beat was only in his head. Vince had been the drummer in local bands since he was fourteen.

As far as Skye could tell, May's attitude was somewhere in the middle—still excited to be a part of the contest, but worried she might miss something while she was stuck in traffic.

"Mom, I have a question for you." Skye figured that at the

rate they were going it would take them at least fifteen minutes to get to the restaurant, which meant this was a good
time to ask her mother about something that had been bothering Skye for the past few months. She was especially worried after her mom's performance at the press conference.

"So, ask it already."

"Why are you suddenly so intent on marrying me off?"

May hadn't been this determined to get Skye married in
a long time. Had Skye's biological clock started ticking so
loudly that even her mother could hear it?

May twisted the knob on the radio until she found the
weather. "I don't know what you mean by 'suddenly.' I've
always wanted to see you married."

"Well, you've wanted me to settle down with some nice
guy and produce two-point-five grandchildren since I turned
twenty-one, but the last few months you've ratcheted your
efforts up about a hundred percent."

"Things have changed."

Skye turned off the radio and focused on her mom's face.
"What has changed?"

"You and Wally." May's expression soured. Although she
wanted Skye married, she wasn't keen on her marrying
Wally, who was several years older, divorced, and not
Catholic.

"What about Wally and me?" Skye asked.

"I'm worried that by the time you get Wally out of your
system, Simon will have found someone else. I saw that
nurse from your school, the one who dated Vince for a
while, talking with Simon at church. And that new woman,
the one who moved to town last summer with that wild
daughter, was flirting with him at the gas station the other
day."

"Mom, I don't want him back." Skye had dated Simon
Reid, the funeral home director and county coroner, on and
off for the past three or so years. Her mother's news that
other women were flirting with him caused a twinge of jealousy, but Skye pushed it away. "I'm happy with Wally. Not
that I necessarily want to marry him." She didn't want May
to start planning that wedding either.

"You're going to be thirty-five this December!" May exploded. "It's time you settled down. Do you want to go to your kids' graduation in a wheelchair?"

"Mother!" Skye blew out an angry puff of air and crossed her arms. "A lot of women nowadays have kids well into their forties."

May muttered something about old eggs not producing a good omelet, then stared out the windshield. After several minutes of icy silence, she spoke as if nothing had happened. "Did any of the other finalists look sort of familiar to you?"

Deciding to let the Simon/Wally marriage issue go, at least until the contest was over, Skye teased, "Besides you, Vince, and Charlie?"

"Yes, smarty-pants, besides us."

Skye pictured the other twenty contestants, then shook her head. "No, I can't say anyone stuck out. I take it one did to you?"

"Sort of, but I couldn't place her. She's the one with short black hair that looks like a wig, and glasses with rhinestone frames. Her name is Imogene Ingersoll. I was only able to speak to her briefly—she was on the way to the bathroom—and she said we hadn't met. I didn't get a chance to talk to her again."

"Well, we'll all be together for the next couple of days, so maybe it will come to you, or she'll remember something."

"Maybe." May frowned. "But it's like a sore tooth. I keep poking at it."

"I hate when that happens."

May sighed, then asked, "What did you think of the other contestants?"

"It's hard to tell. I never got to speak to most of them."

"Yeah, we should have had a plan." May stomped on the brakes as the only stoplight in town changed from green to yellow. "We could have divided them up into four groups and gotten the scoop on each of them."

"Why would we want to do that, Mom?" Skye thought about the mysterious conversation she had overheard coming from the teachers' lounge. That person had wanted information on a contestant too; maybe May could explain why that data was so vital.

"It gives you a psychological advantage." May flipped down the visor and checked her hair.

"How does that help in a cooking contest?" Skye turned slightly so she could study her mother.

May eased off the brake and made a left. "Because if you can psych someone out, they might get so rattled they forget to add an ingredient, or they overcook their dish, or do something else that ruins their recipe."

"But that's not fair." May's primping prompted Skye to smooth her own wayward curls and apply a fresh coat of apricot gloss to her lips.

"All's fair in cooking and baking."

Her mother's attitude of "anything goes" made Skye wonder whether she should mention to someone in charge that one of the finalists had bought her way into the contest. After a few minutes' consideration, she realized that she had no idea who either of the two people she overheard was, and she could end up reporting the incident to the very person who was involved. She had been trying to learn that every problem was not hers to solve. This seemed a good place to start.

May eased over the bump leading into the restaurant's lot, then abruptly put on the brakes. "Shoot. The lot's full."

"Where are we going to park?" Skye asked. Her gaze swept the double rows on both sides of the building. All four were solidly packed.

May frowned. "We might have to park at Vince's salon and walk back."

Great. Skye looked down at her new Ann Taylor zebra-striped pumps. She had splurged during a recent shopping trip in Chicago. Loretta had talked her into getting them, even though Skye knew there were limited places she could wear them without crippling herself. Now their pointy toes mocked her. Talk about shoes that *weren't* made for walking. She'd do better taking them off and carrying them than trying to hike a mile in the three-inch heels.

Skye was about to suggest her mother double-park—after

all, everyone at the restaurant would be leaving at the same time—when she spotted a police car backed into a space right next to the restaurant's door. As she watched, Wally unfolded himself from the driver's side and approached the Olds. He had muscles in all the right places, and she enjoyed seeing him move.

She rolled down the window. "Hi, handsome. What are you doing here?"

He leaned in for a quick kiss, then answered, "I figured you might have some trouble finding a place to park, so I saved you a space." He leaned further into the car. "Hi, May. I'll pull out so you can pull in."

May nodded, but otherwise didn't respond.

Wally's smile cooled at May's cold shoulder, but it warmed back up when he turned to Skye and said, "Come ride with me. I need to talk to you for a minute before you go in."

"You don't have time." May's hand clamped down on Skye's wrist as she opened the car door. "We're on a tight schedule. You'll make everyone late."

"It'll be fine, Mom." Skye freed herself and stepped out of the car. She definitely had to make it clear to her mother that she needed to be nicer to Wally. After the contest they'd have a little daughter-to-mother talk, and May had better straighten up. "Go inside and save me a seat."

For a moment Skye was afraid that May would run them over when they crossed in front of the Olds, but she only revved the engine.

Wally helped Skye into the passenger side of the squad car, then slid into the driver's seat, started the engine, and pulled out. He was silent as he maneuvered the cruiser into the lot's lane of traffic and around the corner. He parked next to the Dumpsters in a space that said, RESERVED FOR DELIVERIES.

Skye bit her bottom lip. What was up? She studied Wally. He was a handsome man who filled out his crisply starched police uniform in exactly the right way. His warm brown eyes melted her heart, and his shiny black hair edged in silver made her itch to run her fingers through the waves. He also had a gorgeous year-round tan. But his most attractive feature was his kind and generous nature.

Now his expression was serious and unhappy. He half turned, took her hand, and opened his mouth, then seemed to change his mind and instead said, "Did I tell you how beautiful you look?"

Skye shook her head. "How could you? This is the first time you've seen me today."

"Mmm." He brought her hand up to his lips and nibbled on her fingers. "You taste good, too."

"That's because I haven't started cooking yet," Skye teased.

Wally continued to nibble. "When's your next time off from school?"

"Well . . ." Skye wasn't prepared for the question, and she stammered, "If you mean more than one day, that would be the end of school, which is June eleventh. Why?"

"We should plan a trip together." Wally's lips were now on the inside of her elbow.

"That'd be fun." Was this what he had needed to talk to her about? Skye glanced at the dashboard clock. She had to get inside pretty soon, or May would send the cavalry to find her—and her orders *wouldn't* be to hold their fire until they saw the whites of Wally's eyes. Skye prodded. "So, you had something important to discuss?"

"Right. Sorry. I know you don't have long. It's just that I wanted to tell you . . . that is, before someone else did . . . that, uh . . ."

He hesitated, then opened his mouth, but before a single word escaped his lips the radio squawked to life. "Chief, there's been an accident over by the I-55 exit. Car versus semi. Traffic is completely stopped, and the ambulance and fire truck can't get through."

"I'll be there in five." Wally had let go of Skye's hand to work the radio. Now he leaned toward her and opened the door for her. "Sorry, sugar—I'll explain when I pick you up for the dinner tonight. And remember, don't believe anything you hear until I get a chance to talk to you."

It almost felt as if he had pushed her out of the squad car.

Skye's shoulders drooped. What in the world did he have to tell her? Whatever it was, she was pretty sure it wasn't something she wanted to hear.

Scumble River might be a small town, but it wasn't quite small enough for the entire population to fit inside the Feed Bag, particularly since the maximum-seating-capacity sign read seventy-six. Still, it looked as if the residents had given it the old college try. When Skye entered the only way she could get to her table was by edging sideways and holding her purse above her head.

Once seated, Skye noticed that Tomi Johnson, the owner of the Feed Bag, was not her usual cool and in-control self. May reported to Skye that when Tomi had been introduced to Grandma Sal, the restaurateur had practically kissed the food manufacturer's ring. Now Tomi was rushing around bringing Grandma Sal bites of this, samples of that, and hanging on the CEO's every tidbit of praise.

In fact, Skye noted that a lot of Scumble River's citizens were acting out of character. They seemed more impressed by Grandma Sal and the contestants than they had been in the past by TV stars and supermodels. Why was that? Could it be that at some level the townspeople knew that nourishment was more important than glamour? Of course, it probably didn't hurt that Grandma Sal's picture was plastered on nearly every product her company sold, and many people saw her face at least three times a day.

The contestants were seated at four tables of six. Skye observed that Vince and Charlie had elected to sit separately, each the only rooster among five hens. Both men had self-satisfied looks on their faces that Skye's palm itched to slap off. She restrained herself, reasoning that once the cooking started and they burned their entries, those smug expressions would be erased with the first wisp of smoke.

Grandma Sal's staff had its own table, as did the judges and the media, which claimed the three back booths. The other diners were all locals, most of whom appeared to be more interested in catching a glimpse of Grandma Sal and the contestants than they did in eating. Skye was happy to see that Tomi had clipped an index card to the menus that read, MINIMUM ORDER PER PERSON $5.00. NO SHARING. NO DOGGIE BAGS. The restaurant owner deserved to make a profit from all this hullabaloo.

Skye had just bitten into her BLT when Butch King, their table's token male, tipped his head toward May and remarked, "So, both you and your daughter are from Scumble River?"

May nodded. "I grew up in Brooklyn, but ever since I got married I've lived here." Skye saw her mother peek at the man's left ring finger, which was bare, and flinched when she added, "I think a woman should live where her husband's work is, as long as it's not too far from her mother."

The man looked amused. He winked at Skye and said to May, "You sound like my mom. She was so happy when I tied the knot and moved into the apartment next to her."

"How wonderful."

Skye did not like the expression that had settled on her mother's face. She could tell that May was already picturing a house next to hers in the adjoining cornfield.

Hastily swallowing, Skye jumped into the conversation before her mother started drawing up the blueprints. "Where are *you* from, Butch?"

"Laurel." Butch cut a piece of his chicken-fried steak and forked it into his mouth.

"I was surprised that the contest was open only to Stanley County." Skye took a sip of her Diet Coke. "I had heard that Fine Foods has been enlarging its market."

Another contestant joined the conversation. "The scuttlebutt around cooking-contest circles is that this will be the last year there's a local contest. Fine Foods used to be strictly a Midwestern company, but the last couple of years it's been expanding to Southern and Western markets. There's a rumor that Grandma Sal is in negotiations with some big food conglomerate. If that company buys Fine Foods, the products will go nationwide and so will the contest."

"I wonder if that will affect the factory here." Skye worried that a lot of locals could be out of jobs if the company was sold.

No one seemed to have an answer, and a few minutes later May asked, "What made you decide to enter, Butch?"

"I didn't." His smile was boyish. "I'm a firefighter, and the guys at my stationhouse love my spaghechili, so they sent in the recipe."

"Spaghechili?"

"It's a combination of my Italian grandmother's spaghetti recipe and my Mexican grandmother's chili recipe." Butch grinned. "I came up with it when I didn't have enough ingredients for either to feed the whole crew."

"Very clever," Skye complimented him.

"Clever, my eye," May muttered. "That's not a recipe; that's leftovers."

"Uh," Skye said quickly, forestalling May's next comment, "so you're a Laurel firefighter? Do you know our police chief, Wally Boyd?"

"Sure. He's a great guy."

"My mom works for him as a dispatcher."

"I'm a police, fire, and emergency dispatcher." May's eyes narrowed. "My paycheck is signed by the mayor, not Wally."

"Oh, I see." Butch looked at Skye, then May. "I've probably heard you on the radio."

May nodded, then said, "I'll bet you know Simon Reid too, the county coroner."

"Right." Butch handed the waitress his plate and ordered lemon meringue pie for dessert. "Not well. He sort of keeps to himself, you know?"

"He's friendlier once you get to know him." May shook her head at the waitress's offer of dessert. "He's Skye's boyfriend, so we know him in a different way, of course."

"No, he isn't," Skye blurted out. "He and I stopped seeing each other six months ago. Actually I'm dating Wally now, but Mom refuses to believe Simon and I have broken up for good."

May harrumphed, nudging Skye. "Butch doesn't care about your love life."

Skye felt her face redden. "But you said . . ." Why did May always do this to her? Why did she start something, then make Skye feel like the one in the wrong? Skye stuttered to a stop. Anything she said to defend herself would make it worse. "Of course, sorry." When everyone else resumed the conversation, she hissed in her mom's ear, "You brought up the subject of Wally and Simon, so back off."

May harrumphed again, then turned her attention to another tablemate. "What about you, Monika? Did Grandma Sal say you were from Brooklyn?"

"Yes," the attractive blonde answered before pushing aside her nearly untouched plate. "I'm lucky it's only eight miles from here."

"I have a lot of relatives in Brooklyn," May said. "Do you know the head librarian, Jayne? She's one of my cousins."

"Yes." Monika reached into her purse and took out a Ziploc bag. "She's one of my clients."

May peered at the woman as she opened the plastic sack and started snacking from it. "Didn't you like your lunch?"

Monika hesitated, then explained, "I have severe food allergies and can't eat anything with dairy or gluten. I ordered a chicken breast broiled without butter, but they breaded it, and then I was afraid the fries had been in the same oil used to deep-fry other foods with breading."

"Such a small trace would be a problem for you?" May probed, a look of disbelief on her face.

"Yes, even a tiny bit could cause me to become extremely ill and possibly die."

"You poor thing." May patted the woman's hand.

Skye wrinkled her brow. If she had a food allergy that severe, would she be brave enough to come to a cooking contest, where someone's innocent crumbs could kill her?

As May had predicted, they were running late, but it wasn't Skye's fault. The responsibility lay with Grandma Sal, who was turning out to be a girl who just couldn't say no. All the townspeople in the restaurant and all the Feed Bag employees wanted an autograph and their picture taken with her. Skye had never seen anyone sign boxes of cake mix, tubes of biscuits, and packets of dry pasta before.

Finally, about three o'clock, a full hour after they were scheduled to have been finished with lunch, Grandma Sal's staff started moving the contestants out of the restaurant and into their cars. Everyone was instructed to follow Grandma Sal's limo to the factory, where they would be given a brief tour and then have a chance to do a trial run of their recipes.

Skye and May were in the last group to be ushered from their table.

As they stood to follow the contest staffer, May whispered to Skye, "Here are the keys. I'll meet you at the car. I have to go to the bathroom."

"Okay." Skye noted that a couple of women were lined up to use the only ladies' room, and wished she had brought a book to read.

Skye followed her tablemates out the door. Once they were in the parking lot everyone scattered toward their vehicles. Skye sorted through the huge ring of keys May had thrust into her hand. She had just found the car key and inserted it into the passenger-side door when she heard the first scream.

CHAPTER 4

Butter and Flour
Your Pan

Skye froze. Did that sound like her mother?

The second scream propelled her into action. Over her shoulder she yelled to the few remaining people in the parking lot, "Call nine-one-one. I'll go see what's wrong."

Skye burst through the restaurant's door and skidded to a stop, searching for the problem. A third scream drew her to the back of the restaurant, where two women were engaged in a shoving match.

When Skye got closer she saw that one of the brawlers was Cherry Alexander. The redhead pushed her opponent and yelled, "You give it back to me right now!"

Cherry's shove moved the other combatant into view, and Skye cringed as she saw her mother raise both fists and shout, "I told you, I don't have your silly *secret* ingredient!"

Cherry pulled back her arm, aiming a slap at May's face, but Skye grabbed the petite woman's wrist and said in her best playground-monitor voice, "No hitting. We're all adults here, and I'm sure we'll find whatever you lost."

"Get out of my way." May tried to thrust Skye aside, but her five-foot-two, one hundred twenty-five pounds was no match for her daughter, who had five inches on her, and quite a bit more weight. "I can fight my own battles."

"I'm sure you could beat each other to a pulp with no trouble whatsoever, but that would mean you would be kicked out of the contest." Skye raised an eyebrow. "Is that what you really want?"

As if someone had lowered the flame on a gas stove, both women went from boiling over to simmering in the space of a heartbeat.

"She started it." May thrust out her chin. "She accused me of stealing."

"If you didn't take it, who did?" Cherry theatrically rubbed the wrist Skye had released. "And I'd better be able to whisk tomorrow with this arm or I'm suing you."

Skye wanted to slap the asinine woman, but instead asked, biting off her words, "What did you lose?"

"You'd like to know, wouldn't you?" Cherry's gaze darted among the women gathered around her.

Until then Skye hadn't noticed that the people who had still been in the parking lot had all come inside. Their presence reminded her that she had told them to call for help before going to investigate the scream. Now she asked, "Did anyone call nine-one-one?"

A woman nodded and held up a bright red cell phone. "They said they'd be right here."

"Shoot." Skye was angry with herself for jumping the gun. "Call them back and tell them we don't need them after all."

"Don't you dare!" Cherry forced her way past Skye and pointed at May. "I want this woman arrested."

Before Skye could react, the restaurant door slammed open and Officer Roy Quirk strode into the room. He immediately spotted Skye and asked, "We got a call about a woman screaming. What's up?"

Quirk was Wally's second in command and, since Skye had been hired as a psychological consultant to the Scumble River Police Department, one of her colleagues.

Skye pointed toward Cherry. "This woman claims her

secret ingredient has been stolen, and she's accusing Mom of taking it."

Quirk spoke into the radio clipped to his shoulder, then approached Cherry and asked, "Ma'am, what exactly is missing?"

"I'm not saying." Cherry huffed, "Don't any of you understand the concept of *secret*?"

"Well, ma'am, how can I look for it if I don't know what it is?"

"It's in a white paper sack." Cherry crossed her arms. "And no one had better open the bag if they find it."

Quirk turned to May. "Is it okay if I look in your purse?"

"Sure." She thrust the large black satchel into the officer's arms. "I don't have anything to hide. I don't need a secret ingredient to win. I have talent."

Quirk opened the purse and upended it on a nearby table. He named the objects as he returned them to the bag. "Wallet, checkbook, comb, lipstick, pillbox, tissues, glasses, pen, pad of paper, and roll of mints."

Before handing the purse back to May he asked Cherry, "Are any of these your secret ingredient?"

"No," Cherry said curtly, her eyes burning with contempt and determination. "But that doesn't prove she doesn't have it. I want her strip-searched."

"Now, ma'am, we can't do that." Quirk pushed his hat back and scratched his head. "May, would you be willing to let this lady pat you down?"

May started to shake her head until Skye pointed out, "You both realize that if we don't resolve this matter here, you'll have to go to the police station, and you'll miss the tour and the chance to do a dry run of your recipes. Heck, maybe you'll even be disqualified."

"Both of us?" Cherry squealed, wheeling toward Skye. "She's the crook; I'm the victim. Why would I be disqualified?"

Skye exchanged glances with Quirk, who nodded his consent for her to go on. "If you make a formal report and we find nothing, we could arrest you for malicious mischief." Skye had no idea if this was really true.

"Fine, just forget it," Cherry said. "Once again the criminal goes free."

"Oh, no. You're not getting away with letting all these people think I'm a thief." May's jaw was rigid. "Cherry can pat me down, but if she doesn't find any paper bag, she has to apologize."

Everyone looked at Cherry, who finally shrugged and said, "Very well."

As she stepped toward May, May held her arms perpendicular to her body and warned, "No funny business, now. I don't play for that team."

As soon as they arrived at the factory, Cherry cornered Grandma Sal's son and started complaining about her missing secret ingredient, which had not been found on May or anywhere else in the restaurant.

Skye stepped within listening range as Jared Fine tried to soothe Cherry by saying, "Don't worry, ma'am; we'll get you a replacement before tomorrow. Everything will be all right, I promise. Just tell me what it is you lost."

Cherry stomped her foot. "No. I'm not revealing the ingredient until I've won the contest. And I don't want you to go looking on my entry form and telling anyone, either."

"Then I'm not sure what I can do for you, ma'am." Jared backed away. "If you change your mind, let me know."

Cherry seethed. "It's not something you can pick up at any old grocery store. It needs to be special-ordered, you moron."

"Sorry, ma'am," Jared said. "Read your contest rules. We aren't responsible for missing ingredients that cannot be purchased locally."

Cherry pulled out her cell phone and stomped off, glaring at May as she passed her.

Skye realized that Jared had caught her eavesdropping. She made a face and joked, "Sounds like Cherry has a couple of issues."

"A *couple* of issues?" Jared shook his head. "She has the full subscription."

Even though they had wasted a good half hour searching

for Cherry's secret ingredient, they had still arrived at the factory in time to join the last tour group. Skye and her mother donned the hairnets and hard hats they were handed and followed the group into the production area.

Their tour was being led by Brandon Fine. The handsome young man seemed less sullen than he had when he was first introduced at the press conference, and Skye wondered what had improved his mood. Maybe he had just been bored, or hungry, or had to go to the bathroom that morning. Skye certainly had experienced all three.

As they walked, Brandon said, "This is an older factory. Much of what you see is original equipment from when it was first built." He gestured to the left and said, "This is where the raw materials—such as sugar, powdered eggs, corn syrup, cocoa, and seasonings—are stored."

Skye poked her head into the enormous room and saw huge bins and sacks the size of refrigerators stacked on wooden pallets.

Next they were led to an area where Brandon pointed down. "The metal plate you see in the floor is actually a scale. While your recipes may call for two cups of flour, ours call for two hundred pounds."

As if on cue, a man wheeled an empty stainless-steel container onto the scale. He reached up to a pipe running above the tub and turned a valve handle, then walked over to a panel with digital numbers. Underneath the display was a series of switches. He flipped one, then another, and oil began to flow into the container.

May poked Skye in the ribs with her elbow. "Good thing your father isn't here to see this. Next thing you know he'd be running pipes for his beer into the living room."

The worker caught Skye's glance and snickered as he continued to add ingredients to the tub. When he was finished, he looked around and muttered, "Where did Shorty get to? I can't move this thing by myself."

"Never mind, Moose," Brandon said. "I'll give you a hand." He joined the factory worker, and they rolled the container over to what looked like a giant milk shake machine.

As the group followed, Brandon said, "There is now over five hundred pounds of raw material in this vat."

As the ladies oohed and aahed, he reached up and grasped a switch.

Moose yelled, "No!"

But Brandon flipped the toggle to the ON position, and the huge mixer growled into life, catching the dangling cuff of Brandon's shirt in its beaters.

Before anyone else could react, Moose slammed down a big red button and all the machinery in the immediate vicinity went still.

The sudden silence was startling. No one said a word for a long moment; then voices rose in concern. Brandon waved away offers of help, inspected the damage to his shirt, and said, "Everything's fine. Moose, have them turn the power back on."

As soon as the machinery roared back into service, Brandon said, "It will take over thirty minutes to mix this batch, so we'll move on to the extruding area."

May held Skye back and whispered, "What do you think would have happened if they hadn't turned off the power?"

"He would have lost his arm, maybe his life." Skye tugged on her mother's hand. "Come on. We'd better keep up. I don't want to take a misstep and become part of the frosting."

As they hurried past Moose, they heard the factory worker muttering to himself, "Those spoiled-brat gran'kids know just enough to be dangerous. We told 'em not to let 'em lead the tours."

Skye and May joined the group in watching what looked like unending rows of cake pans passing on conveyor belts. As the pans went under short lengths of hoses, batter was extruded into each one; then the pan moved into a long oven.

Skye commented, "Sure wish we had this setup for the next school bake sale."

"Yeah! And the family reunion, too," May added.

They ended the tour in the packaging area, where rows of women in white uniforms and hairnets placed the finished product into boxes, sealed the flaps, and stacked the boxes into cartons. There was another section of the factory in the far rear of the building that Brandon explained was called the Boneyard because it contained the out-of-date equipment and broken machinery that Grandma Sal couldn't bear to throw out.

As the tour group was led away, Skye noted that none of the workers was under fifty years old, and she bet that many of them had been doing that same job since they had graduated or dropped out of high school. What would they do if the company were sold to some big conglomerate that moved the factory away or modernized it or otherwise eliminated their jobs?

From the packaging area they were escorted back to the front of the factory, past a row of offices, then through a narrow corridor that led to an outside exit on the left side of the passage and a door leading into the warehouse straight ahead, where all the cooking would be done.

Four sets of six stoves had been arranged in two rows. Next to each stove were four feet of counters, a minifridge, a cupboard, and two drawers. Brandon explained that they'd run two miles of cable to provide the electricity needed for the setup. He also warned them that the room would be at sixty-five degrees to start with, but would warm up quickly once the cooking started and the spotlights were turned on.

The judges and the media were placed behind the kitchen stations. On the right the judges were shielded from sight by several folding screens, but on the left the media had an unobstructed view of the contestants.

In front of the cooking spaces, chairs for the audience had been positioned in rows with a central aisle. Skye was impressed by the professional arrangements and amazed at how efficiently the contest space had been designed. Before returning to Scumble River she had lived in apartments with less well appointed kitchens.

Contestants were grouped by their food category, which meant that Skye, Charlie, and Vince were all on their own. There was no way May could subtly help any of them with their recipes.

Because Skye and May were in the last tour, the other finalists had already begun to cook. Skye cringed when she heard her mother's voice.

"Brandon."

"Yes, ma'am?"

"Do you really think this is fair?" May gestured to the contestants busy at their stoves. "They've all had a head start."

"But, ma'am, this is just a trial run to make sure you have everything you need for tomorrow." Brandon glanced at the media area, a frown creasing his forehead. "It isn't timed or judged."

Skye followed his gaze and was relieved to see that the reporters' attention was focused elsewhere. She felt sorry for Brandon. First Cherry and her secret ingredient, now May and her sense of injustice. Skye bet this wasn't how this privileged young man usually spent his days.

"We're still at a disadvantage." May crossed her arms. "We all should have started at the same time."

"I'll mention that to Grandma Sal." Brandon backed away. "I'm sure she'll come talk to you about it."

May harrumphed, but allowed herself to be led to her cooking area.

Skye found her own stove, located between that of Butch the firefighter, and Janelle the prison cook. She nodded to them both as she stepped into her space, then let out a startled yelp.

The woman standing in front of the stove whirled around. Long fake red curls cascaded down her back to the low-riding waist of her skintight jeans. Lime Skechers matched the baseball cap worn backward on her head. She casually reached into her orange-and-green-striped tank top and adjusted a black satin bra strap, then shot Skye a wide grin.

Skye stood frozen. What in the world was Bunny Reid doing at Grandma Sal's Soup-to-Nuts Cooking Challenge? Bunny was many things—Skye's ex-boyfriend's mother, a retired Las Vegas showgirl, and the manager of the town bowling alley—but she wasn't a cook. The only recipes she knew were the ones that called for crushed ice and a maraschino cherry.

Brown eyes twinkling, Bunny threw her arms around Skye and said, "I thought you'd never get here. I was just about to start cooking without you."

Freeing herself from the older woman's hug, Skye managed to ask in a neutral tone, "Bunny, this is quite a surprise. What are you doing here?"

"I'm your runner." She pointed to her sneakers. "See? I'm all set to get you anything you need."

"Oh." Skye stepped up to the counter, wondering if there was any way to trade runners. She didn't want to hurt Bunny's feelings, but since she herself was a novice cook, she really needed a helper who had actually stepped foot in a kitchen before.

Bunny trailed Skye like a piece of toilet paper stuck to her shoe.

Without turning around, Skye said, "Uh, you know, Bunny, since you and I are friends, I think maybe your being my runner is sort of cheating. The other contestants won't have their friends helping them."

"Honey, you really are *too* nice." Bunny tugged her closer until they were face-to-face, her body language turning suddenly hard. "You've got to be more ruthless in this world."

"No!" Skye nearly screamed. All she needed was cutthroat Bunny working for her. That would be like having a wererabbit for a pet. "I like to play by the rules."

"In that case there's no problem." Bunny relaxed her pose and hoisted her jeans up a fraction. "They asked all the runners if they knew the contestants, and almost all of them did to some degree or another, so they said it didn't matter."

"Great." Skye gave Bunny her best fake smile, all the while thinking, *Rats!* Excuses raced through Skye's mind, but she couldn't come up with any other good reason to object to Bunny as her helper. She was stuck with the redhead, and the last chance Skye had of producing an edible casserole had just hopped out the window.

Sighing, Skye took the recipe card and a pencil out of her purse, then stowed the bag in the nearly empty cupboard.

Handing the card and pencil to Bunny, she said, "Read the ingredients off to me. I'll find them; then you put a check mark next to them on the card."

"Okay." Bunny dug a pair of small reading glasses out of her pocket, settled them on her nose, and asked, "Ready?"

"Ready."

"Chopped chicken." Bunny looked at Skye over the top of her lime green frames.

Skye opened the minifridge and took out the Ziploc bag of cubed cooked breast meat. "Check."

"Elbow macaroni."

Skye reached into the low cupboard, but couldn't quite grab the box, which had been pushed to the back. Sighing, she got on her knees and stuck her head inside.

She had just curled her fingers around the package when she heard someone yell, "Son of a B! Who switched my sugar for salt?" The voice belonged to her mother, and May sounded as if she were ready to have a stroke—or all set to give one to someone else.

Skye sprang up and hit her head on the shelf. Flailing backward, she threw her arms in the air, trying to regain her balance, but failed and ended up sprawled on the wooden floor as macaroni rained down on her head like rice on a bride.

Before she was able to get to her feet, May's shouts bounced off the walls of the warehouse. "I know you did this, Cherry Alexander, and you're not getting away with it."

CHAPTER 5

Sift Dry Ingredients Together

As Skye plucked noodles from her cleavage, she toyed with the idea of pretending she hadn't recognized her mother's voice or, even better, that she hadn't heard the screams at all. Which would have been a good plan if, just as Skye became pasta free, another yell didn't rip through the warehouse.

This cry was a wordless screech that somehow sounded more ominous than the ones before, and Skye gave up any idea of remaining uninvolved. Crunching over the dry macaroni, she ran toward May's assigned area.

Bunny followed, peppering her with questions. "Who's Cherry Alexander? Why would she switch salt and sugar? What's May going to do?"

Skye wished she knew. She was afraid May's retaliation might involve plucking poultry and heating up asphalt. Two things May did not tolerate were anyone insulting her children, and anyone messing with her cooking. And as Skye knew from personal experience, rather than forgive and forget, May's specialty was to reprimand and remember.

When Skye reached the Special-Occasion Baking area, she recoiled. Cameras of all descriptions were pointed at the crowd gathered around her mother's stove. May stood in the center of the group waving a wooden spoon in the air. Two of Grandma Sal's employees, Charlie, and Vince were all dancing around her like orderlies at a mental hospital trying to put a straitjacket on a patient.

Another group restrained Cherry. Unfortunately they had not taped her mouth, and she was screaming, "First she steals my secret ingredient, and now she accuses me of sabotage. I demand she be kicked out of the contest."

Skye saw her mother's face go from red to magenta, and hurried forward. Stopping just out of wooden-spoon range, Skye raised her voice. "Mom, put down your weapon."

May sneered. "The only place I'm putting this is up Miss High-and-Mighty's a—"

Skye cut her off. "Just calm down and think. We'll find out who did this."

"I know who did it, and she's standing over there smirking." May pointed the spoon at Cherry, who did indeed have a smug expression on her face.

Before Skye could respond, a sweet female voice managed to project itself over the melee. "Oh, my heavens. What in the world is going on around here?"

The crowd around May and Cherry split open like a cracked egg, and Grandma Sal walked between the two angry women. Skye prayed fervently that no yolks would be broken.

Both May and Cherry tried to explain at once, but Grandma Sal raised a work-roughened hand and pleaded, "One at a time. My hearing's not so good anymore."

Hmm. That was odd. The older woman's ears had seemed to work just fine earlier. Skye thought she saw a roguish twinkle in Grandma Sal's eyes.

Both May and Cherry tried to speak again, and this time there was a quaver in Grandma Sal's voice as she begged, "Please, ladies, don't ruin my contest. If you do, it might be the last one we ever have."

Skye barely stopped herself from snorting. Grandma Sal was certainly laying it on thick, but it looked as if one of the angry women was buying it—at least up to a point.

May put the spoon on the counter and moved toward Grandma Sal. "We wouldn't dream of ruining your wonderful contest."

Grandma Sal clasped May's hands. "Thank you, my dear. That's so sweet of you."

"But . . ." May tightened her grip on the older woman's fingers. "We do have to punish the person who tried to ruin my recipe."

"Of course we do." Grandma Sal maintained her smile as she freed herself from May's grasp. "*If* it was intentional, but I'm sure it was just a mistake." She spoke to the crowd. "One of the reasons we have this trial run the day before the contest is to iron out any kinks, to find the mistakes and make everything perfect for the actual competition."

May narrowed her eyes and opened her mouth, but Grandma Sal gracefully cut her off. "When you are stocking twenty-four kitchens, there are bound to be mistakes, but let me assure you all that there was no malice involved. It was just an error that could happen to anyone."

The crowd broke into applause, and Skye read defeat in May's face. Sighing with relief that the incident had been averted, Skye turned to go.

She got about halfway back to her kitchen when she heard a male voice roar, "Dammit to hell! Who switched my sweet peppers for jalapeños?"

Skye closed her eyes and willed reality to change. If something was about to happen, please let it be Vince or Butch, not Charlie, whose ingredients had been messed with. Vince would grin and make the best of it, and Butch seemed like a laid-back guy, but Charlie would rampage through the warehouse like an angry hippo, chomping anyone who got in his way.

While Skye hesitated, another voice shouted, "My casserole is ruined. Who screwed with my timer?"

Within the next few minutes several other contestants added their complaints to the general din, including Monika Bradley, who had discovered that wheat flour had been substituted for her white rice flour. As she explained to

Grandma Sal, in her case the switch would not only ruin her recipe, but also had the potential to kill her.

Whoever was sabotaging the finalists' recipes had moved from mere mischief to possible manslaughter. The question was—why?

It had taken hours for Grandma Sal's employees to straighten out the chaos. Those whose stations had been messed with had to be soothed, and new ingredients had to be obtained for everyone.

About half of the contestants were still trying to finish their recipes at six o'clock, when Grandma Sal made an announcement. "Due to the dinner being held here at seven this evening, we are asking you all to go home now so we can get the tables set up in time. Because of the technical problems we ran into this afternoon, you will all be allowed in early tomorrow morning to practice your recipe again. Your areas will be available to you from six until nine a.m. At that point the kitchens will be cleaned and restocked, and the contest will start at ten, as previously planned."

There was a smattering of applause, a few grumbles of complaint, and a couple of murmured conversations.

As Skye was putting away the ingredients she had taken out, her mother hurried up to her.

"Aren't you ready yet?" she asked. "I need to get home right away. I just talked your brother into doing my hair for tonight."

Briefly Skye wondered what Vince would do with May's short, wavy hair. Both its length and degree of natural curl precluded any new style Skye could envision, but she knew better than to ask. Hair was a touchy subject with her mother, and for once she pitied her brother, who was May's golden boy 99 percent of the time, but not when her coiffure was concerned.

Careful not to become involved, Skye said, "Go ahead without me. I need to clean up here."

"Can't your runner do that?" May's brows drew together. "Who is she, by the way? I got the middle school Home Ec teacher; isn't that great?"

"Great." Skye was not about to share with her mother that Bunny Reid was her runner. May had taken an unreasonable dislike to Bunny from the moment the redhead had arrived in Scumble River. "Mine's looking for a broom." Skye fervently hoped that Bunny would stay away until May left. May's favorite nickname for Bunny was the Trollop, and that was one of the nicer things she called her. "I'm sure she'll be back to help soon. You go ahead."

"How will you get home if I leave you?"

"Someone will give me a ride." Skye spotted her godfather chatting with someone she couldn't see. She pointed to him. "Uncle Charlie can drive me."

May's gaze followed Skye's finger and she nodded. "Okay. I'll tell him not to leave without you." May kissed Skye on the cheek. "Don't take too long here. You have to get dressed for the dinner, too."

"I won't. See you tonight, Mom."

"Do you want Dad and me to pick you up?"

"No, Wally's taking me."

May walked away shaking her head.

Bunny returned just as Skye finished cleaning up. They'd gathered their belongings and were approaching the warehouse door when two teenagers rushed through it. The boy was well over six feet tall, skinny, and wore horn-rimmed glasses. The girl was nearly his complete opposite—six inches shorter, well rounded, with long, wavy brown hair.

Skye's stomach tightened in concern. What were Justin Boward and Frannie Ryan doing here, and why were they running? Did it have something to do with their personal lives—Justin and Frannie had recently started to go steady—or was it about the student newspaper? Justin and Frannie were the coeditors of the *Scoop* and very competitive in their reporting.

The teens skidded to a stop in front of Skye and Bunny, and Justin said breathlessly, "Xenia is missing, and we think she kidnapped Ashley Yates."

Several questions crowded Skye's lips, but she finally managed to push one out in front of the others. "Why?"

"Because of the lawsuit," Frannie answered. "Xenia was way pissed when she heard Ashley's parents were threatening to sue the paper over the article she wrote."

Xenia's article had examined the politics of popularity, using Ashley as a prime example of the price girls were willing to pay to be one of the "in" crowd. Xenia had listed all the things Ashley had done to both gain and keep her popular status, including having sex with the entire boys' basketball team, one right after the other, in their locker room the night they won the championship.

"How would kidnapping Ashley make it better?" Skye asked before she could stop herself.

Both teens shrugged, and Skye could have slapped herself for asking such a stupid question. No one knew why Xenia did anything. Skye wasn't even sure Xenia did.

Backtracking, Skye asked what she hoped was a better question. "What makes you think Xenia kidnapped Ashley?"

Justin and Frannie looked at each other. Finally he gave an almost imperceptible nod, and Frannie said, "The last post on her blog."

Before Skye could respond, Bunny jumped in. "A blog is like a diary that you write on the computer and let everyone see. All the kids do it."

"I know what a blog is," Skye retorted. "What I can't understand is why anyone would write on one that she had kidnapped someone."

Justin studied his sneakers and mumbled, "She didn't exactly write that, but we put two and two together and figured it out."

"Are you sure you did the math right?"

Frannie joined Justin in his intense interest in his shoe. "We're pretty sure, especially after Xenia's mom called looking for her."

"Why is that?" Skye had never pictured Xenia as a teen who reported her every move to her mom.

Justin explained, "Since we were off school, Xenia and her mom were going into Chicago to see a matinée of this play Xenia really, really wanted to see, then go to this super cool new restaurant for dinner. But she never showed up.

They were supposed to leave their house at eleven this morning, and when Mrs. Craughwell knocked on Xenia's bedroom door to see if she was ready, she didn't answer. Mrs. Craughwell went in and she wasn't there, and she hasn't shown up all day."

"Oh." *Shit!* It sounded as if Scumble River's newest wild child might indeed have added kidnapping to her already long list of criminal acts. For a nanosecond Skye wondered if maybe Xenia herself was the kidnapping victim, but she quickly realized how unlikely that would be. No way would Xenia trust anyone enough to put herself in a position to become a victim.

Still, Skye held out one last hope that neither girl had been kidnapped. "Okay, the big question is whether Ashley is missing or not. Has either of you called her house to check?"

Frannie nodded. "I pretended to be one of her cheerleading friends." The teen's cheeks reddened. "I'm pretty good at imitating voices. Her mom was mad. Said she'd been looking for Ashley all day."

"Okay, so both Xenia and Ashley are missing," Skye acknowledged. "What did you say to Mrs. Yates?"

"Uh." Frannie swallowed hard. "Well, the thing is, I didn't know what to say, so I might have suggested that the cheerleaders had an all-day practice and a slumber party tonight. Which is why I was calling, since I couldn't remember where the party was. And that Ashley might have forgotten to mention it, since it was sort of a last-minute deal."

The muscle under Skye's right eye twitched, but she kept her cool. She reminded herself that Frannie had just been trying to keep things calm until she could talk to an adult she trusted. She wasn't really trying to cover up a crime. "I don't suppose Xenia's blog said where she was keeping her victim or anything useful like that?"

"Not that we could tell." Justin dug in his jeans pocket, pulled out a crumpled piece of paper, and thrust it into Skye's hand. "Here. I printed out the post for you."

"Thanks." Skye smoothed out the sheet and, with Bunny

peering over her shoulder, read; *Crybabies should b careful. If u can't stand the heat, u need 2 b kooled off. Kept on ice. Get my drift?*

Skye felt even worse after reading the brief message. "Sounds like she was planning on stashing Ashley in a freezer somewhere."

"We thought of that," Frannie said, "but where is there a freezer big enough to hold a person, where no one would notice that a frozen cheerleader had been added to their inventory?"

"I don't know." Skye started toward the door again. "But I do know we need to talk to the police."

After extracting a promise from Bunny not to tell anyone about the Xenia/Ashley situation, Skye sent her runner home. Skye didn't like the glint in Bunny's eye as she hurried out the door, but there wasn't much she could do about it.

Next, she found her godfather talking to a petite brunette half his age. At six feet tall, he towered over the woman. They were deep in conversation when Skye interrupted to tell him that Frannie and Justin were driving her home. He acknowledged her with a muttered, "Great," but his gaze never left the woman's face, and before Skye could add anything, he whispered something in the lady's ear that made her giggle and pat his arm.

Having taken care of Bunny and Charlie, Skye led Justin and Frannie out to the parking lot and borrowed Justin's cell phone—one of the few that mysteriously seemed to work anywhere in Scumble River. "Thea? This is Skye."

"Hi, honey. How's the cooking contest going? Your mom is so proud that you and Vince are in it with her." Thea Jones was one of the dispatchers who worked with May.

Thea was a grandmotherly type who knew everyone in town, and Skye acknowledged that there was no way to cut through the social chitchat if she wanted to keep Ashley's disappearance quiet, so she summarized the day's events, ending with, "We just finished, and I'm heading home to change for the dinner, but I wanted to ask Wally something first. Is he around?"

"Sorry, sweetie. He's not here right now. He's probably at home getting ready for your big dinner party."

"Thanks. I'll try him there. Bye." Skye hit the END button before Thea could ask any more questions, grateful she hadn't had to go through the whole "how are you, how's your family, isn't the weather nice" ritual.

While she dialed Wally's home number, Skye said to Frannie, "Start driving toward town."

From the seat of Frannie's father's pickup truck, Skye watched the trees sweeping by as her call went through. When she got Wally's answering machine she tried his cell phone, but he didn't answer that either. She left another urgent message, checked her watch, then said to Frannie, "Head toward my house. He's supposed to pick me up there at quarter to seven, and it's already six thirty."

Justin and Frannie were strangely quiet as they drove. Skye considered questioning them to try to gather additional information about Xenia, but decided to see what Wally thought before she did anything more.

It was only a few minutes to the old Griggs place, which Skye had inherited that past summer. The house was a little isolated, and a lot run-down, but Skye had felt an immediate connection with Alma Griggs, and had been touched when the elderly woman's will revealed she had entrusted Skye with her home.

During the six months Skye had owned the house, she'd been trying to fix it up. After hiring one horrible contractor, she had been lucky to find a great woman who had whipped the outside into wonderful shape. Skye admired the new siding, windows, roof, and sidewalks as Frannie pulled into the driveway.

The instant the truck stopped, Skye jumped out and headed up the steps, pausing on the wraparound porch to dig through her purse for the keys. Justin and Frannie caught up to her as she swung open the front door.

Inside, Skye had had the contractor fix the plumbing and wiring, but she had run out of money before she got to the cosmetic repairs, so she had been trying to do those herself. So far she had managed to paint the entrance hall, parlor, dining room, and kitchen, but the hardwood floors still need refinishing, and the drapes had to be replaced. She hadn't even begun to touch the upstairs, except for removing a loathsome moose head from the wall of the master bedroom.

Now, as she stood in the freshly painted foyer, she tried to decide what to do about the present situation. Should she change into the clothes she had planned to wear for the dinner? Should she even attend the dinner? She had no desire to sit through a formal banquet, but if she didn't May would demand to know why, and that would mean news of Ashley's disappearance would be all over town. Maybe Wally would want her to go to the party just to keep things quiet. If that was so, she'd better get dressed. He was due in less than five minutes and was rarely more than a minute or two late.

Turning to the teens crowded behind her, Skye pointed to the kitchen and said, "Why don't you guys help yourselves to some sodas and snacks while I change? When the doorbell rings, make sure it's Chief Boyd; then let him in. I'll be back in a few minutes."

"What are you changing clothes for?" Justin demanded, looking her up and down.

"Shut up," Frannie hissed, elbowing him in the side. "I'll explain later."

Skye ignored both teens and took the stairs two at a time, shutting the bedroom door behind her. Kicking off her shoes, she wiggled out of her slacks and yanked her blouse over her head. Luckily she had already selected a dress to wear, and she grabbed it from its hanger.

As she pulled it over head and started to shimmy into it, she heard the phone ring. The dress was a straight black sheath, and required some time to get on. Hurrying was not an option, and before she was able to poke her head out of the draped neckline, there were two more rings.

Skye rushed to the phone by her bedside, another improvement she had finally made to the house. Previously the only phone was in the parlor.

Grabbing the receiver, she heard Wally say, "Skye—"

Then an extremely loud buzzing sound interrupted, and she couldn't make out a word.

She shouted into the mouthpiece, "Hang up and call back."

After returning the receiver to its cradle she waited, wondering if this was one of her ghost's latest tricks. She and Wally had just about given up trying to spend any time at Skye's house. It seemed that whenever they started to get intimate, something would short out the power, cause the plumbing to spew like a fountain, or blow up. Secretly— she had never shared this thought with anyone—Skye thought the ghost of the previous owner was behind the mischief.

Mrs. Griggs had taken quite an interest in Skye, and Skye was pretty sure that Mrs. Griggs didn't want Wally around. Skye wasn't sure if that applied to all men she might date or just Wally, since she'd been broken up with Simon before taking ownership of the possessed house.

The phone rang again, but this time when she tried to answer it nothing happened—no voice, no buzzing, just empty air, so she hung up. When it didn't ring again, she tried Wally's home and cell phones, but couldn't reach him on either.

Grinding her teeth, Skye finally gave up and went back to dressing. It took her only a few minutes to finish. She slipped on black patent-leather sling-backs, brushed some bronzer on her face and mascara on her lashes, combed her hair into a smooth pageboy, and stuffed her jewelry into her evening bag to put on later.

Skye looked at her watch as she descended the stairs. It was a few minutes past seven and she hadn't heard a doorbell. Unless the teens had let Wally in before he had even rung the bell, he was late, which wasn't at all like him.

What could be keeping him? Perhaps if she had been able to hear him when he phoned she would know.

CHAPTER 6

Cream, Sugar and Butter

Skye listened in exasperation to Wally's message on her answering machine. "Skye, sugar, what's wrong with your phone? I sure hope you get this. I'm really sorry, but I've had an emergency come up and I can't take you to the dinner." There was a pause and she could hear a muffled voice in the background; then Wally said, "I'll call you tomorrow morning before you leave for the contest." There was silence, but she could tell he hadn't hung up; then he added, "Oh, I almost forgot to tell you, my cell phone's not working. Bye."

"Damn!" Now what was she supposed to do? Skye wished Trixie hadn't gone away for spring break. Come to think of it Trixie had a knack for being away when things at school imploded.

Skye's head felt as if it were about to fly off her shoulders. Did Wally's emergency involve Ashley's disappearance? Clearly he hadn't gotten either of her earlier messages. Should she go to the police station? Should she go to the dinner? Or maybe she'd go to bed and let everyone deal with their own problems. "Shit! Shit! Shit!"

Justin had sidled into the parlor without Skye noticing. "Uh, Ms. D, are you okay?"

"I'm fine." She took a deep breath and forced herself to smile calmly. "Just a little frustrated."

Frannie edged in and stood next to Justin, taking his hand. "Are you mad because Chief Boyd broke your date?"

"No." Skye sank into the sofa, feeling strangely like crying. "I'm upset because I'm not sure what to do."

"You'll think of something," Frannie soothed. "Take a deep breath."

Skye looked at the girl and realized that Frannie had come a long way since she first met her over two years ago. Back then Frannie had been insecure and obsessed with her own problems. Now, as Skye looked into the teen's confident and caring brown eyes, she saw the woman Frannie would become.

"You're right." Skye inhaled and instantly felt a bit calmer. "Thank you."

"So, what are we going to do?" Justin paced in front of the settee. "If Xenia kills Ashley, the superintendent will get rid of the paper for sure."

Skye fought a flicker of irritation at Justin's self-absorption, reminding herself that he was almost a year younger than his girlfriend, and had had a much harder life.

While Frannie had a loving and supportive father, Justin had pretty much raised himself. Mr. Boward was in nearly constant pain and lived from day to day, which had caused Justin's mother to sink further into a depression that rarely allowed her to leave the house.

"There's not a lot I can do until I can reach the chief," Skye said, and stood up. "Maybe the emergency he was talking about was Ashley's disappearance." She turned to Frannie. "When you talked to Mrs. Yates, did you get the impression she was going to call the police?"

"No. Probably not after I made up the story about the cheerleaders having a slumber party."

"Shoot. I had forgotten about that." Skye scooped up the cordless phone and strode into the kitchen. "So she won't be expecting Ashley until sometime tomorrow?"

Frannie nodded.

"Okay. First I'll call the police station and see if Ashley

or Xenia has been reported missing. I doubt Xenia's mom will involve the cops, considering her daughter's history, but I want to make sure."

Skye punched in the nonemergency number for the PD and said, "Thea? It's Skye again. Have you heard from Wally?"

"Isn't he with you?" Thea's voice rose in alarm. "You're both supposed to be at the dinner. Your mom will be real upset if you aren't there."

"I'm on my way. Wally left me a message saying he had an emergency, but I really need to talk to him."

"Sorry, he doesn't have a radio with him and isn't in a squad car. How about his cell?"

"He said it's not working. I guess I'll try his house again." Skye bit her lip, then asked, "By the way, you haven't had any reports about a missing teenager or two, have you?"

"No. Who's missing?" Thea demanded.

"Uh, I'm not sure. Oh, someone's on my other line. Gotta go." Skye hung up, feeling guilty. No one else was phoning. She didn't even have call waiting.

She turned to Justin and Frannie, who had been listening. "Well, that settles that. Mrs. Yates has not called about Ashley, which means I'll have to tell her Frannie was lying."

Both teens protested, but Skye remained firm. As much as she didn't want to risk the student paper, she knew Mrs. Yates had to know the truth. With Wally AWOL, Skye had no choice. She couldn't ask one of the other officers to look for a girl they didn't have an official report on and whose parents had no idea she wasn't where she was supposed to be.

A few minutes later, after reaching Mrs. Yates and explaining Frannie's deception, Skye held the handset away from her ear. Ashley's mom was not taking the news well. Not that Skye had expected her to. Skye made soothing sounds as the woman ranted and raved, and threatened another lawsuit. Just before she hung up, Mrs. Yates said she was phoning the police.

Although Skye was relieved that at least now someone would be looking for Ashley, she still had to bite back a pithy comment or two about parents keeping control of their own children, and not expecting the school to do the parents' jobs for them.

The call to Mrs. Craughwell went even more poorly. She did not believe Xenia was involved and claimed her daughter was in her room as they spoke. Of course, even if Xenia was there, it didn't mean she hadn't kidnapped Ashley earlier and stashed her somewhere. The best Skye could do was make another phone call to the police and leave a message about Xenia's blog entry.

All of this took surprisingly little time. After Skye sent Justin and Frannie home, she looked at her watch and saw it was only seven forty-five. If she left right away, she could still make the dinner. There was nothing else she could do for Ashley or Xenia, and according to the schedule, cocktails were at seven and the food would be served at eight. Skye would be just in time for the soup, which might be soon enough to keep her out of hot water with May.

"Babe, I promise, I'll totally tell her as soon as this contest is over. She'd grease us both if she barneyed because we messed with her mind." A low, smoky male voice drifted over the racks as Skye stepped into the center of the coatroom, an area in the back of the warehouse that had been partitioned off with two folding walls, and furnished with a dozen or so metal frames with poles suspended horizontally between them.

Skye stood in the middle of the rows. She hadn't realized anyone else was in the room until she heard the voice. Should she cough to indicate her presence, or should she just quietly leave? The tricky part would be moving silently among all the dangling hangers.

Before she could decide, a distraught female voice said, "You always have some excuse. I can't go on like this. Either you tell her about us by this Sunday, or I'll tell her."

"No!" the man shouted, then took on a cajoling tone. "Sorry, babe, I didn't want to tell you this, but I can't bail on her. We have an ironclad prenup. She'd get everything, including custody of the baby."

"But what about us?"

Skye cringed, hating to eavesdrop on these future guests of *The Jerry Springer Show*. She took a step backward and froze when she bumped into a rack, causing a tinny clunk.

"Did you hear that?" he demanded.

"Hear what?" the woman asked between sobs.

There was a long moment of silence while Skye fought to remain quiet.

"Guess it was nothing," the man answered, then said, "I'd better get back to the table. We'll dial in on all this tomorrow while the queen's busy cooking. Her Highness will be wondering what's taking me so long. I swear, she even times me when I take a leak."

A soft giggle hiccuped through the tears. "You're so funny, Kyle."

Skye raised an eyebrow. So, half of the amorous couple was Cherry Alexander's husband, Kyle. She wondered who his lover was.

"And you'd better get back before Juanita complains to Cherry about having to do your job and hers too."

"I didn't leave the baby with Juanita."

Ah, the nanny. How clichéd. Skye shook her head. Did every rich father sleep with his child's nanny?

"What?" Suddenly the male voice was no longer cajoling. "Who's watching him?"

"He's in the car."

"By himself?"

"Yes." The girl's voice quavered. "He's in his car seat asleep and the doors are locked."

"You skank!" All traces of Kyle's prior charm had drained away, and his tone was now utterly harsh. "Never, ever leave my son alone again."

"But . . . but, Kyle. What about us?"

"Just get out of here, Larissa. We'll talk later."

It took Skye a moment to realize that the couple would have to come her way to get out of the coat area, and another second to figure out what do. Hoping that their own movement would be blamed for the noise, Skye wedged herself between two racks, pulling the coats in front of her as camouflage. Thank goodness she was wearing black.

Larissa came first. She was crying too hysterically to notice if an armed Roman gladiator popped up in front of her. Kyle was close on the girl's heels, looking straight ahead, nearly pushing the distraught nanny out of his way. Luckily for Skye he was too angry to care who might be around.

Once the couple left, Skye found a hanger, hung up her coat, and smoothed her hair and dress. As she made her way into the large area that had been set with circular tables, she shook her head. She would never have guessed that surfer-dude Kyle would turn into Romeo Kyle, then morph into protective-father Kyle. That scene had sure been an eye-opener.

The tables were packed, and servers were scurrying around delivering bowls of steaming soup, bringing baskets of fragrant bread, and filling glasses with wine. Skye's stomach growled. She hadn't had anything to eat since a BLT six hours ago.

She scanned the chairs, looking for her mother and dad, but couldn't spot them. Finally, one of the servers asked, "Can I help you find your table, ma'am?"

"Are there assigned seats?" Skye was a little surprised, wondering how Grandma Sal's staff had decided who sat with whom.

"Yes, ma'am. Are you a contestant, media, judge, or Grandma Sal's staff?"

"Contestant."

"The contestants are seated two to a table with their guests and their runners and their runners' guests." The young man pointed to a group of twelve tables in the front of the room. "Starting from the right side, the places are arranged alphabetically."

"Thank you." Skye nodded at the server and walked toward the area he indicated.

She found her place at the third table. Her mother and father sat with the middle school Home Ec teacher, whom Skye was acquainted with, and a man Skye assumed was the teacher's husband. On the other side of her parents were two empty seats, and next to the vacant chairs were Bunny and her son, Simon.

Skye paused only a second before turning to leave, but it was a second too long. May saw her before she moved.

As Skye searched her mind for options, she saw her mom stand up, wave her arms, and yell, "Over here!"

What in the world had Vince done to their mother's hair? All the natural curl had been gelled out, and it was plastered to her scalp like a rubber Halloween wig. May looked as if a vat of cooking oil had been poured over her head and left to congeal.

"Why are you so late?" May demanded as Skye slipped into her chair. "You certainly don't look as if you spent the extra time primping."

"Thank you, Mom. You look nice, too." Skye fought to keep the sarcasm out of her voice and to prevent her gaze from drifting to her mother's new 'do. "I'm not late. I just had a rescheduled arrival time."

"You sound like those teenagers you spend too much time with." May's tone was disapproving.

"Hi, everyone." Skye ignored her mother. "Sorry I wasn't here on time."

The others said hello and murmured that her tardiness wasn't a problem.

"I was worried something had happened." May reached up and tucked a stray curl behind her daughter's ear. "What kept you?"

Skye had taken the empty chair nearest her mother, as her other choice was the vacant seat next to Simon. Now she wondered if she had really chosen the lesser of two evils. "A situation with the school newspaper came up, and it took me a little longer to deal with it than I estimated."

"What situation?" May narrowed her eyes.

"Oh, nothing I couldn't refer to someone else."

The others had remained silent through the exchange, but as May paused in her interrogation and Skye sipped a spoonful of soup, Bunny piped up, "Where's your date, Skye?"

Skye closed her eyes and counted to ten. "He had an emergency and had to cancel." Sitting at a table with both Bunny and May was almost like having two mothers to irritate her. It was odd how different the women were, but they could certainly both drive her crazy. Of course, considering how this day was going, all it would take was a short putt.

May dabbed her lips with her napkin. "He seems to have a lot of emergencies popping up lately."

"He is the chief of police." Skye counted to twenty. At this rate she'd be up to hundred before the entrée was served. "He's bound to be occasionally called away."

As usual, Skye's father, Jed, was silent while the women talked, and the other two tablemates appeared determined to appear as if they hadn't heard a word of the discussion.

Skye saw Simon open his mouth, but then close it without speaking.

They all finished their soup, and the server replaced their bowls with salads. May lowered her voice and asked in a hopeful tone, "Are you and Wally breaking up?"

"Not that I know of. Have you heard something?" Skye matched her mother's low volume. "Or is this just wishful thinking on your part?"

"You rush in here an hour late, disheveled and dateless. It's not much of a stretch."

"Everything's fine between us," Skye assured her mother, but wondered herself what was going on. Determined to change the subject, she raised her voice and asked the middle school Home EC teacher, "Barb, what made you decide to volunteer to be a runner?"

"When I didn't final in the contest, I thought maybe seeing the whole process up close and personal would give me a hint about what to enter next year." The stylish brunette leaned forward. "How about you, Bunny? Are you looking for ideas for next year's contest, too?"

"No. I'm not very good in the kitchen." The redhead jerked up her strapless aqua minidress, fluffed her curls, and fluttered her lashes at the teacher's husband. She giggled. "I'm better at keeping the bedroom sizzling. After all, I'm still a hot babe. But now it comes in flashes."

Simon's handsome face reddened, and Skye gave him a sympathetic look that clearly said, *Mothers!*

His hazel eyes softened and he smiled, nodding his head in agreement.

After the entrées were served, and everyone turned to their food, Simon leaned close to Skye and said quietly, "Frannie mentioned that some disgruntled cheerleader's parents are suing the school newspaper. Does that have anything to do with why you were late?"

Skye hadn't intended to let anyone know what had happened, especially before she could talk to Wally, but she found herself nodding.

"Anything I can do to help?" His soothing tenor made Skye relax for the first time since Justin and Frannie had told her about Ashley's disappearance.

"I don't think so, but thanks for offering."

Once they finished their entrées and the tables were cleared, the room was darkened and a masculine voice boomed over the loudspeakers, "We have a special treat for you tonight. Instead of a traditional dessert, our factory has constructed the largest chocolate fountain in the country." A spotlight aimed at the center front of the room flared to life, illuminating a tublike vessel about the circumference of a child's wading pool and nearly as tall as a refrigerator. From its four spouts chocolate flowed in a continual stream.

After a second of silent appreciation, applause and excited chatter broke out among the audience. Flashbulbs went off as newspaper photographers took pictures. Even TV cameramen jockeyed for good shots.

Once the noise and activity decreased, the voice said, "Tables one through four are invited to come up and get your dessert now."

May was the first one out of her seat. From the table near the fountain she piled her plate with slices of banana, small squares of angel food cake, and a small mountain of strawberries.

Simon was behind Skye, and as he made his selections

he murmured to her, "I can think of something I'd rather drizzle chocolate over than this stuff."

Her face flooded with warmth, but she pretended not to have heard him. They had broken up at the end of last summer because she thought he had cheated on her. At the time he had refused to explain himself, and Skye had not learned until Thanksgiving that the woman she had discovered him with was his half sister, not a girlfriend. By then Skye had become involved with Wally, and Simon's explanation involving family secrets was too late.

Since finding out Simon's big secret, she had seen him here and there, but hadn't spent any time with him. Skye considered their relationship over, and she wasn't ready to be just friends. Was Simon saying he felt otherwise? Was he just flattering her or was he intimating that he wanted her back?

Before she could figure out his intentions or decide what to do about them—she really was very happy with Wally—a voice came over the PA system.

Clearly the person speaking didn't mean for the whole place to hear him when he said, "What do you mean, you might not sell Fine Foods? You can't pull out of a deal like this. They'll sue us, you crazy old woman."

Grandma Sal's voice was easily recognizable. "I haven't signed anything, and behavior like this won't get me to. You'd better watch your manners and remember who owns the majority of Fine Foods."

"I've slaved my whole life for this company. You'd better not try to screw me out of my share now."

"It's not your name and face on the products; it's mine, and I have to do what I think is right for both the business and its employees."

"And I have to do what I think is necessary for me. I'm warning you that if you get in my way on this deal, I'll be forced to get rid of you."

CHAPTER 7

Add Egg Yolks

No human being should be forced to get out of bed at five in the morning. Skye stuck an arm out from under the covers and thumped her squealing alarm. She usually woke to the sound of music, or at least a deejay's serene baritone, but she had purposely changed the setting to buzzer, knowing that anything less wouldn't rouse her at this ungodly hour.

May was picking her up at ten to six. She'd insisted they needed the full three hours allotted for practice, and while Skye didn't disagree, she knew her mom hadn't taken into consideration the fact that no amount of preparation would make Skye's cooking edible.

Skye had tried to talk May into meeting her at the factory, intending to arrive later in the morning, but May knew her too well and had vetoed that suggestion. At the time it had seemed too much trouble to argue, but now that she actually had to get up at the crack of dawn, Skye wished she had insisted on driving herself.

It was too late to change things now, and Skye set a new personal record for showering, dressing, and gulping down a cup of Earl Grey tea. She was waiting on the porch when her mother pulled into the driveway. She slid into the passenger side of May's Oldsmobile and slumped back on the seat, closing her eyes.

"Good morning." May chirped. Skye winced.

"Morning," Skye mumbled, refusing to call anything that started this early "good."

"Isn't this a beautiful day?"

"If you like the wind whipping down the plains." Skye squirmed in her seat. "My poor tulips have been stripped of all their petals."

"You sound grumpy." May expertly backed out of the long drive. "What's wrong? Are you sleepy, hungry?"

"No. And I'm not Happy, Dopey, or any of the other Seven Dwarfs either."

"Then what's up?" May ignored Skye's feeble attempt at humor.

"Nothing. I'm fine. You know I'm not a morning person. Just give me a chance to wake up."

May huffed, but was silent for only a few seconds before saying, "Who do you think that was arguing with Grandma Sal over the PA last night?"

Skye forced open one eye. "Who else could it be but her son, Jared?"

"Yep, that's what everyone else I talked to on the phone this morning is thinking too."

It didn't surprise Skye that May had already polled people about the incident. Her mother's group of friends got up before the birds, and had a better communication network than AT&T.

May was silent for another couple of seconds, then changed the subject, a dark look clouding her usual sunny expression. "All I can say is that if Cherry Alexander messes with my ingredients today, I'll make cherries flambé out of her."

"Mom, you don't know that Cherry was behind the salt/sugar mixup."

May ignored Skye's interjection. "Yesterday my cake turned out flat as a training bra. That won't happen again. Today I'll check everything as soon as I get there, and no one will get near my kitchen."

Skye closed both eyes again. "Sounds like a plan, Mom."

Before Skye could doze off again, May commented, "You and Simon seemed to be pretty cozy last night."

Skye shrugged, keeping her eyes shut. Simon was not a subject she was ready to discuss before she was fully awake and armed with all her senses.

May continued, "Barb and her husband commented on how well you two danced together."

Darn! After the dinner the front area had been cleared for dancing. A local band had been hired to provide the music. In a moment of weakness and—Skye might as well admit it—pique at Wally's absence, she had agreed to one waltz with Simon.

Skye shrugged again, then realized she'd better nip May's fantasies in the bud before they grew into Barbie's Dream Wedding. "Simon and I have had a lot of practice dancing together. It doesn't mean a thing. After all, he danced with several of the women present."

"They were all married or old enough to be his mother." May put on her turn signal and slowed down, then eased the big car into the nearly empty factory parking lot.

As soon as May stopped the Olds, Skye leaped out and hurried toward the warehouse entrance. She had to get away from her mother and clear her mind. It was time to become one with the casserole.

May lagged behind, hefting a box and two canvas bags she'd taken from the trunk. Skye watched as her mother struggled under her load. What in the world did she have in the box, not to mention the bags? Grandma Sal's people were providing all the ingredients, pans, and utensils, although they had said it was okay to bring your own.

Skye was torn between giving May a hand and completing her escape. Just as she was about to go back and help, someone dressed in a dirty factory jumpsuit, wearing both a hairnet and a net over the lower half of his face, rushed past May. Skye couldn't hear what her mother said, but the worker stopped, turned around, and took the box from her mom's arms.

Skye's mouth hung open as she saw the person close the

lid of the trunk and allow May to lead the way. Her mother was truly amazing. She could guilt nearly anyone into doing nearly anything.

Smiling, Skye turned back to her original goal, and sprinted the last few steps to the warehouse entrance. As she reached for the handle the door smashed into her. She teetered backward, trying to regain her balance, but before she recovered her uncle Dante rushed out of the building shouting something unintelligible. In the process he slammed into her and she fell onto her derriere.

May was his next victim. Dante hit her like a champion in a belly-bucking contest. The two bags she was carrying flew upward, spreading kitchenware in an impressively large arc. A sudden gust of air caught the lighter articles and carried them away.

The person carrying May's box dropped it and took off running like the space shuttle blasting into orbit.

As Skye struggled to her feet and hurried over to her downed relatives, she wondered if May's helper could out-run the wind. "Are you okay, Mom?"

"I'm fine." May had already gotten to her knees and was retrieving the cooking items from the grass.

"Uncle Dante." Skye squatted down level with the mayor, who was still sitting, stunned, on the sidewalk. "What happened?"

At first his response was gibberish, but finally Skye made out a few words. She heard him say, *woman*, *dead*, and *chocolate*.

The last explained the wet brown stain on Dante's ample shirtfront, but that still left the most important question: Who was dead? Was it Grandma Sal? After all, they had all heard her being threatened by her son last night.

Her heart pounding in alarm, Skye looked around. Her mother hadn't heard Dante's mumblings—she was still picking utensils out of the grass—and no one else was in sight. The guy in the jumpsuit had not returned, and Skye figured he was probably late for work or didn't want to get involved with the crazy people. She checked again, but no one else had materialized, which left her in charge.

She brought her attention back to her uncle and asked, "Who's dead? Are you sure they aren't just hurt? Did you call for help?"

Dante was rubbing at the chocolate on his shirt, muttering something that sounded suspiciously like, "Out, out damn spot," and didn't seem to hear Skye's questions or feel her shaking him.

Deciding that he would be of no help for quite some time, Skye reached around him and unclipped the cell phone from his belt. Dante frowned momentarily, but didn't stop in his stain-removal efforts.

Rising to her feet, she dialed 911. Due to May's absence, the PD was shorthanded and Thea was on duty again, but this time Skye cut off her social chat and said, "Thea, Skye here. We have a problem at the Grandma Sal's factory. Send the police and an ambulance. I'm not sure exactly what the situation is. My witness isn't coherent at the moment."

The dispatcher instantly snapped into professional mode. "Someone will be there in a few minutes. Don't hang up, in case you need help."

"Fine." Skye left the line open, but wanted her hands free. She had no pockets and was afraid that if she put the phone into her tote bag she'd never find it again. Shrugging, she slipped it into her cleavage. The little antenna sticking out from her chest looked a tad strange, but there was nothing normal about this situation.

Skye's mother had finally retrieved all her belongings and noticed that Dante was sitting on the sidewalk in a nearly catatonic state. Now that her whisk was safe and her measuring spoons out of harm's way, May focused on trying to snap her brother out of his stupor, but he still wasn't putting together coherent sentences.

Since Skye was the new Scumble River Police Department psychological consultant, she would no doubt be assigned to debrief her uncle once Wally arrived, but for now she felt that securing the scene of the crime was more important.

She positioned herself in front of the door, determined to keep anyone from entering before the police arrived. Dante's

exit had jammed the door into an open position, and the
wind was blowing debris from the yard inside. She chewed
her lip, wondering if she should close the door.

The longer Skye waited, the more she second-guessed
herself. Maybe she should have checked to see what Dante
was mumbling about before calling 911. What if he'd had a
psychotic break, and there was nothing wrong inside the
building?

Before the police had employed her she would have gone
in and scoped out the situation, but now she felt obligated to
be more restrained and professional.

While she was considering her next move, an earsplitting
scream from just beyond the warehouse doors prodded her
into action, and without thinking Skye rushed inside. As she
ran she dug through her purse until she found the pepper
spray she always carried. Holding the canister at the ready,
she followed the sound of the screams.

Last night the party had taken place in the rear of the
warehouse. Although the tables had been cleared, they were
still arranged as they had been for the dinner, facing the back
wall near the dessert station and dance floor.

As Skye wound her way through the table maze, she saw
that the dance floor was clear, but to her left, standing frozen
by the chocolate fountain, was Diane White, the cookie
blogger. She stood in the famous *Home Alone* pose, hands to
cheeks with mouth and eyes rounded into giant Os.

Looking past the shrieking woman, Skye saw a pair of
five-hundred-dollar Vera Wang sandals sticking up from the
chocolate fountain. They weren't moving. Skye approached
Diane warily, not sure what role the blogger had played in
this particular tragedy. Was she the innocent witness, or was
she the diabolical killer, sneaking back to clean up her
tracks?

Skye was pretty sure the woman in the fountain had been
murdered. Suicide by chocolate or natural death via cocoa
was a bit of a stretch, even for Skye's active imagination.

"Diane, calm down. Everything's fine. The police will be
here any minute." When the blogger continued to shriek,
Skye's palms itched to slap her, but luckily for the finalist

the Scumble River police force arrived, and Skye stepped back and allowed them to handle the hysterical woman.

Wally, gun drawn, raced into the warehouse, followed by Anthony, one of the part-time officers who also had his firearm at the ready. Both men aimed their weapons at Diane, who swallowed a scream in midscreech and promptly began to choke.

Without taking his eyes from the suspect, Wally asked Skye, "Are you okay?"

"I'm fine."

"What about her?" He indicated the coughing woman.

"I heard her start to scream a minute or two ago, which was several minutes after Dante came running out of here covered in chocolate and muttering about a dead woman."

Wally nodded. "Anthony, pat her down, then get her out of here and have the paramedics take a look at her, but don't let her leave."

The officer complied. He didn't find any weapons on the blogger and took her outside.

As soon as they were gone, Wally rushed to Skye and took her in his arms. "Are you sure you're okay?" He smoothed the hair off her forehead. "Thea was hysterical. She said you didn't answer her, and all she could hear on the phone was screaming."

Guiltily Skye reached into her bra and withdrew Dante's cell. "I . . . ah . . . forgot I had it on. Once the yelling started I followed my instincts."

As a pair of EMTs ran in, Skye reluctantly withdrew from the safe haven of Wally's arms. He kissed her on the temple, gave her one last squeeze, and then joined the paramedics at the chocolate fountain.

Suddenly Skye felt dizzy and sank into a nearby chair. Her view was a bit obstructed, but it was clear from the snatches of conversation she heard and the body language of the EMTs that the woman in the fountain was dead.

There was a short argument between Wally and one of the paramedics, who was obviously inexperienced. The newbie wanted to remove the body from the chocolate, but Wally insisted they wait for the coroner.

Skye cringed. It was obvious to her that Wally's legendary patience was growing thin. She could see the irritability on his face and the way his shoulders twitched. Unfortunately the EMT didn't seem to notice, and Skye was afraid that Wally would take a swing at the guy, whose persistent questions were as annoying as a two-year-old demanding a toy at Wal-Mart.

Fortunately, before Wally decided to deck the guy, Simon rushed in, and, as county coroner, took over.

Skye watched Wally step aside and speak into the radio clipped to his shoulder. She guessed he was calling the county crime scene techs. For a while Scumble River couldn't get assistance from the county because the sheriff blamed Skye and Wally for opening an investigation into his conduct on a previous case. But a few weeks ago the old sheriff had finally been removed, and his temporary replacement was a reasonable man who didn't hold a grudge.

A quick glance at her watch told Skye that it was nearly six thirty. She knew it would take at least three-quarters of an hour, maybe more, for the techs to arrive. They were based in Laurel, the county seat, which was forty-five miles of secondary roads away.

Pulling herself together, Skye rose from her seat and walked over to Wally. "Is there anything you want me to do while we wait for the techs to get here?"

"I've called in all off-duty and part-time officers, and they're keeping the perimeter intact and rounding up anybody they find nearby. Luckily only you and your mother were here promptly at six for the practice. The other contestants have been showing up a few at a time, and my officers have been able to stop them at the gate."

"Except for Diane," Skye reminded him. "I wonder when she arrived."

"Good question. May said that you two got here just a few minutes before the mayor came running out." Wally paused until Skye nodded her confirmation. "Dante and the screamer are still not making any sense."

"Do you want me to try to talk to them?"

"Might as well give it a try." Wally nodded toward the

chocolate fountain. "I'd like to know if they saw anything or only stumbled across the body. Ms. White was too clean to have committed the murder—unless she did it naked and then re-dressed."

"Now there's a picture I could have done without." Skye winced.

"Sorry." Wally patted her arm. "We've called for Grandma Sal to come out and identify the body."

"Do you want me to look?" Skye hated to do it, but knew that the sooner they knew who the victim was, the better their chances of solving the case.

"It would be a help, but you don't have to. We can wait." Wally put an arm around her shoulders.

"No, I can do it." Skye gazed into the warm depths of Wally's eyes and gained strength from them.

"Okay." Wally led her to the chocolate fountain.

Simon had laid the victim out on the floor. The rest of the crime scene belonged to the county techs, but the body was the coroner's domain. He was taking a temperature reading to help determine the time of death, and Skye tried not to notice the sharp probe going into the body's liver. Instead she concentrated on the face. She leaned forward and looked closely. As she had suspected from the expensive sandals, the chocolate-covered corpse was Cherry Alexander.

CHAPTER 8

Add Vanilla

"Uncle Dante?" Skye found the mayor sitting on a bench, clutching a gray wool blanket around his shoulders and staring into space.

It wasn't like her uncle to remain on the sidelines—he was too fond of the limelight to wait for someone to seek him out. His normal MO would be to charge into the crime scene, try to order Wally around, and generally make a nuisance of himself. Clearly he wasn't okay.

May sat next to her brother, patting his hand and murmuring soothing words. When Skye approached, May looked up with a worried crease between her eyebrows. "I saw Simon go in. Who's dead? What happened?"

"Cherry Alexander," Skye answered, then wondered if she should have kept that information to herself. "Don't tell anyone else. Treat the info as if you heard it while at work—confidential." Skye answered her mother's last question: "We don't know what happened. How's Dante? Has he said anything?"

"I can't get him to talk. I even tried to get a rise out of him by mentioning that this would probably be the end of the good publicity for Scumble River, but he still didn't respond."

"Have the EMTs looked him over?" Skye didn't see an ambulance in the parking lot.

May shook her head. "They had their hands full with that cookie blogger. She was screaming and twitching and causing all sorts of commotion. I heard they thought she was having a stroke or a seizure or some such thing, so they're transporting her to the hospital."

It crossed Skye's mind that Diane might be putting on an act in order to get away from the cops. "Did Anthony go with her?" It would be a lot easier to escape from the hospital than from the police station.

"I think so." May's voice was taut, her fingers twisted in a knot. "They asked if Dante was okay, and I said he wasn't hurt, so they gave me a blanket for him and then left. Did I do something wrong?"

"I don't know." Skye squatted in front of her uncle and studied him closely. His breath was coming in small, fast gasps, his skin was blotchy, and the area around his mouth had a bluish cast. Skye chewed her lip, then handed Dante's cell phone to May. "Mom, you'd better ask for another ambulance. I think he's going into shock."

May fumbled a little, but eventually managed to turn the phone on and dial. "Thea? It's May. We need another ambulance at Grandma Sal's."

Once Skye was sure May was making the call, she tuned out her mother's voice and focused on her uncle. "Dante, everything is okay now. The police are here and you're safe." She pressed him back so that he was lying on the bench and elevated his feet by putting them on May's box of utensils. "Just forget what you saw and relax." She kept her voice a hypnotic tone as she loosened his shoelaces, belt, and tie. "Think of your favorite place."

Dante didn't react. He appeared to be conscious, but completely unresponsive.

"The ambulance from Brooklyn is on its way," May reported.

"Good." Skye unbuttoned Dante's shirt, then without looking away asked May, "Do you have a gallon-size Ziploc? One that hasn't been used?"

"Yes." May dug through the canvas bags next to the bench, found the unopened box, and extracted a bag. "Here's a brand-new one."

"Hold it open," Skye instructed as she eased her uncle's shirt off him and carefully put it into the bag. "Close it up and don't let it out of your sight."

May nodded, closed it, then stared at the plastic sack as if it might sprout wings and fly away.

Skye turned back to her uncle, and as she pulled the blanket higher around Dante's shoulders she noticed that his undershirt was soiled, too, and this spot didn't look like chocolate. She lifted the white cotton tee and examined his upper torso; there was a jagged wound smeared with dried blood just above his belly button. The chocolate on the front of his outer shirt had masked the bloodstain. Dante had been stabbed!

Skye was torn between staying with her uncle and finding Wally to report this new development, but before she could decide she heard an ambulance siren. In minutes a man and woman rushed over to them and began issuing orders and firing questions.

As Dante was being wheeled away, he suddenly became alert and grabbed Skye's hand, saying, "Don't let them cancel the contest. Promise me you'll make Grandma Sal keep it going."

She was saved from answering when the EMTs lifted the gurney into the ambulance.

"Here, take this." Skye's mother shoved the Ziploc bag containing Dante's shirt into her daughter's hands. "I'm going with him." May grabbed her purse and hurriedly climbed in beside her brother, clutching his cell phone and muttering, "I need to call Olive and Hugh, and you need to get hold of your father." She aimed the last bit at Skye.

"No!" Skye swallowed back a frustrated shriek. "Call Olive, but don't tell her what happened. Just say that Dante's injured and going to the hospital. Do *not* say anything else and do *not* call anyone else."

May nodded distractedly, and Skye wondered if her mother had even heard her. Since May was armed with a cell phone and knew how to use it, Skye decided she needed to fill in Wally ASAP, or the news of Dante's wound would be all over Scumble River before the chief of police even knew about it. Wally had been a little cranky lately, and Skye didn't think being scooped by the town gossips would improve his mood.

Skye passed Simon and his assistant, Xavier Ryan, wheeling a gurney bearing a black body bag down the sidewalk toward the parking lot. She nodded to both men, but kept walking.

While she had been with her uncle the county crime scene officers had arrived, and the warehouse was buzzing with voices and activity. She found a tech she knew and handed him Dante's shirt, explaining how it came to be in her possession. He put the Ziploc into his own evidence bag, noting the information she had given him on the outside.

Circling the crime scene, Skye made her way over to the table in the rear corner of the dining area, where Wally was seated, talking to Grandma Sal and Jared. JJ and Brandon were at a table in the opposite corner of the room. Both young men had cell phones pressed to their ears, but neither seemed to be having much luck with reception as they took turns yelling, "What? Say that again. No, I said dead, not bread."

Skye caught Wally's eye, then made a questioning face. Should she join them or wait somewhere else? He nodded and indicated a chair next to him.

Skye sat down, and Wally introduced her. "This is Ms. Denison, the psychological consultant for our police department."

Grandma Sal smiled. "You're also one of our finalists. Right?"

"Yes, ma'am."

"Then maybe you can help me convince my boy here that the contest must go on."

Skye was caught by surprise. That was the last thing she had expected to hear the older woman say. "Well, I hadn't given it much thought." In fact, she had figured that Grandma Sal would be horrified by the murder, and would want to put as much distance between it and her company as possible.

Grandma Sal's son spoke up before Skye could say more. "Going on with the contest would be disrespectful to Ms. Alexander, and put an undue burden on the rest of the contestants. We certainly can't expect them to do their best under these conditions."

Wally looked at Skye. "What do you think? The techs say they'll be done by this afternoon, and I would like to keep everyone together until we figure out what happened here. If we cancel the contest, all the participants will scatter. I can't order that many people to stay put. Their lawyers would be all over me."

"I think the challenge should go on, for several reasons." Skye paused to gather her thoughts. "First, as you say, it's better for the investigation if everyone stays around. Second, it isn't really fair to the finalists who have worked so hard to get here to have it canceled. And third, going on with the contest will provide some closure to the people involved. Perhaps you could even give out an extra prize, the Cherry Alexander Award for something or other."

"Perfect." Grandma Sal clapped her hands. "We'll push everything back a day. I'm sure no one will mind sticking around an extra twenty-four hours." She turned to her son. "Jared, you and the boys make sure everyone gets the word that we're going ahead, and the cooking starts at ten a.m. tomorrow. You can use the phones at the factory, and I'll meet you there when I'm done here."

Her son shook his head, but stood up and walked over to JJ and Brandon. Neither of the "boys" looked pleased with Jared's news, but both followed him out the door.

Wally asked Grandma Sal a few more questions, then rose and held out his hand. "Thank you for your cooperation."

Grandma Sal shook Wally's hand, nodded to Skye, then headed toward the exit.

As soon as Grandma Sal was out of sight, Skye said, "We need to talk."

He picked up his pen. "Shoot."

"When I went out to check on Dante, I found a stab wound on his stomach. He's on his way to the hospital."

"Son of a bi . . . !" Wally stammered to a stop. His jaw worked for a while, but he finally said, "What happened?"

"He's in shock and not able to communicate, except to order me to make sure the contest goes on."

"He and Grandma Sal are two of a kind."

Skye shook her head. "Let's just hope they aren't a 'dying' breed."

"So, he didn't mention that he'd been stabbed, and you have no idea how he got the wound?"

"That pretty much describes the situation."

"Any guesses?"

"It depends." Skye shrugged. "We arrived here at six o'clock on the dot, and Dante came running out of the warehouse maybe thirty seconds later. Was Simon able to give you a time of death for Cherry?"

Wally consulted his notes. "Reid said the body temp was ninety-seven-point-four. Bodies cool at about one and a half degree per hour, and she was one-point-two degrees below normal. Which means she could have been killed just a few minutes before you were knocked over by Dante."

"I take it that the chocolate fountain wasn't heated at the time?"

"No."

"But then"—Skye narrowed her eyes—"why wasn't the chocolate hard?" She had noticed it was in liquid form when she was trying to calm down Diane.

"Grandma Sal said the fountain chocolate is like the syrup you pour over ice cream. It never solidifies."

"Okay, then it's my guess that Dante wrestled with the killer and was cut by him or her. Was Cherry stabbed or drowned or both?"

"The only injury Reid found was at her hairline above her right eye. There were lacerations and a depression in the skull, indicating she had been hit on the head with something like a hammer or mallet." Wally tapped the table with his pen. "Unfortunately, Reid can't say yet if it was the blow or the chocolate that killed her."

"Why not?"

"Drowning is a diagnosis of exclusion. If the medical examiner doesn't find any other cause and there's fluid in her lungs, he'll call it a drowning."

"Maybe once they wash the body they'll be able to tell us more. Hard to see bruising while she's covered with chocolate."

"Yep. Let's hope Reid missed something." Wally pushed back his chair. "I guess I'd better get to Laurel Hospital and see if the mayor is talking yet."

Skye followed him as he headed out and waited as he had a word with the techs and his officers, but as he reached his squad car she put a hand on his arm and said, "We really need to talk. Did you get my message about Ashley Yates's disappearance?"

"Yes. Quirk moved on it last night. He didn't find her, but her mother admitted that this isn't the first time Ashley has gone missing for a couple of days."

"Really?" *Gee*. What a shock that Mrs. Yates hadn't mentioned that to Skye, instead blaming the school. "But how about Xenia and her blog?"

"Xenia was home, just like her mother claimed, but— surprise, surprise—when Quirk questioned her she claimed the blog wasn't hers, and it has since disappeared into cyberspace." Wally's expression showed his disbelief. "Quirk's got the county computer expert looking into that."

"Good. Xenia bragged to the other kids about the blog, so I'm sure she's lying about it not being hers. Not to mention she's quite a hacker, which is how she got her story about Ashley into the newspaper without Trixie or me catching it. So she wouldn't have any trouble getting rid of the blog if she wanted to." Skye let go of Wally's arm. "Was that why you couldn't make the dinner last night? Was that the emergency you mentioned?"

He shook his head, the expression on his face strained. "No. That was something else."

She opened her mouth to ask what, but Wally was already sliding into the driver's seat and closing the door.

He rolled the window down and, as he started the engine,

said, "I don't have time to get into it right now. Are you free tonight?"

She nodded, a feeling of alarm making her chest hurt. What was going on? Was he breaking up with her?

"Okay. Unless something else happens I'll be at your place around seven, and I'll bring supper." He stuck his arm out the window and took her hand, raising it to his mouth for a kiss.

The touch of his lips sent a flame into the pit of her stomach, and the warm expression in his brown eyes curled around her heart.

She sensed his reluctance to let go, but when he did he said, "Everything will be fine. I promise."

As Skye watched the cruiser drive away, it occurred to her that Wally had said he'd come to her house. That was odd. Although they'd never voiced their concern, it seemed that every time she and Wally even touched each other anywhere in her house, something exploded or caught on fire or flooded. Since Thanksgiving they'd been spending most of their time together at his house.

Why did he suddenly want to meet at her house? She frowned. Was Wally planning to tell her something that would end their relationship for good, and so had no intention of touching her? She blinked back a tear and forced herself to think positive thoughts.

When Skye finally turned away, she realized that she needed a ride. Her mom had left with Dante, taking the keys to her car with her. And all newcomers were being turned away at the factory's gates, which were being monitored by the police.

Shoot. She'd have to go over to the plant, ask to use a phone, and get someone to pick her up. But who? She had no idea where Uncle Charlie or Vince was, since they were also contestants and would have been turned away at the gate a couple of hours ago. Her dad refused to answer the phone.

Skye thought for a moment. Heck, anyone she called for a ride would expect her to tell them everything that was going on, which she couldn't do. Maybe her best bet was to go to the gate and see if anyone she knew turned up. It would be easier to be evasive with an acquaintance than a friend.

Slinging her tote bag over her shoulder, she started toward the main road, about a quarter mile away. She kept to the pavement, not wanting to get her new running shoes dirty. About halfway there she noticed a swathe of white caught in the bushes that lined the driveway. It was probably just garbage, but something about it seemed familiar.

She stepped closer, trying to avoid the mud. Just as she reached out to touch it, it fluttered in the wind, and Skye realized she was staring at a discarded factory jumpsuit that was smeared with chocolate, and maybe blood. *Oh, shit.* This must belong to the man she and May saw running in the parking lot that morning. Darn. In all the confusion she'd forgotten to tell Wally about the guy—and he *could* be the killer!

What to do now? Better to let the techs get it, but did she dare leave it? What if it blew away? Okay, she'd wait until someone came in or out, and ask them to get a tech. This kind of situation made her wish for a cell phone.

Twenty minutes later her plan to wait didn't seem like such a good idea. Finally an elegant black Lincoln limousine coming from the direction of the factory purred into view. Skye waved it to a stop, and leaned in as the passenger window eased down. Inside were Grandma Sal, Jared, JJ, and Brandon.

Skye explained her dilemma and asked them to go back and get a crime scene tech. After a bit of an argument as to whether it would be faster to call the Scumble River PD and wait for the message to be conveyed to Wally, or just to drive back the quarter mile, driving back won.

That decision led to a discussion about who should do what. In the end Brandon and JJ got out of the car to stay with Skye while Jared and his mother were driven back for the tech.

While they waited Skye tried to make conversation. "Do you both work for the family business?"

JJ, the pudgy, blue-eyed blond, ducked his head shyly. "I'm Grandma's assistant."

"Where'd you go to school?"

"I graduated from Loyola a year ago with a degree in business."

"Good school." Skye turned to the dark-haired one. "How about you, Brandon?"

"I'm the head of the company's legal department."

"Does that mean you do *all* the legal work for the company?"

"No." Brandon smirked. "I supervise the people who do it."

"My, you seem so young for such a responsible position."

"Yes. Pays to have family connections. Right, JJ?"

The young man nodded.

Skye nodded too, having benefited from nepotism herself when Uncle Charlie got her the school psych job in Scumble River. Still, she'd bet JJ was making five times what she did, and Brandon probably made ten times her salary.

Skye was uncomfortably aware that they were standing in silence. Neither young man seemed able—or willing—to chat.

She searched for something more to say, wishing the tech would arrive. "Sounds like you're both tried-and-true Chicagoans. Do you get out to the Scumble River factory very often?"

"We work mostly out of the Chicago building." JJ stared at his shoes. "Grandma comes out here a lot, and she insists we maintain duplicate offices for all the departments here, but they're rarely used."

"Why does she do it, then?" Skye asked, intrigued at the way big business was run compared to the school, where she was lucky to have a single cramped office, let alone a spare one.

"Grandma says she feels closer to Grandpa here than anywhere else," JJ answered.

Brandon rolled his eyes. "She gets to be the queen bee out here. That's why she likes it."

Skye sighed with relief as the unmarked county car

pulled up, followed closely by the Fines' limo. Skye showed the tech what she had found. She was about to explain that someone wearing a factory jumpsuit had been running past the warehouse that morning, but something stopped her and she decided to tell Wally first.

The Fines offered her a ride home, and she gratefully accepted. As she sat cradled in the soft leather seat of the luxury car, she wondered what it would be like to know that you were going to inherit millions and millions of dollars. Of course, everyone said that money couldn't buy happiness. Still, she might enjoy the chance to see for herself.

CHAPTER 9

Slowly Add Dry Mixture to Creamed

Skye wasn't surprised to find several messages on her answering machine when she got home. Most of the callers wanted to know what had happened, and a couple asked how Dante was, but the one she returned immediately was from Frannie, who had called to ask if Ashley had been found.

Skye cradled the receiver between her shoulder and ear so she could change into jeans and a sweatshirt as she phoned the teen. There was no answer at Frannie's house, and Skye was in the process of looking up Justin's cell number when her doorbell rang.

She hurried down the stairs, looked out the peephole, and opened the door. "I was just calling you."

Frannie and Justin stood on her welcome mat. Frannie looked upset, and Justin's expression said that he was itching to punch something really, really hard really, really soon.

"What's up?" Skye ushered them inside and steered them toward the kitchen.

Frannie flung herself in the chair Skye offered, but Justin ignored the proffered seat and paced.

Skye raised an eyebrow, then ducked her head into the refrigerator to hide her expression. As she gathered meat, cheese, and condiments she asked, "Are you hungry? I'm starving. That's the problem with getting up at five a.m.—you're ready for lunch by ten."

Frannie giggled politely, but then drooped back into her original dejected posture.

Justin sneered and kept pacing.

Skye knew from past experience that Justin wanted her to beg him to talk. She also knew that if she did, he would close up tighter than a shrink-wrapped CD case.

Instead she asked, "So, who wants a snack?"

Frannie's well-mannered, "No, thank you," was a sharp contrast to Justin's negative growl.

Skye shrugged and assembled a sandwich. She was just cutting it on the diagonal, because even TV chef Alton Brown said sandwiches tasted better that way, when Bingo sauntered into the kitchen.

The cat had an uncanny ability to appear when food was being prepared or eaten. He could be anywhere in the house, from the attic to the basement, and still manage to arrive before Skye could take the first bite.

This time Bingo ignored Skye and her sandwich, walked over to where Justin was pacing, and started doing figure eights between his ankles.

Skye watched carefully while pretending to be engrossed with shaking potato chips into a bowl. Justin had come a long way from the angry and depressed eighth grader she had originally seen for counseling, but she still wasn't sure he wouldn't lash out, given the right circumstances.

At first the teen snarled at the feline, but Bingo ignored him and revved up his purrs to jet-engine volume. Finally Justin stopped moving, and the cat immediately sat down on his feet, looking up at him with a questioning meow.

Skye took a quick peek at Frannie, who had straightened and was staring with her mouth slightly open.

The scraping of a chair on linoleum brought Skye's attention back to the boy and the cat. Justin was sitting with Bingo on his lap. The teen's expression was still angry, but his shoulders had relaxed and his hand rested lightly on the cat's soft black fur.

Skye nonchalantly made her way to the table, putting the bowl of chips in the center and sitting down with her plate. Just before taking a bite she asked again, "What's up?"

Frannie glanced at Justin, who shrugged and kept petting the cat.

Slumping once again, Frannie sighed and said, "It's Xenia."

Skye's throat tightened, but she forced herself to say lightly, "What about her?"

"She's being a real bitch," Justin blurted out.

"In what way?" Skye wanted to ask how being a bitch was new behavior for the girl, but controlled the urge. She couldn't say that about one student to another, no matter how great the temptation or accurate the observation.

Frannie took a chip and crumbled it in front of her. "She's claiming that she didn't write that blog, and is acting like we betrayed her by even thinking she had kidnapped Ashley. She's turned a bunch of the kids on the newspaper staff against us."

Ah. Skye nodded her understanding. Both Frannie and Justin had had friendship issues in the past. Neither had been accepted by the "in" crowd, and they had gotten to the point of forming their own circle of friends only within the last couple of years. Add to this that their group consisted of the other newspaper kids, and Xenia's duplicity took on a whole new meaning.

Before Xenia's arrival in the fall, Frannie and Justin had been the undisputed leaders of that crowd, but Xenia had challenged them at every turn for that position.

Justin broke off a piece of potato chip and offered it to Bingo, who sniffed, took a delicate lick, then regally accepted the offering.

Skye took the opportunity to swallow before saying, "When the truth comes out the kids will see who their real friends are. Xenia has a lot of charisma, but it isn't something that can sustain a relationship for long."

Frannie nodded. "That's true. Remember, she tried to get everyone on her side when she first came here, but it didn't last long. This is just another lame attempt to be elected editor next year."

"Easy for you to say." Justin shook his head. "You'll be away at college next year. I'll be the one stuck with her."

Skye's internal warning bell went off. This was the first time either Frannie or Justin had acknowledged that Frannie would be leaving next fall, and the pair would be separated.

She stole a peek at Frannie, who swallowed a couple of times before saying, "Maybe you and Xenia will team up and not miss me at all."

Justin scowled but didn't verbalize his reply.

Finishing the last bite of her sandwich, Skye pushed the plate away. "You do realize that Mrs. Frayne and I have to approve whoever is elected student editor?"

"You wouldn't say someone couldn't if he or she was elected, would you?" Justin asked.

"In a flash, if we thought they'd cause trouble." Skye poured three glasses of Diet Coke and put one in front of each teen, keeping the third for herself. "But that's next year, and a lot can happen between now and then. So, any idea where we can look for Ashley? Or did you both forget she's still missing?"

"I didn't forget, but there's nothing I can do about her, and it's not as if we were her pals or anything." Frannie shook her head. "When she came into the newspaper office to complain about Xenia's article, she looked right through me. Then, when she thought she could use me, she tried to pretend we were best friends. So I asked her my name, and she didn't have a clue. Heck. We've been in classes together since third grade."

"Yeah." Justin nodded his agreement. "Ashley thinks she's such hot shit, but she only stinks."

In a sympathetic but firm tone, Skye said, "Be that as it may, we can't let Ashley get hurt just because we don't like her. It's our duty as decent people to help find her if we can."

Justin shrugged. "Whatever."

Frannie snorted.

Skye took that as agreement. "Let's start with the blog message you showed me. Maybe I'm not reading it correctly. Let's see if your interpretation is any different from mine." She grabbed a couple of legal pads and a few pens from the junk drawer and reseated herself at the table. "The message read: 'Crybabies should be careful. If you can't stand the heat, you need to be cooled off. Kept on ice. Get my drift?' Right?"

Both teens nodded.

"Okay. Is there any other meaning to the word *crybabies*, beside whiner or complainer?"

"The kids use it to mean tattletale, but that's sort of the same thing," Justin offered.

"Has anyone told on someone lately?"

"No." Frannie frowned. "No one I can think of." She looked at Justin, who shook his head.

"Any ideas on what the blogger meant by the next section?" Skye underlined it with her pen.

"Just, if you can't stand the problems you've caused, you should fix things." On her scratch pad, Frannie doodled monsters with huge open mouths and pointy fangs.

"How about the 'cooled off and kept on ice' part?"

Justin looked away, then muttered, "Some of the wannabe gang kids use that term to mean kill and get rid of the body, but I think Xenia might mean it more like keeping Ashley away from her friends until she cools off and stops her parents and their lawyer from harassing the paper."

Skye's breath had gone out with a whoosh when Justin mentioned murder, but she was able to inhale by the time he finished his thought. "And the last bit? Anything with the word *drift*?"

Both kids shook their heads.

"Have you had any ideas since yesterday about where Xenia might be keeping Ashley?"

More head shakes; then Frannie added, "We've looked in all the places we knew that either of them hang out."

"We even checked the school—you know, like the cafeteria's freezer and the pantry, and the closets and lockers—in case she was hiding her in plain sight." Justin leaned forward, and Bingo jumped off his lap with an annoyed yowl.

"Ashley pretty much hung out with the cheerleaders, and

they pretty much hung out at each other's houses during the winter and at the rec club beach during the summer." Frannie put her hand down to pet the cat, but he stalked away.

"Where would one teenager hide another?" Skye muttered almost to herself. "It would have to be either completely isolated, like a hunting cabin, or a place with so many people going back and forth that no one would notice a couple more."

"Xenia is new in town. She doesn't have any uncles or cousins around here with shacks in the woods," Frannie pointed out.

"Right, so it's got to be the other choice." Skye and the teens were silent, thinking. Finally she said, "I'll call Officer Quirk and see if he's had any luck."

It took her a while to track Quirk down, but she finally got through to him. "Roy, this is Skye. I'm calling about Ashley Yates. Is she still missing?"

"Ten-four. Parents have not reported her return."

"I've been going over the blog message with a couple of my students, and we wondered if Xenia had access to any hunting cabins or fishing shacks." Skye wanted to double-check before crossing that possibility off her list.

"That's a negative. And we've searched the school and both the vic's and the suspect's garages."

"Any other ideas?"

"No, we put out an AMBER Alert right away, but there haven't been any legitimate tips."

"Thanks, Roy." Skye didn't want to keep him any longer, knowing how busy he'd be with the morning's murder.

She relayed her conversation to Frannie and Justin, who remained quiet.

Finally she stood up and said, "Sorry, guys, but I have to get ready for an appointment, so you'll need to be going."

The teens shuffled to their feet and headed toward the front door. Skye heard Justin whisper the word *date* to Frannie, who giggled.

Once the kids were gone, Skye phoned the hospital to see how her uncle was faring.

Her mother was put on the phone "Uncle Dante is fine.

He lost some blood and is a little shocky, but the wound was superficial."

"That's a relief." Skye hadn't realized until just then how worried she'd been about her uncle. "Did he say how it happened?"

"No. Wally's been trying to get him to make sense, but no luck. The doctors say Dante should be back to normal in a couple of hours."

"Okay. Thanks, Mom." Skye looked at her watch as she hung up. It wasn't even noon yet. She had seven hours before Wally was supposed to show up. She could probably finish painting the sunroom. And maybe as she painted, an idea about Ashley's whereabouts might pop into her head.

By the time she spread the drop cloths, taped the windows, and picked up a brush, she was feeling calmer. Skye loved the delicate moss green color she had chosen for the walls. She couldn't wait until the painting was finished and she could have the new hardwood flooring laid and the floral window treatments hung.

She painted in contented silence, not even putting on a radio, letting her mind wander from mystery to mystery. Who had killed Cherry Alexander and why? Where had Xenia hidden Ashley, and how had she managed to subdue the cheerleader? What did Wally have to tell her, and why at her house instead of his, their usual meeting place?

Hmm. If the body had been Grandma Sal, after that argument that went out over the PA system last night, Skye would have thought her son did her in. But there was no way Cherry could have been mistaken for Grandma Sal.

What did she know about Cherry? She was self-centered, annoying, and married to a surfer dude who was boinking Mary Poppins. All of that certainly gave the husband and the nanny motive.

Skye got down from the ladder, balanced the brush across the open paint can, and grabbed a pen and paper from the end table. She made a note of her thoughts about Kyle and Larissa.

While she was at it, she added the guy in the soiled

jumpsuit who had helped May that morning. Who was he, and what was on his clothes?

This time when Skye got back to painting, Xenia and Ashley popped into her mind. Had Xenia drugged Ashley? But surely someone would notice one teenage girl hauling an unconscious friend around. Especially since Xenia's preferred mode of attire was gothic-punk sex kitten.

Was there any way Xenia could have persuaded or tricked Ashley into going with her? But what did Xenia have that Ashley would want? Certainly not her spiked dog collar or stiletto granny boots.

Okay, forget how; concentrate on where. Skye paused to move the ladder, then picked up where she had left off. Where? It took several minutes, but suddenly an idea came to her mind. Could "kept on ice" equate to ice cream?

The local soft-serve drive-in, the Dairy Kastle, closed at the end of September and didn't unbolt its wooden shutters until the beginning of May. Surely they would have a freezer, even if it wasn't running.

As Skye finished the last wall and put away her equipment, the idea of Xenia keeping Ashley at the Dairy Kastle grew stronger and stronger. Xenia wouldn't hesitate to break into a locked building. The drive-in was on the edge of town, and the gas station that was next to it was out of business, so Ashley could scream her head off and no one would hear. Yes, Xenia could be hiding Ashley at the Dairy Kastle.

Skye hurried to the parlor and grabbed the phone, dialing as she ran upstairs. *Shit!* Quirk was still at the warehouse questioning suspects, Wally was in Laurel informing Cherry's husband of her death, and the dispatcher couldn't help her contact either one. Thea said that there was no officer at the police station at that moment, and asked whether it was an emergency, or if Skye would like to leave a message.

Skye wanted to declare it an emergency, but somehow couldn't bring herself to do so. After asking Thea to tell Quirk to call her, she tried to let the idea go, but couldn't.

She looked at the clock. It had taken her a little over five hours to finish the sunroom and talk to Thea at the PD, so she still had two hours until Wally was due. She'd check out the Dairy Kastle herself.

Should she get ready for their date first or go look first? Look first. If Ashley was there it wasn't fair to keep the girl locked up any longer than necessary. Besides, Skye might get dirty if she had to smash down a door or something. Good thing she hadn't gotten paint all over herself.

Considering that she might have to break through a lock, she gathered a hammer, screwdriver, and flashlight from her basement workbench, then grabbed her keys and coat and took off.

At the edge of town most of the businesses were closed, and not just for the winter. Many buildings had been razed, but there were enough deserted relics left intact to make the area creepy.

Skye parked nearest the back entrance of the drive-in and got out of the car. She shivered despite the warmth of her wool pea jacket. The door was locked, not that she had expected anything else. Still, it would have seemed silly not to try.

She used the handle of the screwdriver to knock, calling, "Ashley, are you in there?"

Silence.

Skye knocked harder and yelled again.

Maybe the teen was gagged. "Ashley, if you can hear me, make some noise."

Nothing.

Skye listened intently; still no sound. Okay, what if she couldn't move? What if she was unconscious? But breaking down a door based on nothing but a hunch was not a good thing. She'd better wait and talk to Wally or Quirk.

Turning, she took a step toward her car. Suddenly she heard a rattle and dashed back to the building. She put her ear to the cold metal. Nothing. Nothing. Then she heard it again: a distinctive rattling sound. If that was Ashley, it would be unconscionable to leave her locked up for one more minute.

The lock was a dead bolt—nothing a credit card would open. There had to be another way in. She circled the building and discovered that the front serving windows were covered with wooden shutters nailed on in four places.

Moments later, using the claw end of her hammer and working patiently, Skye lifted off one of the wooden rectangles. The darkness inside was too deep to penetrate even with her flashlight, so she hoisted herself up on the metal counter and swung her legs over the other side.

She slid down to the floor and called reassuringly, "Ashley, it's Ms. Denison. Don't be afraid. I'm here to rescue you."

The only response to her announcement was another rattle. She thumbed on her flashlight and aimed it toward the sound. There in the back of the twelve-by-twelve space, between cans of strawberry sauce and buckets of peanuts, two glowing yellow eyes stared at Skye.

She screamed, scrambled back over the counter, and ran for her life.

CHAPTER 10

Mix until Smooth

Skye checked her watch as she tore up the stairs. Less than a half hour before Wally was due to arrive. Shedding her clothes in the middle of her bedroom floor, she dashed into the bathroom and turned on the shower.

Even with the new plumbing it took forever for the water to get hot, and as she waited the humiliating memory of her latest escapade nagged at her. What would Wally say when she told him she had broken into the Dairy Kastle to save Ashley, who wasn't there, then had been frightened away by a rat?

She knew exactly what Simon would say. His lecture would begin with the consequences of breaking and entering, segue to the fact that she had not found Ashley, and end with a scientific explanation as to why she couldn't possibly have seen a rat. He would have coolly pointed out that the rodent she'd had eye-to-eye contact with was merely a harmless field mouse. All of which made her glad she wasn't dating him anymore.

But the million-dollar question: Would Wally react any better? A couple of months ago she would have said yes, but lately he'd been behaving oddly.

Skye hurried through her shower, debating whether she really even had to tell him about her little adventure. She had returned to the drive-in and nailed back the shutter, so she doubted anyone would know the building had been broken into. Maybe she could "forget" to mention how she had spent the latter part of her afternoon.

As she blew her hair dry, a little voice nagged at her, insisting that if this was the man she might want to spend the rest of her life with, keeping secrets from him was not a good idea. Even though the voice sounded a lot like her mother's, she listened anyway.

This meant she had to figure out the best way of imparting the news, and time was running out. As she applied bronzer and mascara, she rehearsed how she would tell Wally about her afternoon activities.

She finished polishing her speech as she wiggled into a pair of black jeans, then chose a baby pink off-the-shoulder knit top that displayed her cleavage to its full advantage. She hoped her décolletage would sweeten her words, or at least take the sting out of them.

The doorbell rang as she was slipping on pink Skechers, but she took time to put on lipstick and take one last glance in the mirror before going to answer it. Wally's recent history of breaking dates suggested he was taking her for granted lately. It wouldn't hurt him to cool his heels on her front porch for a few minutes.

After passing her own inspection, Skye made her way downstairs, took a quick look out the peephole, and opened the door. Her welcoming smile faded as she noted that Wally was in uniform. That he hadn't changed meant either he was still on duty or had been so busy he couldn't get home before coming over. Either scenario did not bode well for a relaxing evening.

At least he held a pizza box. She was starving, and the only ingredients she had on hand were those that went into her contest entry. And she was pretty sure they were both sick and tired of Chicken Supreme.

Wally silently handed Skye the pizza, strode through the door, and shed his jacket. He hung it and his gun belt on the foyer's coatrack, then took the pizza back and tossed it on the table.

Finally he turned toward her and said, "It seems like years since we've spent more than five minutes together." Without waiting for her response, he swept her into his arms and added in a lower, huskier tone, "Damn, I've missed you so much."

As his lips claimed hers, Skye caught a glimpse of his expression. Passion and something she couldn't quite read warred in his dark eyes. Deciding not to worry about it for the moment, she put her arms around his neck and buried her hands in his thick black hair. She loved the crisp feeling of the strands as they feathered through her fingers.

His kiss sent the pit of her stomach into a wild Tilt-A-Whirl ride, and she pressed closer, her body tingling from the contact.

Wally groaned and parted her lips, his tongue exploring the recesses of her mouth.

He tasted sweeter than her favorite chocolate, and she wanted to devour him. She forgot about the murder, the kidnapping, and all her other worries and enjoyed the moment.

Wally's fingertips were icy as his hands crept under her shirt, but his palms were fiery hot when they cupped her breasts.

She caressed the planes of his back, and they moved as one toward the stairs.

Skye blindly stepped backward, expecting to encounter nothing but hardwood floor. Instead her shoe came down on a throw rug, which somehow wrapped itself around her ankle, causing her foot to slide out from under her.

She was about to do the splits in slow motion, but Wally grabbed her upper arms, trying valiantly to keep both of them upright. There was an instant when it seemed he had succeeded; then the rug slithered farther away, and Skye toppled over.

At the last minute Wally thrust himself sideways to avoid landing on top of her, and for a split second their fall seemed frozen in time, like some bizarre ballet routine. Then, as her back and head hit the edge of the stairs, the hurt swept away all of her fanciful thoughts.

Skye had no idea how long she lay there absorbed in

pain, but when she was able to focus she looked to where Wally lay sprawled motionless on the hardwood floor. In saving her it appeared he had hit his head on the newel post. Her heart stopped, and she couldn't swallow the lump that had risen in her throat.

Whimpering, she raised herself on one elbow. "Wally, sweetheart, are you all right?"

It seemed like forever, but he finally sat up, fingering the back of his head. "I'm fine. How about you?"

"I'm not sure." The room was spinning, and she was slightly nauseous.

He immediately leapt to his feet. "Stay right there." Staggering a little, he rushed to her side. "I'll call an ambulance."

"No. Wait." She put her hand out. "Help me up."

"You shouldn't move if you're injured."

Skye ignored him and got to her knees. The pain in her back made her gasp, but she forced herself to her feet. "See? I'm fine. Just a little shaken up."

He wrapped an arm around her waist and they hobbled into the parlor. Lowering themselves onto the settee, they both let out sighs.

"What the hell happened?" Wally cradled Skye against his side.

"It's this house." Skye shook her head, and the pain shooting through her skull made her realize that movement of any kind was a bad idea. "For some reason it doesn't want us to be together."

"That's ridiculous." Wally touched the bump on the back of her head. "Maybe we should let a doctor take a look at you. You're not being rational."

Skye jerked away from him, the stab of pain that surged up her spine reminding her once again that quick movements equaled suffering. "Don't start that rational stuff on me, or I'll think you're channeling Simon. And we wouldn't want that, would we?"

"That was a low blow." Wally scowled.

Skye raised an eyebrow. "If the personality trait fits . . ."

"Okay, forget rational. It doesn't feel like the house hates me. There aren't any cold spots. The lights don't flicker. The doors don't lock me out."

"Maybe not, but I swear that rug was not at the foot of the stairs when I came down to let you in, and it's not the only time something bad has happened." Skye scrunched up her face, thinking. "There was the first time we kissed in this house and the kitchen faucet did an impression of Old Faithful." Skye held up her index finger. "Then there was the mirror that smashed to smithereens the first time you tried to take my bra off, and the space heater that blew up the next time things got hot and heavy between us." She wiggled three fingers at him.

"It's an old house," Wally stated, but sounded less sure as he added, "Things are bound to go wrong."

"Right. So, why have we spent all our time together at your house since the explosion?"

He shrugged. "Coincidence."

"And since we're on the subject, why didn't you want to meet there tonight?"

"Well . . ." Wally's face clouded with uneasiness. "That's one of the things I wanted to talk to you about."

Suddenly Skye didn't want to hear what he had to say. "I'm starving. I bet you are too." She hated surprises. "How about we heat up the pizza and talk while we eat?" She popped up off the settee, ignoring the ache in her back. "I'm pretty sure the house will let us eat in peace. It just seems to dislike it when we touch."

"Okay." He looked puzzled by her abrupt change of mood, but stood up. "I'll grab the pizza from the hallway and meet you in the kitchen."

"Great. You want a beer or are you still on duty?"

"They'll only call me if something comes up with the murderer or the missing girl, but I guess I'd better stick to Diet Coke just in case."

Skye nodded and scurried into the kitchen. She set the dial on the stove at three-fifty to preheat, then got two glasses from the cupboard. She was already pouring the soda over ice when Wally came in carrying the now-cold pizza.

After she wrapped it in foil and put it in the oven to re-heat, she sat down and immediately started telling Wally everything she could think of regarding the murder and Ashley—up to the point where Skye had broken into the Dairy Kastle.

He listened and took a few notes, but the only thing she had to say that got a rise from him was her news about the person who had helped May that morning, and finding the factory jumpsuit. "Do you think your mom got a good look at the guy when he was helping her with her box?"

"I doubt it." Skye pursed her lips. "The lower half of his face was covered with that net thing the workers use if they have beards or mustaches, and he had another hairnet on his head. The only thing exposed was his eyes."

"What color were they?"

"He was never close enough for me to see." Skye bit her lip. "Mom may have noticed."

"Did you tell anyone about seeing this guy?"

"No. I forgot to tell you this morning, and then I wanted to talk it over with you first."

"Good." Wally absentmindedly started to pat her hand, but snatched his away as if he had been burned.

Skye lifted her chin. "I thought you didn't believe the whole haunted-house thing."

"I don't." The tips of his ears turned red. "I just didn't want to distract you." He cleared his throat and added, "We'd better make sure May doesn't tell anyone either. If it was the killer, we don't want him to think she can identify him. It was a him, right?"

"I think so, but Mom probably got a better impression than I did." Skye wrinkled her brow. "I guess the reason I thought it was a male was the net thingy on his face. But I couldn't see if he really had a beard or mustache, so maybe that was just used as a sort of mask."

"I'll talk to May first thing tomorrow." Wally made a note. "Your dad picked her up at the hospital just as I was leaving, and she said they were going to stop for supper at the new Culver's in Laurel, then head straight home, so she shouldn't tell anyone between now and then."

"Are you kidding?" Skye snickered. "May is gossip central. She'll probably hit the phone as soon as she gets home. No way would a Culver's butter burger and a custard keep her from broadcasting on the Scumble River ten-o'clock news. You'd better call her right now."

Wally's hand went to the clip on his belt where his cell phone should have been, and he cursed when he realized it was not there, then got up and grabbed the kitchen phone.

Skye tuned out his conversation as she set out plates, napkins, and silverware.

As soon as he hung up he said, "May hasn't told anyone and promises she won't. She didn't see the color of his eyes, and isn't sure if her helper was a he or a she."

Skye blew out a frustrated breath, then took the pizza from the oven and put it on the table.

After they practically inhaled the first pieces, she asked, "Did you ever get Uncle Dante to tell you who stabbed him? And why he was at the warehouse, anyway?"

"Dante said he was there as a favor to Grandma Sal to help make sure everything went smoothly and that no one played any more pranks."

Skye made a disbelieving noise.

"*Anyway*, he was supposedly inspecting the cooking areas, heard a noise in the back of the warehouse, went to check on it, and saw feet sticking out of the chocolate fountain. When he bent down to look more closely, someone threw a tablecloth over his head, spun him around, and stabbed him in the stomach." Wally took a swallow of Diet Coke before continuing. "By the time he got clear of the tablecloth his assailant had run away, and when he saw the blood he started to feel woozy, so he ran out of the building looking for assistance."

"Shoot." Skye licked her fingers. "So, Dante was no help at all."

"Right. His attacker could be anyone. Dante's not a big man, so most women could handle him in that situation." Wally helped himself to another slice. "The county crime techs found the tablecloth when they drained the fountain, but say they doubt there's any trace evidence on it after being submerged in chocolate."

"Did they find any other evidence?"

"Nothing yet. The ME has the body, and we should get word tomorrow on cause of death, but he did confirm she'd suffered a blow to the head."

Skye wiped her mouth with a paper napkin. "So, what's the plan?"

"Once I knew that it would be a while before Dante was in any shape to talk, I went over to Cherry's house to break the news to her husband. But contrary to my instructions, someone leaked Cherry's identity to the press. Reporters had descended and told him about her death. At which point Alexander became hysterical, his doctor was called, and he was given a sedative. So he's on the top of my list to interview tomorrow morning."

"You'll probably want to chat with Larissa, the nanny, too," Skye suggested. "She and Mr. Alexander are having an affair. I overheard them arguing about it at the dinner last night. She wanted him to leave his wife for her."

"Right." Wally made a note. "I also need with talk to the other contestants again, and anyone else having to do with the contest who we didn't get to today."

"Do you want me to do anything?" Skye's face lit up. "Maybe I should drop out of the challenge to help you."

"No, I think you'll be more valuable hanging around and hearing what everyone has to say." Wally took her hand and kissed her wrist. "Besides, I don't want your mom any madder at me than she already is."

"Chicken." Skye picked up a slice of pepperoni and popped it into his mouth. "Will we have a lot of problems with the media? I remember when that model was killed at Thanksgiving. They were so obnoxious they even stole people's garbage."

"Grandma Sal's PR people are handling it. They're putting out a statement saying that Cherry Alexander was discovered dead this morning, but so far there is no cause of death. We're holding back the whole chocolate-fountain part."

"But Cherry was a best-selling author. Won't the media be looking for a better story?"

Wally devoured the last piece of pizza, which Skye had slipped onto his plate, figuring he probably hadn't had any lunch. After he finished he said, "An author isn't really a celebrity. Unless they're Stephen King or Danielle Steel or someone like that, most people don't even recognize them. You read a lot. Did you recognize Cherry?"

"No. But from the title she mentioned while we were waiting for the opening ceremony, she writes tell-all books about celebrities, which I don't read."

Wally shrugged. "Well, if the media is more interested than I'm guessing, Dante said the mayor's office would take care of any spillover Grandma Sal's people can't handle."

"That's a relief. The press was a darn nuisance on our last case." Skye thought about the Thanksgiving murder for a moment, then asked, "Any news on Ashley's disappearance?"

He shook his head. "The county and state police are looking for her, and all the area police departments have her picture. But no one's seen a thing."

"Well, I had an idea this afternoon, but it didn't pan out." Skye looked at him from under her lashes. He seemed only mildly interested, so she quickly gave him the rehearsed and sanitized story, ending with, "But she wasn't there, so I nailed the shutter back."

"Too bad." Wally wiped his fingers, crumpled up his napkin, and threw it on top of his empty plate. "But what was causing the noise if it wasn't her?"

"Just a mouse." Skye kept her face down so he couldn't read the real answer in her eyes. She didn't want to go into the whole rat versus mouse issue. "Still, I feel like an idiot for tearing over to the drive-in when she wasn't even there."

"Why would you feel like an idiot for following a logical lead?" Wally cupped her cheek. "You would feel a whole lot worse if she was found there later and you'd disregarded your hunch."

Skye turned her face and kissed his palm. This was why she was with Wally and not Simon. Simon's insistence that she act as coldly logical as he was drove her nuts. Wally's acceptance of who she was, with no desire to change her, made her feel cherished.

Wally scooted back his chair and started to clear the table. Skye ran hot water in the sink—she hadn't been able to afford to install a dishwasher yet.

"So we're all caught up on the murder and Ashley, right?" Wally asked.

"I think I've told you everything I wanted to." Skye squirted detergent into the water. "Xenia's blog—which she now claims isn't hers—my idea that fell flat, and the runner wearing the jumpsuit. Yep, that's it."

Skye plunged the dishes and silverware into the bubbles, trying to come up with more information to stall him, but before she could think of anything Wally said, "There's something I need to tell you, and I'm not sure how you're going to take it."

Skye's stomach clenched. Had his ex-wife come back? Had he met someone else? Was he sick?

When she didn't speak, Wally continued. "I know you've wondered what's been up these couple of months. Why I've had to cancel out on you so many times."

She nodded, but couldn't force any sounds past the lump in her throat.

"Well, you know how I don't like to talk about my family or my past?"

"Yes." Her voice quavered, but she managed to squeak out the single word.

"I told you it was because after my mom died, my dad and I didn't have anything in common, since he didn't like me going into law enforcement, right?"

"Right."

"Well, that's true, but not the whole truth." Wally's eyes were wary.

"Okay." Skye dried her hands on a dish towel and walked back to the table. She had a feeling she needed to sit down for this.

"The reason my dad was so upset with me for becoming a cop rather than getting my MBA was because I'm an only child, and there was no one else to take over the family business."

"I can understand that. My dad feels the same way about Vince not taking over the farm. He's been a little better about it the past few years, since he's seen how happy Vince is with the hair salon, but it still bothers Dad."

Wally moved closer to Skye, taking her hands. "Imagine how your dad would feel if the farm wasn't five hundred acres, but five thousand."

"Your dad owns five thousand acres?"

"He owns a lot more than that." Wally squatted in front of Skye. "I'm from a little town in west Texas. My grandfather was a rancher, and then when my dad was in his late teens, oil was discovered on their land. My dad parlayed the oil money into an international company with concerns in almost every kind of manufacturing."

Skye's mouth opened, but nothing came out. What do you say when your boyfriend tells you his father is a multi-millionaire?

CHAPTER 11

Beat for Two Minutes

Skye jerked her hands from Wally's grasp, pushed back her chair, and jumped to her feet. She felt light-headed, and the room seemed to spin out of focus. Her mind raced as she tried to figure out what to do, what to say. She needed to be alone for a couple of minutes to pull herself together. The bathroom. That was it. He wouldn't follow her in there, and she *was* slightly queasy.

As she fled the kitchen she said over her shoulder, "I need to use the restroom. I'll be right back."

She staggered up the stairs and into the master bath. Once inside she slammed the door, snapped the lock, and leaned against the thick wood as if guarding it against a marauding Mongol horde.

When she was sure Wally hadn't followed her, she moved from the door to the sink and got a damp washcloth for the back of her neck. She still felt a little shaky, but her heart rate had returned to normal and the pizza was no longer threatening reappearance.

A few seconds later her brain kicked back into gear and began working again. The first coherent thought it produced was a question. *If Wally's a gazillionaire, but has never revealed that fact before, why is he bringing it up now? And, most important, does that change anything between us?*

Skye had a bad feeling that it might. After all, she was a farmer's daughter from Podunk, Illinois. Wally's father was the CEO of an international conglomerate, and probably had homes in Paris, London, and St. Kitts.

Not to mention how poorly the whole rich-boyfriend thing had gone the last time Skye found herself in this situation. Been there, done that, had the T-shirt repossessed right off her back. Her ex-fiancé Luc had proved to be a shallow, bigoted, self-centered bastard. How often did a guy have to dump her for being a country bumpkin before she caught on?

No, wait. That wasn't fair to Wally. She'd known him for eighteen years, and she'd never seen any trace of Luc's awful characteristics in him. He was thoughtful, fair, and always put others' needs ahead of his own. Could money change that in a person?

And, hey, he didn't say his father had died and left him the money. He and his father weren't even on good terms. Maybe Mr. Boyd had cut his son out of his will, and that was what Wally had been leading up to.

She was being silly, jumping to conclusions. Just because Wally had finally told her about his family didn't mean that his father had persuaded him to resign as the Scumble River police chief, move back to Texas, and take over the family business. Did it?

Skye stared in the mirror. A thirtysomething woman with too-generous curves and hair that tended to revert back to Shirley Temple curls at the slightest hint of humidity looked back at her. Her only remarkable feature—large emerald green eyes—clouded with worry.

She bit her lip. No matter how hard she tried, she couldn't see herself on the arm of a tuxedo-clad millionaire attending charity balls and making small talk with all the other trophy wives. Did Dior even make an evening gown in her size?

Praying that Wally wasn't about to shuck his old life, including her, and become a star on *Lifestyles of the Rich and Famous*, Skye splashed cold water on her face, freshened her lipstick, and treated herself to an extra spray of Chanel. Then she squared her shoulders and went back downstairs.

She found Wally pacing in the sunroom. When she entered, he rushed over to her. "Are you okay?"

"I'm fine." She perched on the edge of the chair. "I'm sorry I took so long. You sort of threw me for a loop, and I needed time to think."

"And have you?" His dark eyes were intense.

"Yes." Skye sank back, feeling a little dizzy again. "And I am ready to hear the rest of what you have to tell me." She paused, and when he didn't say anything she prodded, "There is more to this than just a sudden urge to tell me about your family, right?"

Wally nodded and sat back down on the settee, then became interested in one of Bingo's squeeze toys. He studied the little rubber mouse as if he had never seen one before. Finally, without looking up from the plastic rodent, he said, "It all started the beginning of January. My father called to wish me a happy New Year, then mentioned he was in the area on business and asked if we could get together."

"That would have been the first time you canceled a date with me."

"Yeah." Wally turned the molded toy over and ran his finger along the seam. "I figured this was a onetime visit on his part; he'd never been to Scumble River before, and I didn't see any reason to go into my whole complicated family situation with you."

"Yeah. You wouldn't want to do that unless you were in a serious relationship." Wally tried to protest, but Skye cut him off. "Except it wasn't a onetime visit. He's been back . . . let's see . . ." She thought backward, counting the missed dates on her fingers. "He's been here five more times, including last night, right?"

"Yes." Wally gripped the mouse, and its loud squeak in the silent room startled them both. "He dropped by twice in February and twice in March."

"And you still didn't think to mention him to me or introduce us?"

A muscle below Wally's right eye twitched, and he said, "I just don't trust him. I was afraid he'd do something to hurt you, or that knowing him would make you think less of me."

She ducked her head so he couldn't read her face as she considered what he'd said. Did she believe it? Or was there something else he wasn't telling her? She braced herself and asked another question. "What about last night?"

"That was different." Wally finally put down Bingo's plaything and looked at Skye. "Previously he's called from Chicago and then driven down, or I've met him in Joliet for dinner. Yesterday afternoon after I got off work I took the Thunderbird to the gas station near I-55 to fill it up so it would be ready for our date that night, and there he was, filling up his rental car. I figured he was going to surprise me, so I explained how I couldn't cancel our date this time, since you were counting on me as your escort, and he said that was fine; he'd see me today for lunch."

"So, what happened?" Skye tilted her head. "I mean, you did stand me up, so . . ."

"Well, he seemed to be acting odd, like he hadn't really expected to see me and didn't want to. And he almost looked as if he were in disguise."

"How so?"

"He had shaved his head and was wearing cheap mirrored sunglasses, and his rental car was a Ford Escort."

"I'm guessing he has a beautiful thick head of hair like you, usually wears designer sunglasses, and always rents a high-end automobile." Skye tapped the armrest of her chair. "Could he be sick? Maybe he didn't shave his head. Maybe his hair fell out because of chemo treatments?"

"I considered that, too. In fact, I thought maybe the reason he'd been in Chicago so often was for treatment. That could explain his suddenly wanting to see me too."

"But?"

"But then I saw him pull into a cabin at Charlie's motor court and throw a tarp over his car."

"Hmm." Skye scrunched up her face, thinking. "That is odd. First, how did he get a reservation? Charlie's been booked up for this weekend since January. And second, why would he protect a rental car with a tarp?"

"Unless he was trying to hide from someone." Wally ran a hand through his hair. "So, I decided I'd better watch him."

"Did he do anything suspicious?"

"Nope. He didn't leave the motor court. I watched until eleven, when the lights went out, and he was there the next morning when I got the call about Cherry's death. I drove past on my way to the factory."

"What did he say when you had to cancel lunch with him today?"

"Not much. Said he'd catch me next time. But I was afraid he might show up at my house tonight before I could tell you about him, which is why I suggested we meet here."

"I see." Skye tucked her legs under her and got more comfortable. "You know, it's pretty weird that he would drive all the way down here from Chicago without checking to see if you were free. It had to take him at least ninety minutes to two hours, depending on traffic, and then he wasn't upset when you couldn't see him. Is he usually that easy-going?"

"No. He expects everyone and everything to revolve around his convenience."

"Since he said he'd catch you next time, I'm assuming that means he's left town."

"That's what you would think, isn't it?" Wally's brows met over his nose. "But I had a funny feeling about it, so I came past the motor court on the way here, and his car was still there."

"Why would he stick around and not tell you? Unless he meant he'll see you tomorrow."

"That can't be it. If nothing else he's always extremely precise in what he says."

"When you've gotten together these past few months, what has he talked about?" Skye plucked a pen and pad from the end table. "Was there a theme—the good old days, your childhood, current events?"

Wally bent forward and put his elbows on his knees. "A lot of it was just general stuff. We hadn't seen each other in years, and it seemed to me he was mainly trying not to start an argument."

"You never asked what he was doing in Chicago so

often?" Skye's massive curiosity couldn't imagine leaving that question unanswered.

"No. I figured it was business, and I didn't want to get him started on how much I had disappointed him by not taking a job with the family company."

"Maybe he's thinking of remarrying. Did he sound you out about how you'd feel about a stepmother?"

Wally shook his head. "My father has a lot of traits I don't particularly care for, but he loved my mother with a passion that never faded. He would never remarry. No other woman could take her place."

"Never is a long time. He's been a widower for what, eighteen, nineteen years?" Skye tried to put it delicately. "A man has needs."

"Tell me about it." Wally raised a brow, and his chocolate brown eyes invited her to fall into their depths. "I'm not saying he didn't have an occasional lady friend, but the Boyd men are like wolves—there is only one true mate for us. And once we find her, no matter how short a time we have together, there is no one else."

Skye caught her breath. Wally had been married for over ten years before his divorce two years ago. Was Darleen his true mate, and Skye just someone to meet his needs?

Before she could figure out how to phrase that question, Wally had pulled her up from her chair and settled her on his lap, tucking her curves neatly into his own contours as if they were two pieces of a jigsaw puzzle.

The muscles that rippled under his uniform shirt as he lifted her quickened her pulse, but she tore her gaze away and raised it to his face. Smooth olive skin stretched over high cheekbones, and his strong features held all the sensuality he usually kept hidden. He was a devastating package, and Skye yearned to tear off the wrapping.

Lightly he fingered a tendril on her cheek, then slid his hand down to caress her neck and bare shoulders. Hypnotized by his touch, she tingled under his fingertips, her growing arousal erasing all her questions and doubts.

Suddenly, as if he couldn't wait any longer, he crushed her to his chest. Her body tightened from the contact, and she wound her arms around his neck and lifted her face to his, basking in his hungry gaze. His kiss was urgent, devouring her and making her forget everything but him.

He freed one hand and was sliding her shirt off when she heard the first yowl. Skye stiffened, but either Wally hadn't heard it or he was ignoring it.

A few seconds later an even louder howl, this one sounding almost like a baby's scream, penetrated his passionate fog, and he tore his mouth from hers. "What in the hell was that?"

A third yowl ripped through the house, followed by a thud and another howl.

Skye scrambled from Wally's lap. "I think that's Bingo, but he's never sounded like that before." She raced in the direction of the noise, which seemed to be coming from above them.

Wally followed her as she ran up the stairs and into her bedroom. They both skidded to a stop and gaped at the agitated feline. The black cat's fur was standing on end, making him appear twice his normal size. He was arched by the balcony doors, hissing at what Skye at first thought was an elderly woman, but a moment later realized was just a bunch of rags being blown against the glass by the wind.

As they stared, Bingo gathered himself up and launched himself at the door. His bounce off the pane and onto the floor produced the thud they had heard in the sunroom.

Skye leapt forward and tried to grab the cat, afraid he could hurt himself or break the window.

When Bingo evaded Skye's grasp, Wally snatched up an afghan draped over a chest at the bottom of the bed, snapped it open, and threw it over the cat, scooping the disturbed feline up like a sack of fireworks about to go off at any minute.

Skye took the squirming cat from Wally's hands and cuddled him to her chest, murmuring reassuring words.

Wally strode over to the doors and flung them open, surveying the balcony. He stepped outside and picked up the bundle that had been beating against the glass and examined it. It was a faded housedress wrapped around a tree branch.

Skye joined him. "Where do you think that came from?"

"It must have blown off someone's clothesline. It's been really windy the past couple of days."

"It sure has." Skye turned and leaned against the railing. "I noticed it was really bad at the factory this morning."

"That's the one thing I hate about Illinois springs." Wally put an arm around her and cuddled her to his side. "The high winds drive me crazy."

"Yeah. I can take the snow and the cold, but the wind gets on my last nerve." She shivered. "You know, for a minute there, when we first ran into the bedroom, I could have sworn it was Mrs. Griggs pounding on the balcony door."

"You have quite an imagination," Wally teased.

"True, but that's the kind of dress she wore, and I find it odd that one so similar not only got wrapped around such a large branch, but also found its way to my balcony."

"You live on the river in the middle in a flat area. All sorts of trash blows through here."

"Maybe." Skye shrugged.

They were quiet for a few minutes; then Wally said, "I bet this is old Mrs. Calvert's dress. She's your nearest neighbor, and she wears clothes like this."

"Sure. It couldn't possibly have been another of the house's attempts to keep us apart."

"Of course not."

"It's getting cold out here." Skye separated herself from Wally. "I'm going back."

"Yeah." Wally opened the door for her and stepped inside as she crossed the threshold.

Bingo had recovered from his trauma and was curled in a ball on top of the bed, snoring lightly. Skye gave him a pat as she walked by, and Wally followed suit.

Once they were resettled in the sunroom, Skye felt restless. Wally tried to resume their kissing, but she shrugged him off and paced. Finally she said, "Let's get out of here for a while. The paint smell is driving me crazy."

"Okay. Where do you want to go?"

She was about to suggest they get a drink somewhere, but caught back the words when she remembered that Wally was still in his uniform. Where could they go? There weren't a lot of entertainment options in Scumble River.

"How about McDonald's?" Wally asked. "I'll buy you a hot-fudge sundae."

"Perfect."

McDonald's was crowded. It was a favorite hangout for the teens, several of whom greeted Skye. It was nice to see that quite a few of them also said hi to Wally, and that none of the kids seemed to feel awkward in their presence.

After getting their sundaes, Skye and Wally settled into a back booth. They were still in the process of taking the lids off their ice-cream containers when Skye stiffened and put her finger to her lips.

Wally shot her a questioning look.

She jerked her chin to the booth on the other side of theirs, then cupped her ear.

He nodded and leaned forward.

A group of girls from the high school was seated there, and two were arguing. Skye immediately identified the dominant voice as that of Bitsy Kessler, a preppy cheerleader who wrote an advice column for the school newspaper. Skye didn't recognize the other girl.

Bitsy's tone was scornful. "I can't believe you losers think that Ashley has really been kidnapped. I'll bet you still leave milk and cookies for Santa, too."

The other girl murmured something too low for Skye to hear, but Bitsy's next words were loud and clear. "Yeah, right. Poor little Ashley. The victim of the Scumble River Snatcher. She's probably holed up in a motel room with some guy, laughing her ass off at all of us."

"Why would you think that?" the other girl challenged.

"Ashley's the biggest social climber since Cinderella. This whole negative article in the newspaper and her parents' insisting on suing over her little indiscretion with the basketball team pissed her off.

"It just pointed out that her family is so blue-collar. You don't see Paris Hilton's mother suing when her sexploitations are printed in a newspaper. All the knockoff Vera

Bradley purses and last-season Emma Hope sneakers in the world can't change who your parents are. Even her North Face jacket is last season's from a secondhand shop."

"But how does running away help?" The other girl sounded confused.

"What better way to get back at everyone? Her parents are worried sick. The girl who wrote the nasty stuff about her is suspected of the kidnapping. And the superintendent is threatening to shut down the newspaper. All things Ashley would love to see happen."

Skye shot Wally a meaningful glance.

His look said it *was* a plausible explanation.

"But where would they be hiding?" Ashley's defender sounded less sure than she had at first.

"Where else is there around here but Mr. Patukas's motel?" Bitsy paused, and Skye heard the sound of a straw sucking up air rather than liquid. "It's not like Ashley would go camping."

Once the teens moved on to another subject, Skye scooped a spoonful of ice cream covered in chocolate into her mouth, then asked in a low voice, "What do you think?"

Wally finished his sundae, wiped his mouth on his napkin, and answered, "Maybe we should stop by Charlie's and see if Miss Ashley is in residence."

"All but one of the cottages are rented for contest personnel, and don't we think your father has that one?"

"Who knows?" He lifted a shoulder. "Someone could have canceled."

"True." Skye plucked the cherry from the bottom of her dish. "Doesn't it seem like the contest and the kidnapping and the murder have all been going on forever?"

"Uh-huh. Hard to believe how short the time really has been. Ashley's only been gone a day and a half, and the murder took place this morning."

Skye popped the cherry into her mouth, slid out of the booth, and walked toward the wastebasket with their trash. "And with that in mind, I think we should get moving and kill two birds with one stone."

Wally followed her to the exit. "You mean . . . ?" He held open the door.

"Exactly. Let's go look for Miss Ashley and then pay your father a little visit."

CHAPTER 12

Set Aside
Beaten Mixture

Skye and Wally pulled into the Up A Lazy River Motor Court a few minutes after ten. The red neon NO VACANCY sign glowed steadily, and of the dozen cabins that formed a horseshoe around the parking lot, the front windows in all but number twelve were pitch-black. Scumble Riverites went to bed when the WGN nine-o'clock news ended, and visitors soon fell into the same routine.

Skye stared at the darkened motel, feeling her investigative fervor waver. "Maybe we should come back tomorrow morning. We don't want to wake people up, do we?"

Wally jerked his chin toward the well-lit office-bungalow that blossomed like a pimple on the lip of the frowning row of cottages. "Looks like Charlie's still up. Let's see what he has to say."

"Right. Surely he knows who he rented his cabins to."

When there was no response to her first knock, Skye hesitated. Maybe Uncle Charlie had fallen asleep in front of the TV. She hated to wake him.

Wally clearly had no such concern and reached around her to knock a second time on the old wooden door. This time they heard the creak of the La-Z-Boy as the footrest was lowered, then heavy steps approaching where they stood. The blue gingham curtain was snatched aside, and Charlie's face appeared in the little window, his round head looking like a jack-o'-lantern floating in the glass.

Abruptly the cotton cloth dropped back into place and the door was swung open. "What's wrong? What are you two doing here at this time of night? Is it May?"

Skye had never quite figured out how her mother and Charlie had become so close. In the past she'd even wondered if they'd once had an affair, but she'd finally realized that Charlie's love for May was paternal, and May reciprocated with daughterly affection. Both fulfilled a need in the other. Charlie had never married or had children, and May's father had died while she was still a teenager.

"Mom's fine, Uncle Charlie," Skye hurried to reassure him. "Sorry to give you a scare. We just have a few questions about a couple of your guests."

Charlie stepped away from the doorway and gestured for them to come inside. "This have something to do with the murder?" He pointed to the sofa and settled himself in his lounger.

"No, with the missing girl." Wally sat down and leaned forward with his hands dangling between his legs.

Skye sat next to him. She watched her godfather as Wally told him what they had heard at McDonald's. Charlie had been one of the very few people in town who had not expressed his views about Skye breaking up with Simon and starting to date Wally. It had been unusual for him not to wade in with an opinion, and now she wondered what he thought and why he had kept silent.

Something flitted through her mind, but before she could figure out what, she tuned in to what Charlie was saying.

"There's no way that girl could be here, unless one of those contest people is hiding her, and I can't quite see Grandma Sal stashing her in her bathtub, can you?"

Skye started to shake her head, but then took a second to think of the people involved before saying, "Well, you know, those media people would hide a teenager in a flash if she could convince them there would be a big story. And Brandon and JJ might have other reasons for sharing their room with a cute cheerleader. But you're probably right about the judges, Grandma Sal, her son, and her daughter-in-law being in the clear."

Before Charlie could respond, Wally asked, "Wouldn't the lady who cleans the cabins for you mention an extra person? I mean, I know you charge more for additional guests."

Charlie nodded. "That's true normally, but Grandma Sal is paying for the whole block of cabins, so I gave her one rate. And I had to hire a couple extra ladies to help with the cleaning, so they might not think to mention something like that. I can give you their names and you can ask them."

"I'll have Quirk talk to them tomorrow morning. What time do they get here?"

"They start at eight."

Charlie picked up a cigar and ran it between his sausage-like fingers. He had given up smoking a couple years ago after a health scare, but Skye knew he still liked to hold a cigar, especially when he was agitated. What could be bothering him?

"Uncle Charlie, have you seen anything out of the ordinary? Maybe an incident that, now that you think about it, might have something to do with the missing girl or the murder?" Skye asked, trying to cover all the bases. Charlie wouldn't lie to her, but he might not volunteer information. She knew her godfather had his secrets.

"No, can't say as I have." Charlie put the cigar down and took a pull on his beer can. "You want a Budweiser?"

"No, thanks, Charlie." Wally leaned a little closer to the older man. "Sorry to bother you so late, but we have one more question."

"Oh?" Charlie picked up the cigar again.

"It's about the twelfth cabin." Skye leaned forward too. "I thought you told Uncle Dante that it had been rented for four months straight by somebody, and that's why you couldn't let the contest people have it."

"Yeah, that's right," Charlie said, narrowing his eyes. "What about it?"

"Well, then, why did you let some guy rent it yesterday?"

"I didn't. I mean, the guy who's in cabin twelve is the guy who's rented it since January." Charlie relaxed. "He got a new haircut and is driving a different kind of car, that's all."

Wally and Skye exchanged a long look; then Wally asked, "What's his name?"

"Brown, Charles Brown."

Another long look passed between Skye and Wally, but this time she spoke. "How did he pay for the room?"

"Cash on the barrelhead. Thirty dollars a night times one hundred and twenty nights: three thousand, six hundred dollars in hundred-dollar bills." Charlie smiled in fond remembrance. "Between Mr. Brown and the contest, the Up A Lazy River is going to have a good first quarter."

"So you didn't see the guy's ID?" Wally stated.

"No, why would I need to?"

"And you didn't think it was a little comical that Charlie Brown was renting your cabin?" Skye asked, exasperated with her godfather's nonchalance. "Did you check to see if he had Snoopy with him?"

"There's nothing funny about thirty-six hundred dollars. And you know I don't allow pets."

For the second straight day, Skye woke to a buzzing alarm at the appalling hour of five a.m. Once again she hurried through her morning ablutions and choked down a cup of scalding tea—burning her tongue in the process, which added to her bad temper.

Why in the world had she agreed with Wally when he had encouraged Grandma Sal to continue the contest? Right now she could still be curled up under the covers, dreaming that she and Hugh Jackman were dancing cheek-to-cheek on a white sand beach in the Caribbean.

But no. Instead she was standing in the cold wind waiting to be picked up by her mother in order to go cook a dish that had yet to come out of the oven in an edible state. And to top it all off, last night had not ended well.

When she and Wally had left Charlie's they'd walked over to cabin twelve, which still had a lamp burning in its front window. But as soon as Wally rapped on the door, the light was snapped off and the drapes drawn. Finally, after half a dozen knocks, each more insistent than the one before, Skye had persuaded Wally to give up.

By then neither had been in the mood for romance, and he had dropped her off at her house with only a quick goodnight kiss. Not exactly how she had expected her Saturday night to end.

Now Sunday morning felt like déjà vu to Skye as she slid into the passenger side of May's Oldsmobile, slumped back on the seat, and closed her eyes.

At least this time May's voice wasn't chirpy when she said good morning.

Skye opened one eye and muttered a greeting.

May drove a mile or so in silence, then said, almost as if she were desperate for a topic, "I didn't see you in church last night. Did you forget you wouldn't have time to go this morning?"

Skye nodded, unwilling to go into a full explanation of what had distracted her. "Maybe I can cut cooking practice short and run over for eight-o'clock Mass."

"If you go to confession God will forgive you for missing Mass, but Grandma Sal won't forgive your macaroni being rubbery no matter how many prayers you say."

Skye knew that May was intent on one of her recipes winning the contest, but she had thought that the state of her immortal soul might sway her mother. Clearly May was willing to take a chance that Skye might burn in hell if it meant taking home the gold.

After a few minutes of blessed silence, Skye asked, "How's Uncle Dante?"

"Fine. They're letting him out of the hospital this morning, and he's holding a press conference at city hall to inform everyone that he nearly lost his life while trying to help Scumble River grow."

"Better tell him to spread the word that he didn't see his attacker."

"Why?" May's head jerked toward Skye. "Do you think whoever did it might try again?"

"Duh." Sometimes Skye forgot that her mother had taken

up permanent residence in the land of denial, and that almost nothing could make her apply for a passport out of that realm. "It's also why you have to keep quiet about the person who helped you yesterday morning. If anyone asks, you don't remember a thing."

"So I've been told." May scowled. "I'm not as dumb as you think, missy."

Skye bit her lip before something sarcastic slipped out. If her mother didn't win the contest she'd be looking for someone to blame, and Skye wasn't about to paint a bright red target on her backside by upsetting May right before she started cooking.

They were both quiet until they pulled into the factory parking lot. Then, as she shut off the car's engine, May asked, "Do you think any of the contestants will drop out?"

"No." Skye stepped from the Olds. "In fact, I heard that Grandma Sal offered Cherry's slot to the runner-up, and that person snapped it up."

"Anyone we know?" May's voice came from inside the trunk of the car as she leaned in to get her belongings.

"I didn't ask." Skye plucked a box from her mother's arms as May emerged. "But probably not." She took a step toward the warehouse, then turned to look at May. "Unless you entered a fifth time."

May shushed Skye. "Keep your voice down. Are you deliberately trying to get us in trouble?"

Skye raised an eyebrow. "I thought we weren't doing anything against the rules."

"We aren't, but I don't want them to write any new ones," May retorted as she hurried through the door.

In the cooking area, Skye put the carton on her mother's counter. Not surprisingly, they were the first to arrive, but even as Skye headed toward her own space, she heard the door open and a voice she recognized stopped her in her tracks.

"Earl, you are stupider than an idiot. If I didn't need it for my secret recipe, I'd knock you into Tuesday with my cast-iron skillet."

Skye cringed. It couldn't be. Slowly she turned her head

and looked behind her with slitted eyes. *Shit!* Just what they needed. As if the murder, the missing teenager, Wally's father, and the contest weren't enough, standing at Cherry Alexander's cooking area, dressed as if she were about to sing a duet with Johnny Cash, was Glenda Doozier.

Kneeling at Glenda's cowgirl-booted feet was Earl Doozier, Glenda's husband and the patriarch of the Red Raggers. Skye ducked behind a stove and edged away from the pair.

The Red Raggers were hard to explain to anyone who hadn't grown up in Scumble River. They were the ones your mother meant when she warned you not to go into certain parts of town. They were the ones who were most often complained about in the newspaper's "Shout Out" column—but only by people who never signed their names, because no one was foolish enough to purposely get the Red Raggers sore at them. In short, they were the ones whose family tree didn't branch—and that single trunk was full of dry rot.

Skye had a special relationship with the Dooziers. In the past she had protected them from bureaucratic school rules, and they had protected her from her own naïveté, but she didn't like to press her luck.

While Earl was firmly in her corner, there was no love lost between her and Glenda. Thank goodness they weren't competing in the same category. Speaking of category, if Glenda was taking Cherry's place, that meant she was in the Special-Occasion Baking group. What on earth could Glenda produce that would be fit for a special occasion? Possum Pie? Roadkill Jubilee? Or maybe a Squirrel Sundae?

Once Skye reached her cubicle she put the Dooziers out of her mind and began to assemble the ingredients for her recipe. While she worked, more finalists began to appear. They came in all shapes, sizes, and ages, but everyone wore the same determined look.

This was *the* day. Either they'd take home thousands of dollars and bragging rights for the next year, or they'd leave with nothing, and be forced to say over and over again, "Oh, I'm not disappointed I didn't win. It was just an honor to make the finals." Those words might quickly become harder to swallow than Skye's cooking.

As the warehouse started to fill with the sounds and smells of food being prepared, Skye slid her practice Chicken Supreme into the preheated oven. She set the timer, checked the clock on the wall, and looked at her watch. The dish had to come out in exactly fifty minutes, just as the cheese started to bubble, but before it started to brown. At that point she would sprinkle the top with buttered bread crumbs and then cook it five minutes longer.

Skye frowned as she adjusted her apron; they still hadn't gotten her one with the right spelling of her name. She was tempted to take a Magic Marker and make the correction herself, but instead she set off to visit her competition and see what everyone was saying about the murder.

She couldn't exactly take notes as she chatted, but she did tuck a small spiral pad in her pocket to jot down anything relevant as soon as she was out of a contestant's sight. She was hoping to overhear discussions, but would start one if there was no alternative.

The first row of six stoves that Skye approached was the Healthy recipe entrants. She noticed that one cooking space was empty. Where was Vince, and how come May hadn't picked him up and hauled his butt to the six a.m. practice? Skye ground her teeth; Vince had always been their mother's favorite.

Pushing away her jealousy, she concentrated on what the other five Healthy recipe finalists were saying. The first conversation she tuned in to was between two women cooking next to each other. One of them was the contestant that May had thought she knew when they first gathered on Friday, Imogene Ingersoll.

This time Skye saw what her mother meant; there was something familiar about Imogene, but thick glasses, heavy makeup, and what was obviously a wig made identification difficult. *Hmm* . . . Skye bit her lip. Maybe Imogene had lost her hair undergoing chemotherapy. A couple of months ago Skye'd given a ride to a student who worked part-time at the

Laurel Oncology Clinic and that might be where she'd seen Imogene.

Skye's focus was brought back to the two when Imogene said, "After they turned us away at the gate yesterday, I thought for sure they'd cancel the contest, or at least postpone it." She tied on her apron while continuing to chat. "I didn't see the message on my cell that the contest was still on until I came home from Mass; then I flew over here."

Skye recognized the other lady as the one with the injured leg. What was her name? She squinted at the apron pocket. Right, Monika. Now she remembered—Monika Bradley, the CPA from Brooklyn.

As Skye watched, Monika nodded. "Yeah, I was surprised, too. But my husband can never let a phone go unanswered, so I got the news yesterday afternoon." She slid a pan into her oven, then said, "I guess the show must go on."

"Well, not to speak ill of the dead, but she wasn't very nice."

"That's an understatement. She reminded me of my cousin's poodle. It was a pretty little thing, all bright eyes and curls, and it would come up and rest against your leg like it wanted to be petted. But the minute you reached down to stroke it, it would bite your fingers clean to the bone." Monika set the stove's timer. "Did you hear her yelling in the restaurant? Someone stealing her secret ingredient, my eye. I saw her put that little sack she was carrying on about in the garbage can. She shoved it in way to the bottom."

"Really? Did you say something to her?"

"Sure." Monika crossed her arms and leaned back against the counter. "At first she denied it, but then I threatened to go to Grandma Sal and she admitted she pulled the whole stunt to try to get May Denison kicked out of the contest."

"No!"

"Yes. Cherry said that May was her biggest competition, and she always tried to get her main rival disqualified."

Imogene pushed her glasses up. "Why didn't you turn Cherry in?"

"Because they were going at each other tooth and nail. I was hoping both of them would get kicked out. If Cherry had ended up winning the grand prize and I had a chance at winning it, I would have turned her in then." She sniffed. "Instead they let the next runner-up take Cherry's place. Damn!"

Skye snickered softly and moved on to the Snack recipe row. Here Charlie was holding court, waving a spatula and talking loudly. He wore his usual gray twill pants, white shirt, and red suspenders. His three-hundred-pound bulk took up nearly every inch of space in his cubicle, and made him look like a sumo wrestler squeezed into a pair of size-A panty hose.

Charlie's booming baritone echoed off the warehouse walls. "If I hear any of you say that again, we'll be suing you for slander."

Skye slipped behind a pillar. She wanted to know what he was talking about, but not enough to be drawn into the fray.

"Oh, shut your yap, you old fool." A birdlike woman marched up to him clutching a whisk. "All I said was that the dead woman had a fight with May Denison. You can't sue me for stating the facts. I'm not saying May killed her."

A dignified woman whom Skye recognized as a math teacher from Scumble River High shook her head. "Besides, Mr. Patukas, I think Ms. Alexander had words with at least a dozen or so people. I saw her yelling at Grandma Sal's son just after we finished dinner."

The others in the area joined in, and Skye quickly scribbled names and motives in her notebook. It seemed as if Miss Cherry had argued with nearly everyone in the place.

Skye looked at her watch; she had ten minutes before her dish had to come out of the oven. Hurriedly she moved on to the Special-Occasion Baking row. Here all was quiet. May was intently making frosting roses on what looked to Skye like a tiny lazy Susan.

Next to her the cookie blogger, Diane White, concentrated on a chocolate creation that looked something like the fusion of a truffle, a tiramisu, and a brownie. Skye licked her lips. As she watched Diane started to sprinkle chocolate shavings on the dish's surface. Just then the blogger's assistant arrived, gliding into the kitchen area.

Diane's back was to the entrance, and when the assistant spoke, the blogger threw up her hands and squeaked in fright. The bowl of chocolate flakes slipped from her fingers, spilling its contents on the ground, and Diane sank to her knees, screaming.

Wow, she certainly was high-strung. Was she afraid she might be the next victim, or was she on edge because she was the killer? She had been poking around the murder scene yesterday. In fact, she'd had to be escorted out due to her hysteria. But maybe that had been a ruse to escape the scene of the crime without arousing suspicion. Could the cookie blogger be a coldhearted criminal?

CHAPTER 13

Beat Egg Whites
Until Stiff

Shit! Skye glared at her watch. If only sheer willpower could make the hands move backward. It was nearly five minutes past the time her casserole was supposed to come out of the oven. Just what she needed—another ruined mess.

But surely anyone would agree that finding out who murdered Cherry was more important than creating the perfect entrée. Skye paused and bit her lip. Well, anyone but her mother. With May's angry yet disappointed face in mind, Skye turned on her heels and raced across the warehouse to the One-Dish Meals area. Making a tight turn at the end of the row, she skidded into her cubicle.

The first thing Skye saw was Bunny sitting on a folding chair painting her nails, wearing a red leather minidress and matching ankle boots laced with white silk ribbons. Not a good look for someone Bunny's age, but the redhead had never appeared more beautiful to Skye. Surely Bunny would have taken the dish from the oven when the timer went off.

Skye's smile faltered when she realized the counter was empty—no sign of the Chicken Supreme. Still, the timer wasn't pinging, so Bunny must have stopped it.

Skye let her gaze slip to the oven just in time to see twin

columns of smoke curl upward like elephant tusks. She yelped, ran forward, and twisted the dial to the OFF position. Seizing a potholder, she flung open the door and grabbed the Corning Ware dish.

This time her scream was louder than a the tornado siren, as the casserole slipped from her hands to the floor; elbow macaroni, chunks of chicken, and cheese splattered the cubicle. Skye gazed at the oozing cabinets and closed her eyes. The orange and white mess was revolting!

As she tried to pull herself together, the smell of scorched Velveeta clogged her throat. Her eyelids flew open and she whipped around to look back at the stove. The smoke had turned from gray to black and was billowing toward the ceiling. Somehow, although the arrow on the dial was aligned to the word OFF, the oven's broiler had been ignited.

Damn! Damn! Damn! Some of the ingredients must have bubbled over while baking and were continuing to burn. Before she could react, the overhead sprinklers chirped, then spurted like exploded water balloons.

Bunny bounced off her chair and popped out of the cubicle like refrigerator biscuits from a tube. Skye covered her head with both arms and dashed after her. The shrieks of Skye's neighboring finalists accompanied her flight.

Within seconds contest staff came running from the four corners of the warehouse. The first to arrive slid into Skye's booth as if he were making a grand slam home run; others followed, looking like cars piling up on I-55 in a snowstorm.

Grandma Sal's son, Jared, picked himself up from the heap and turned on Skye. "What the fu . . ." He caught himself and took a deep breath. Speaking between clenched teeth, he gritted, "What happened?"

He drummed his fingers against the partition as Skye explained, pointing to the offending dial. When she finished he said under his breath, "Great, another prank." Then, looking out at the gathered reporters, who were firing questions faster than a Xerox machine spitting out copies, he pasted a fake smile on his face and announced, "We've had a little mishap. No big deal. It only affected three workspaces, because Fine Foods went to the added expense of wiring the sprinklers in small sections. And, since the contest hasn't started, I'll get a cleanup crew here right away, and these people can get back to cooking."

While Bunny and Skye waited for their area to be put to rights, Skye picked bits of green pepper and red pimento off her arms. Without looking at the older woman, afraid that if she did she might smack her, Skye asked in her best psychologist voice, "Bunny, why didn't you take the casserole out of the oven when the timer went off?"

"Yesterday you told me not to touch it."

"But you did turn off the timer?" Skye wondered how the woman had managed to remain both spatter-free and dry.

"Well, yeah. I had to do that." Bunny adjusted her black-and-white-checked thigh-high stockings. "It was as annoying as a poor man begging for a kiss."

"Didn't you think that the timer might be set to indicate something? Like maybe when the casserole was done?"

"Nah." Bunny resumed painting her nails. "Thinking causes wrinkles."

"So does death," Skye muttered as she continued to scrape burned food from herself.

"What?" Bunny peered up at Skye.

"I said, please get me some wet paper towels."

"Sure. As soon as my nails dry."

"You know, Bunny"—Skye jammed her hands in her pockets so she wouldn't strangle the redhead, but she couldn't resist a verbal jab—"that outfit you have on is a bit on the young side for you. Don't you think?" She attempted to twist the knife. "How old are you, anyway?"

Bunny, clearly impervious to Skye's criticism, deposited the nail polish bottle in her purse and started to wave her fingertips in the air as she replied, "Age is just a number, and mine is unlisted."

At ten o'clock Grandma Sal blew a whistle and the Soup-to-Nuts Cooking Challenge officially started. Each contestant would have six hours to produce three identical dishes. One would go to the judges for tasting, one would go to the photographers for pictures, and the third would be cut into bite-size pieces and put out for the audience to evaluate. It was up to each finalist to determine which of their dishes went where.

Skye knew her mother would be among the most pressed for time. Not only did May have the mixing and baking to contend with, she also had the decorating. On the other hand, she also had a recipe she had successfully produced many, many times, while the best casserole Skye had ever managed to create ended up looking like drowned roadkill on the warehouse's floor.

As Skye set to work putting together her first official Chicken Supreme, her mind drifted to what had been happening in the outside world while she had been chained to a hot stove.

When Quirk talked to Charlie's cleaning crew, had they told him anything about the missing teenager? Had Wally found his father or figured out why he was checked into the motel under the assumed name of a cartoon character? And most important of all, had the police found out who killed Cherry Alexander?

Skye finished the first casserole and popped it into the oven. She couldn't start on the second one until the first was nearly done. May had warned her that each dish had to go into the oven as soon as it was finished. It could not be refrigerated nor sit at room temperature.

This left Skye between thirty and forty minutes to investigate. But what would she do about Bunny?

She glanced beneath her lashes at the redhead, who had settled back into the folding chair and was leafing through an *In Style* magazine. "Hey, Bunny, do you want anything? I'm going to take a walk and get a Diet Coke."

"Yeah, bring me a cup of coffee. Two creams and three fake sugars."

"Okay." Skye slipped out of the kitchen area, then poked her head back, praying Bunny wouldn't decide to come with her. "Listen, if I get held up and the timer goes off, take the casserole out of the oven, okay?"

"Sure." Bunny didn't look up from the glossy page. "I've got you covered."

Skye vowed to be back before the first ding.

Most of the contestants would be too busy to be talking about Cherry's murder, so Skye headed back to the hospitality lounge, a walled-off section furnished with tables and chairs. Coffee, tea, and soft drinks were provided, along with small pastries and sandwiches.

Two women and a man were the only occupants besides Skye. They sat at a table against the back wall, deeply involved in a conversation. Skye immediately recognized the trio as the contest judges.

Skye smiled to herself. This was perfect. She couldn't approach them, but it made sense that they would be in the lounge, since they wouldn't have anything to judge for the first hour or more.

She concentrated on being invisible, silently choosing a can of pop and a bear claw. Careful not to make eye contact, she selected a seat off to one side. She wasn't facing them, but they were in her peripheral vision. Someone had left the Books section of the Sunday *Tribune* on the table, and Skye opened it in front of her face.

As she hoped, the judges paid no attention to her and continued their discussion.

The first thing Skye heard was the male judge, Paul Voss, say, "I doubt they'll ever figure out who killed that woman. The cops here are straight out of *Mayberry R.F.D.* Barney Fife questioned me yesterday and could barely spell my name correctly."

"You needn't sound so pleased," Alice Gibson, the cookbook author, chided him. "All that means is that someone gets away with murder." She poked Paul in the ribs with her elbow. "Unless, of course, you're the killer."

"Very funny." Paul took a swig from a water bottle. "It was probably the husband. It's always the husband. Or the lover, if she had one."

"Whoever it was, they did us a favor," Ramona Epstein, the food editor, said. "That woman was the most annoying contestant I've ever run into."

"True." Alice fingered her napkin. "If flattery and bribes didn't work, she tried blackmail."

Paul straightened. "What'd she have on you?"

"Nothing I couldn't handle." Alice raised an eyebrow. "How about you two? She told me she had something on all of us."

Ramona and Paul both said, "Nothing," at the same time; then Paul added, "Well, we may be happy she's gone, but Fine Foods sure must be upset."

"Why?" Alice asked.

Ramona answered before Paul could. "Because Fine Foods is in the midst of a big buyout deal. This is not the time for Grandma Sal's to look bad in the press."

"So, Fine Foods wants the murderer caught and the case closed and forgotten ASAP?" Alice asked.

Paul nodded. "Sure, it's just like when you sell your house—you make sure the lawn is mowed, the carpet is vacuumed, and the windows are sparkling so you can get the best price."

The two women nodded.

He looked at his watch. "We probably should be getting back to the judging booth. If a dish comes in and we're not there, Grandma Sal will kill us."

After the judges left, Skye wrote down what she had heard. She'd been having some remarkable luck in eavesdropping on conversations about Cherry. On the other hand, what else would anyone be talking about the day after the murder?

Interesting that Cherry had been able to come up with information to threaten all of the judges. Of course, everyone had their secrets, but how had Cherry known about them? Did she have a private investigator on her payroll? *Hmm.* That wasn't as wild an idea as it might seem, considering the type of books she wrote. She'd need someone to dig up the dirt on her latest victim . . . er, subject.

Skye made a note to find out who Cherry was writing about in the book she was currently working on, then checked the clock. She had several minutes until her casserole was due out of the oven, but not wanting a repeat of that morning's disaster, she hurried back to her workspace.

After handing Bunny her coffee, Skye clicked on the

oven light. Her casserole looked perfect. A couple more minutes and she'd top it with the buttered bread crumbs and finish baking it. Meanwhile, she'd start on the next one.

As she worked, she casually said to Bunny, "Have you heard anything about the murdered woman?"

Bunny got up and leaned a hip on the counter. "Not much. She made big money from those tell-all books she wrote about famous people. Her husband is at least twelve years younger than her, screws any woman who is breathing, and his only job is as her manager."

"Wow." That certainly gave him motive. "Where did you hear all that?"

"People talking at the bowling alley." Bunny fluffed up her red curls. "And the husband's been hanging out at the bar, hitting on any female who crosses his path."

"Anyone take him up on his offer?" Skye finished with the second casserole and put the topping on the first one, returning it to the oven so the bread crumbs could brown.

"Not that I saw." Bunny adjusted her bra strap. "He may be good-looking, but there's something missing in him. Even me, with my bad luck with men, can tell that."

"Yeah, I noticed a certain coldness behind his eyes," Skye agreed, then chewed on her bottom lip. Kyle was looking better and better for his wife's murderer.

After a few minutes Skye took her first casserole out of the oven. It looked surprisingly good. The cheese was melted, the sauce bubbled, and no little elbows of macaroni were sticking up, waving their burnt arms. Now the question was whether to send it to the judges or the photographer. Each could award a dish up to forty-five points. The audience had a mere ten points, and it was mostly stacked with friends or relatives of the competitors, so Skye's getting their points was unlikely.

If only she could taste the casserole. But she couldn't, and she had to make a decision soon. Once it cooled off it wouldn't be good for either the judges or the pictures. Okay, she'd send this one to the photographers. It really did look perfect.

After delivering the dish to the photo area, Skye returned

to her workspace and checked her watch. Once again she had nearly half an hour until the second casserole came out of the oven—plenty of time to find a telephone and make contact with the outside world.

She repeated her previous instructions to Bunny and headed out of the cooking area. There were no public phones near the judges or behind the workstations. She spotted a few reporters in the media quarters, but they were all using cell phones.

Skye tapped her foot. She really wanted to talk to Wally. Maybe he had some news about the murder or the kidnapping, or at least what the heck was going on with his father.

She wandered around for another fruitless ten minutes, at which point she was ready to scream. How could there be no public phones in the whole place? Did they really assume that everyone had a cell, or, more important, that a cell would work when they needed it?

Blowing a curl out of her eyes, Skye decided she'd have to go over to the factory. Surely they'd have regular phones there. Unfortunately, a peek at her watch informed her that she had only ten minutes left. Realistically, could she get from the warehouse and back in time not to risk her dish?

No. She'd just have to wait until after she made her third casserole. Maybe she could borrow Bunny's cell phone, but it seemed sort of sleazy, using her ex-boyfriend's mother's phone to call her present significant other. *Crap.* Maybe it *was* time to buy a cell of her own.

The second casserole emerged looking as good as the first. Was there a chance she might actually win? Skye took this one to the judges. Her mother's Chicken Supreme was superb. If by some chance Skye had managed to reproduce the recipe, it could very well be one of the best dishes in the category.

As she assembled the third and last casserole, Skye daydreamed about what she would do with her half of the five-thousand-dollar prize. Two thousand would go for more home repair and remodeling, but she was taking the other five hundred and going shopping for spring and summer clothes. And she could actually go to Von Maur and Nord-strom, rather than Target and Kohl's.

Four hours into the contest Skye put her third dish into the oven. As long as nothing went wrong she'd finish with nearly an hour to spare, but right now she had thirty minutes available, and this time she was finding a phone.

Neither her mom nor Uncle Charlie had a cell, so that left Vince. He was doing May's Healthy Pasta Primavera, and Skye wondered how her brother was making out. As far as she knew Vince ventured into a kitchen only to grab a beer and a bag of pretzels. May brought him lunch at his salon every day, and if he wasn't going out in the evening, he ate supper at his parents'.

Not surprisingly, when Skye arrived at Vince's workstation, a group of women was gathered around the entrance. Skye elbowed her way through the adoring masses, announcing, "I'm his sister. Family business. Step aside."

The throng parted reluctantly, and she finally made her way to the edge of the inner sanctum. She could see Vince bent over his stove, his assistant standing a few steps behind him holding a spoon as if it were a scalpel ready to be slapped into his waiting hand.

Vince's helper was a stunning brunette who Skye remembered worked as a fitness instructor at her mother's health club. Somehow Skye didn't think her presence was a coincidence. The instructor had probably heard May talking about the contest and thought this would be a good time to spend some quality time with her client's handsome son. Girls had been plotting similar schemes since Vince had turned fourteen.

Skye dredged her mind for the assistant's name. Skye remembered that besides being May's fitness instructor, the woman had been the roommate of a suspect in a murder Skye had investigated a little over a year ago. But what was her name? It had something to do with a TV game show. Ah, Price, as in *The Price Is Right*. And her first name was . . . yes, Nikki, since she helped nick those inches away.

Clearing her throat, Skye said, "Nikki, hi, I'm Skye, Vince's sister."

"Shhh." The brunette frowned and put her finger to her lips, then whispered, "He's almost done."

Skye waited impatiently while Vince tossed whole-wheat spaghetti with cottage cheese, then topped the mixture with sautéed vegetables.

He turned with a flourish and bowed to the crowd, holding up his dish for everyone to admire. "Ta-da!"

After the applause died down, Skye finally got her brother's attention. "Do you have your cell phone with you?"

"I did, but Ma took it a few minutes ago. She said she had information that might help solve the murder."

CHAPTER 14

Fold Egg Whites
into Batter

For once Skye was eager to talk to her mother. She was hurrying over to May's cubicle when she noticed the time. Once again the minutes had ticked away, and her dish was in danger of burning if she didn't hustle back to her oven. Interrogating her mother would have to wait.

This was why she hated cooking. It felt as if she were shackled to the stove and, as soon as she got a certain distance away, someone removed a few links from the chain and yanked her back.

As she rushed toward her workstation, Skye plotted her escape. This was her last casserole; as soon as she browned the topping and gave the dish to the contest staff supervising the audience tastings, she'd be free. And once she was liberated she would find May, and then she'd call Wally.

She was nearing the beginning of the One-Dish Meals row when she heard a commotion. Several male voices battled to be heard, but a loud alto drowned them all out. "I'm gonna pop all you upside the head if you don't shut the—"

A tenor cut her off. "Why you bustin' our chops, Janelle? We was stickin' up for you."

Skye tiptoed forward and put her eye to the gap where the

cubicle partitions didn't quite meet. Once she got used to peering through the crack she could see Janelle Carpenter, the prison cook from Granger, surrounded by guys from the opening ceremony's cheering section. They looked even bigger and more menacing close up.

There were four of them, ranging in size from elephant to manatee. Skye guessed that the manatee had been the one to interrupt Janelle, because the cook had hold of him by his shoulders and was shaking him like a dust mop.

"Get outta my face, chump, before I kick your ass. There's only an hour or so left, and I ain't even got my third dish in the oven yet."

The elephant stepped forward. "Can you cook and listen? This is important."

She shrugged, but let go of the smallest guy. "Make it quick. My first one didn't turn out so good, so I had to send it to the audience tasting. The next one looked good, but I wasn't sure if I forgot the salt or not, so it had to go the photographers. That means this one gotta be perfect, 'cause it gotta go to the judges."

"Gotcha." Mr. Elephant nodded. "But you'll want to know this."

"Okay." Janelle's red flip-flops flapped against the soles of her feet as she turned back to the counter. "Go ahead, but you best not be wastin' my time."

The rhino, the second-largest of the quartet, said, "We was jes' kickin'—you know, waiting for more food to be brought out to taste—when this cracker tried to hustle us."

"How?"

"He offered us papes to give our points to his bitch's entry."

Janelle swung around holding a butcher knife. "How many times do I gotta tell you about using that word when you're talking about women?"

"Chill, Janelle, and check out the rest." Mr. Elephant shoved Mr. Rhino aside.

Janelle narrowed her eyes but went back to cooking. "So, what happened?"

"Dude—" The manatee started to talk, but the wilde-beest, the third in line, size-wise, interrupted.

"That punk not only tried to bribe us; he usin' fake money to do it with."

"How you know that?" Janelle looked over her shoulder. "You take him up on his offer? You gonna give someone be-sides me your points?"

All four men backed away, protesting their innocence, but still putting at least a knife's length between them and Janelle.

Mr. Elephant, plainly the leader of the group, cleared his throat. "No, Janelle, honey, you know we wouldn't ever do that to you."

"No?" Janelle's growl could be heard clearly over the whir of her mixer.

"No, babe, that's straight-up."

"Okay, so why you be tellin' me this?"

"Because when we turned him down, the fool tried to make us change our mind by tryin' to intimidate us."

"He have a death wish?"

They all shrugged this time, and Mr. Manatee said, "We just thought you ought to report this guy to the man, since you tol' us not to get into any fights here."

"Why didn't you all report him, 'stead of botherin' me?" Janelle frowned as she smoothed a concoction into her casserole pan.

"Babe," Mr. Elephant answered, "you know the man don' listen to dudes like us."

Janelle slid the dish into the oven and set the timer, then turned and asked, "So, how am I supposed to report this chump if I didn't see him?"

"They won't have no trouble findin' this cracker," Mr. Manatee blurted out. "He a little guy, 'bout five-seven, five-eight, with tats up and down both arms. He don't weigh no more than a buck twenty, twenty-five, and he bald on top, with a ratty old ponytail down his back."

"That all?"

Skye could hear the sarcasm in Janelle's voice, but obvi-ously her crew couldn't, because Mr. Wildebeest said, "No, he got a stomach on him like a big ol' muskmelon, and he's dressed all in camo."

"I'll take care of it as soon as my casserole is done." Janelle waved toward the door. "Now you all get the hell out of here."

Skye jumped back from the peephole and hastily walked away. The herd had described Earl Doozier, right down to his little potbelly. What in the world was he thinking, trying to buy votes, and with fake money? Not to mention threatening guys who would find a Hummer a tight fit.

Of course, the simple answer was that Earl didn't think. His impulse control was less than that of a two-year-old with attention deficit disorder. And, while he had a mind like a steel trap, it had long ago been left out in the rain and rusted shut.

Which meant she'd better find him right away. She needed to stop him before he got Glenda kicked out of the competition, or one of Janelle's guys forgot their vow of nonviolence. Because if Earl didn't stop his nefarious activities, either his darling wife or one of the animal pack would end up kicking his poor scrawny butt from here to St. Louis.

But what about her casserole? If she didn't get back to it soon the sprinklers would be going off again. Still, even though Earl deserved whatever Glenda or the herd dished out to him, he had saved Skye's life on more than one occasion, and it seemed wrong to put a cooking contest ahead of their friendship—no matter how odd and twisted that alliance might be.

Sending a silent prayer that Bunny might actually follow her orders and take the dish from the oven when the timer went off, Skye turned around again, this time heading for the audience.

As she emerged from the glare of the bright lights aimed at the cooking areas, it took her eyes a minute or so to adjust. Once they were focused she saw several people she knew, including aunts and cousins who had come out to support May and her children.

She waved at her relatives and friends, then scanned the rest of the seats for any sign of Earl. It didn't take long to spot him. A crowd had formed a half circle at the rear, and everyone was focused on an unfamiliar woman dressed in jeans and a plaid flannel shirt. She was tall and broad, and easily held the errant Doozier off the ground by the scruff of his neck while hitting him on the nose with a rolled-up newspaper as if he were a naughty puppy.

Edging her way through the crowd, Skye tried to come up with something to say, but as she emerged from the mob all she could think of was, "Put the Doozier down."

It sounded familiar. She thought she had issued a similar command during last summer's hundred-mile yard sale when the goat-cheese guy accused Earl of feeding the guy's kids—baby goats, not children—to the Doozier's pet lion.

The order had worked back in August, but this time the woman looked at Skye as if she were a flea, then turned her attention back to Earl. "Bad man, bad man. No cheating. Stop it right now."

Skye hated having her suggestions ignored. It happened too often in her job as a school psychologist. When parents or administrators disregarded her ideas she could wait them out, as they generally ended up coming back to her for help, but in this situation time was not on her side.

How could she get through to this person? Maybe if Skye blew a dog whistle or offered her a liver treat, the woman would put Earl down. But before Skye could find a muzzle and a leash, Earl wiggled out of the woman's grasp.

Spittle flew from his semitoothless mouth and spattered on the lady's chest as he yelled, "I keep telling you, Miz King, I ain't cheatin'!"

Ms. King bopped Earl again with the newspaper. "What do you call offering people money to assign their points to your wife's recipe?"

Oh, no. Skye tensed, sensing impending doom. Everyone in Scumble River knew you didn't accuse a Doozier of wrongdoing—at least, not to his face and without backup. Clearly this woman was from out of town.

While Skye was trying to figure out what to say or do to defuse the situation, Earl's wife, Glenda, materialized next to her husband, holding a cast-iron frying pan in a threatening grip. Glenda was the epitome of the Red Raggers' ideal woman. She wore a denim miniskirt, the overtaxed material fading to white across her derriere, and a bubble-gum pink halter top that was losing its fight with gravity. She had swept her hair, dyed one shade beyond believability, into a ponytail, and the black roots were an interesting contrast to the rest of the platinum mane.

A movement behind Ms. King dragged Skye's gaze from Glenda. Sneaking up on the group was Hap, Earl's brother. Skye flinched. She hadn't known Hap had been released from prison. He'd been doing a five-year sentence for child abuse and attempted murder—hers. He'd tried to kill Skye when she turned him in for beating his son.

Hap was unarmed, but was scary nonetheless. He was short and skinny like his brother Earl, although not as densely tattooed. While Earl preferred sweatpants and tank tops, Hap liked to dress as if a rodeo might suddenly appear in Scumble River. His tight blue jeans were cinched with a wide leather belt that sported a silver buckle the size of a Frisbee, and his shiny western-style shirt had mother-of-pearl snaps. As he got closer, the stench of his cologne mixed with the alcohol fumes that surrounded him and created an olfactory nightmare.

While Skye had been distracted by Hap's appearance, Earl's twin siblings, Elvis and Elvira, had flanked Ms. King. They both preferred to dress in uninterrupted black, including the switchblades they flicked open and held at the ready. Elvis had dropped out of school, but Elvira was still one of Skye's students. She tried to catch the girl's gaze, but the teen refused to look at her.

Skye knew she had to do something before someone's blood was shed, because without a doubt, no matter who else got hurt, her plasma would be mingled with theirs.

Desperate, she decided to go with the obvious, wishing she had her walkie-talkie and identification card with her. Why hadn't she thought to bring them? This was a crime scene. The only reason she could come up with for her lapse was waking up before the break of dawn two mornings in a row. Skye's mind never did work well when she was sleep-deprived.

Shrugging off the excuses, she said, "Ms. King, I'm the psychological consultant for the Scumble River Police Department. Please put your newspaper down and step away from the Doozier."

Skye wasn't sure if the woman finally noticed that Earl's relatives could have passed for the cast of *The Addams Family* or if she was impressed by Skye's title, but Ms. King stepped back from the little man and turned on Skye. "Are you in charge?" While Skye pondered that question, Ms. King strode over to her and said, "This man is going around offering people money to use their points on his wife's recipe. And if they refuse he intimates that physical harm will befall them."

"Yes, so I've heard." Skye nodded. "I'm here to put a stop to it."

Earl had been backing away from Skye and Ms. King, but when Skye spoke he stopped and bleated, "Now, Miz Skye. You can't do that. There ain't nothin' in the rules that says I can't reward people for doin' a good thing or punish them if they don't."

Skye paused. Why did that sound so familiar?

"After all, ain't you been tellin' me and tellin' me that's what I needs to do with the kids?" Earl answered her unspoken question.

Ms. King glared at Skye and took a step closer. "You told him to do this?"

All eyes swung toward her. The crowd buzzed with comments, all of them malevolent. Skye cringed. With the Dooziers, ignorance was not a barrier to self-expression.

As if to prove Skye's thoughts correct, Glenda pointed her pink acrylic fingernail at Skye. "That's right. She told us it was okay."

Skye gulped. "No. That's not what I meant." They were twisting what she had been trying to show them about positive reinforcement. "Earl, you know that wasn't what I was trying to teach you. Tell them the truth."

Earl squirmed under her stare, but then looked at his

wife, who waved her frying pan, and at the large woman, who shook her rolled-up newspaper at him. "I'm sorry, Miz Skye, but you did say it."

Great, she was about to be torn apart by a mob at a cooking contest because she had tried to teach some parenting techniques to two people who should never have been allowed to breed in the first place. There was some irony in this, but she couldn't quite put her finger on it.

She swallowed—her throat had gone dry—then raised her voice and tried to explain one more time. "Look, everyone, I'm a school psychologist. I was trying to teach them parenting skills. I certainly did not tell them they could use those methods to try to cheat in this contest."

Ms. King glared at Skye. "That's all fine and good, except how do we know how many people he's already bribed? My son is entered in this contest, and Butch deserves to win. If he loses to this . . . this . . . tramp, it will be on your shoulders."

Glenda narrowed her rabbitlike brown eyes. "Who you callin' a tramp, you old cow?" She raised the cast-iron skillet, but before she could bring it down on the other woman's head a flash went off.

Skye whirled around. They had been discovered by the media. Reporters were taking notes, photographers were clicking cameras, and the local TV station was zooming in.

Briefly, Skye considered throwing her apron over her face and making a run for it. But since several flashes had already gone off and the TV camera had been rolling for who knew how long, what was the use? Besides, those people who ran from the courthouse to their limos with their coats over their heads always looked guiltier than if they had walked erect, maintaining an innocent expression and saying, "No comment."

Still, someone should try to do something to mitigate the damage. Grandma Sal and her company had been wonderful to the community for years and years, and this type of media exposure couldn't be good for the Fine Foods brand. Where were the business's PR people? Surely they could handle the situation.

Skye's gaze searched the crowd as her mind rummaged around for an idea. On her second sweep of the throng, Skye narrowed her eyes and shaded them with her hand. Was that Brandon and JJ standing just beyond the media?

Yes. JJ, the pudgy one with the blond curls, had just joined Brandon, the slim, dark-haired one. She made her way toward them, and when she could speak without having to shout, she said, "JJ, Brandon, you need to do something. This will look awful on the six-o'clock news."

Brandon asked, "What happened?"

Skye explained the Dooziers as well as she could, then described the situation with Ms. King, ending with, "Then the mob turned on me, but Ms. King insulted Glenda Doozier, and that diverted everyone's attention."

JJ bit his thumbnail. "We'd better get Dad and Grandma."

Both JJ and Brandon had their cell phones out in a flash.

Skye opened her mouth to suggest that two grown men should be able to handle the situation on their own, but then realized that both these guys were very young for their age, having led protected and pampered lives. Chronologically they may have been in their late twenties, but emotionally they were probably closer to sixteen or seventeen. Frannie and Justin were more mature than these two.

As his fingers flew over the tiny buttons, JJ said, "I'm calling Dad; you get Grandma."

Brandon nodded, pressing a few numbers.

JJ and Brandon were still trying to get a signal on their cell phones when a gunshot rang out through the warehouse. Instinctively Skye went into bodyguard mode and tackled the young men, sending them all to the floor in a gigantic heap.

As Skye worked her way free of tangled arms and legs, having somehow ended up on the bottom of the pile, she heard more screams and shouts. Her first clear view was of running feet and a panicked crowd. Only the thought of her burning casserole motivated her to continue freeing herself rather than pulling JJ and Brandon back over herself like a blanket.

CHAPTER 15

Add Nuts

It had taken Skye several minutes to persuade JJ and Brandon to get off of her. They had been reluctant to stand up, even after they were reassured that there would be no more shooting.

The situation had disintegrated so quickly, she could hardly blame them for being a bit disinclined to leap into the fray. There had been the gunshot, which caused the audience to charge toward the exit like a tidal wave mowing down anyone and anything in its path. Next there was a dramatic showdown between Hap and the factory security guards, who had appeared just in time to witness Hap twirling his pistol in the air and yelling drunkenly, "Yee-haw! Let's get this here shindig started."

Apparently Skye had been mistaken in her initial assessment—Hap Doozier had been armed after all.

The guards must have been used to dealing with inebriated counterfeit cowboys, because they snuck up behind Hap and had him roped and tied so fast they would have won the first-prize buckle if Hap-busting had been a rodeo event.

As they passed her, Skye heard one of the security men shouting into his walkie-talkie, arranging for the police to pick up the errant Jesse James. She smiled in relief when one of the other guards commented that Hap was on his way back to prison, since possession of a firearm was a violation of his parole.

While the Fines and their PR staff worked on getting the stampeded people back inside and in their seats, Skye finally headed to her workspace. By now her casserole was probably a charcoal briquette, and there wasn't enough time to make another, but at least no one had gotten hurt. She told herself again and again that that was all that mattered, hoping May would buy into that sentiment when she heard about the incident.

Earl had been banned from the premises, and the Fines had announced that his Earl dollars were worthless, but Glenda was allowed to remain and compete. She had somehow convinced Grandma Sal that she was an innocent victim of her husband's stupidity—which was not a far stretch from the truth. It appeared that the only casualty of the Doozers' antics might be Skye's Chicken Supreme.

Behind the spotlights and inside the cubicles, everything appeared normal. If the contestants had heard the ruckus on the other side of the warehouse, either they had ignored it or taken a look and were already back at their stoves. There were only fifteen minutes left on the clock, and many of the finalists were putting the last-minute touches on their dishes. Those who had finished were cleaning up.

Skye approached her space with trepidation. She sniffed. No smell of smoke. She checked the floor and partitions. Nothing seemed freshly soaked. Could Bunny have actually come through for her?

Stepping around the corner, Skye held her breath, then exhaled it loudly. The stove and counter looked just as she had left them, but Bunny was gone. Skye checked the oven. Her casserole was gone, too.

It looked as if Bunny had actually taken the dish from the oven and brought it to the contest staff. Hope flared in Skye's chest until she remembered that the casserole needed the bread-crumb topping to be complete. Without it she'd be disqualified.

She sank onto the chair and pushed Bunny's abandoned

magazine off the seat, watching the shiny pages slither to the ground. *Shit!* If only Bunny had followed instructions and just taken the dish from the oven, Skye could have still gotten it topped and into the contest official's hands in time.

But that was Bunny's curse. She always meant well, but things never turned out right for her. It was hard to understand how she remained such an optimist.

Simon would have said it was because most of the trouble his mother caused was for other people. Nevertheless, no one ended up on the shady side of fifty, managing a bowling alley in a small town, dependent on the goodwill of a son she was estranged from, and with a daughter she had met only a few months ago, without making some really bad choices.

Skye felt drained. There was nothing she could do now. The decision to find Earl rather than save her dish had been made and there was no going back. She only hoped that May wouldn't be too disappointed in her.

Willing herself to get up off the chair, Skye started to rise just as the ending whistle blew. The contest was officially over.

Seconds later Bunny flew into the workspace. She beamed at Skye and threw a pair of pot holders toward the counter, not appearing to notice when they missed by several inches and dropped to the floor.

Skye picked them up, stalling for time while she tried to think of what to say. Bunny had tried her best, and Skye didn't want her to feel unappreciated.

But Bunny beat her to the punch, grabbing her by the shoulders and waltzing her around the little cubicle. "We did it! I got it to the officials with ten minutes to spare, and she said it looked scrumptious."

Skye dug in her heels, forcing the older woman to stop dancing, then squirmed out of her embrace. "I appreciate what you did, Bunny, but you should have waited for me. Without the topping the dish will be disqualified, since it doesn't match the submitted recipe."

Bunny frowned. "But—"

Skye cut her off. "It's okay. I know you were just trying to help, but you need to learn to follow directions."

"No, I—"

"I said it was okay. Just don't tell May. I'll let her think I screwed up. She's prepared for that, but to come so close and have this happen would send her blood pressure into the stratosphere."

"Wait." Bunny stamped her foot. "Listen to me. I put the topping on before I brought it over. You had it all ready, and I saw what you did the other two times. So when you were so late, I just sprinkled on the bread crumbs and browned the whole thing for a few minutes in the oven. You won't be disqualified."

Skye opened her mouth, then closed it, then opened it again. Had she heard Bunny correctly? Had she really saved the day?

Gradually Skye's lips began to twitch. Wait until she told her mother that Bunny, May's archenemy, had salvaged the Chicken Supreme entry.

"That's great!" Giggling, Skye enveloped Bunny in a bear hug. "You're a lifesaver. Thank you."

"You're welcome. Too bad you and Sonny Boy aren't seeing each other anymore. You could tell him his mama finally did something right."

Skye swallowed the lump in her throat and gave Bunny a final squeeze before releasing her. "Don't worry. I'll make sure he knows."

"Good." Bunny picked up her magazine and purse. "You don't need my help cleaning up, do you? Charlie offered me a ride home, and I don't want to keep the darling man waiting." Without pausing for a reply, she trotted out the doorway.

Skye shook her head. With Bunny it was always one hop forward and two hops back. It would have been nice to have help with the cleanup, but considering everything, doing a few dishes and mopping a floor was the least Skye could do for the woman who had saved her casserole.

She was just putting away the last utensil when May bustled into the cubicle. Her critical stare examined every inch of the workspace. She closed a cupboard door that had been slightly ajar, then ran her finger over the stove's cooktop.

Impassively she opened the oven door, peered inside, and scraped something off the interior with her fingernail, throwing the debris in the wastebasket before acknowledging her daughter's presence.

When May straightened, she said, "We can go as soon as you bag the trash." She held up a white plastic sack closed with a yellow twist tie. "We can throw mine and yours both in the Dumpster on the way out."

"Don't they have someone to do that?" Skye took off her apron and grabbed her purse from a drawer.

"Yes. Us." May stared at Skye, then looked pointedly at the trash bin. "Didn't you read your rule sheet?"

"Most of it. Why?"

"Because it states that in case of a draw, either in your category or for the grand prize, the cleanliness of your workstation will be the tiebreaking point."

"I saw that, but I didn't see where it said it included garbage duty."

May *tsk*ed. "Better safe than sorry."

Words that had been forming in Skye all during the contest threatened to spill out, but she swallowed them. Maybe her mother was right. It would be awful to lose five thousand dollars because of an unemptied sack of garbage.

From what Skye could tell when she and her mother emerged from the cubicle rows, the other finalists seemed to have all left. The judges and photographer remained, as did a large part of the audience, who were milling around tasting the last few dishes.

As Skye and May headed for the back door, Skye said, "Vince told me you borrowed his cell phone to call Wally, because you remembered something that could help catch the murderer. What was it?"

May lowered her voice. "I remembered that the person who helped me with my box was left-handed."

"How did you notice that?"

"You know how when you reach for something you usually do it with your dominant side? This guy took my tote bag with his left hand; then, when he carried the box, he switched it to his right and had the box in his left hand."

"That's great, Mom." Skye tried to think of anyone involved who was left-handed. She hadn't really paid attention, but she would now. "Did Wally have anything to say? Anything new in the investigations?"

"I left a message with Thea. She said she hadn't heard a thing, and that both Wally and Quirk had been in the field the whole day." May held the door for Skye, then followed her daughter to the Dumpsters.

Skye heaved her bag into the huge black bin, then took her mother's and did the same.

As they walked toward the car, May stopped and picked up a piece of crumpled paper nearly buried in a footprint in the dirt beside the sidewalk. She looked around but there were no trash cans, so she half turned to go back toward the Dumpsters.

"Just give it to me, Mom." Skye held out her hand. "I'll throw it away when I get home."

May handed it over, and Skye thrust it into her jeans pocket.

They got into the car in silence, both exhausted from cooking for nearly eleven straight hours. Skye rested her head on the seat back and closed her eyes, not opening them until she felt the car turn into her driveway.

May pulled the Olds up to the front walkway and asked, "Do you want Dad and me to pick you up for the square dance and pork-chop supper?"

"Are they still having that?" Skye had been certain that the event would have been canceled to show respect for the dead finalist.

"Yes, didn't you get the flyer?" May rummaged in her purse and handed Skye a sheet of paper, but instead of letting her read it, May continued, "It says that they checked with Cherry's husband and he said to go ahead. That Cherry wouldn't want them to call it off."

Skye raised an eyebrow. Kyle must know Cherry better than anyone else, but Skye's impression of the author had been more prima donna and less humanitarian.

"Do I have to go?" Skye knew the answer before the words left her lips.

"Dante went to a lot of work organizing this event, and it would be disrespectful to him, Grandma Sal, and the whole community for you not to show up." May's lips thinned. "Especially since Dante's attending, and he only got out of the hospital this morning."

"I'll take that as a yes." Skye opened her door and slid out.

"You're a grown woman. I certainly can't tell you what to do."

Skye muttered under her breath, "Since when?"

"So, shall we pick you up?"

"No, thanks. I'll drive myself." Skye waved at her mom and started to shut the car door. "Thanks for the ride. See you tonight."

May shouted through the closed window, "It starts at seven. Don't be late." Without waiting for a response, she tooted the horn and drove off.

Bingo met Skye as she walked through the front door. His purr-o-meter was turned to high, making his sides vibrate like a bagpipe playing "Amazing Grace." She scooped him up, rubbing his ears and under his chin.

After thirty-two-point-one seconds of petting, he wiggled out of her arms and trotted toward the kitchen. About halfway down the hall he stopped and looked back to make sure she was following.

Skye had paused to put down her purse and apron, but reassured the feline, "Go ahead. I'll be there in a minute. I doubt you'll starve before I arrive."

Bingo flicked his tail twice—to show he meant business—then continued toward his food dish.

Skye risked the wrath of the feline by poking her head into the parlor as she passed. The indicator light on her answering machine beamed a steady red. No one had tried to contact her.

Darn. She was hoping to hear that some progress had been made on the missing teen, the murder, or even the mysterious disappearing father. In any case, as soon as she fed Bingo she'd call Wally. She knew he was busy, but she needed to update him on all she had heard during the contest.

Bingo was waiting by his food bowls when Skye walked into the kitchen. One bowl held a heaping portion of dry cat food; the other had been licked so clean it looked as if it had just come out of the dishwasher.

According to the vet, Bingo was allowed one small can of wet cat food a day, at the most. He could have as much of the dry as he wished. Unfortunately, what he desired was an unending supply of the canned, and for the dry to disappear in a puff of smoke and never come back.

Most of the time Skye stood firm, parceling out his Fancy Feast a third of a can at a time, once in the morning, once when she got back from work, and the last before bed. But on days like today, when she had no idea what her schedule would be, she gave him the whole can before she left the house, which resulted in a demanding feline when she got home.

She should ignore his plaintive meows, the sad slump of his tail, and the hungry looks—just as she should ignore her own craving for chocolate and cookies. Normally she was about 50 percent successful with either endeavor, but today had been extremely stressful, and she decided both she and Bingo deserved a treat.

After putting half a can of grilled tuna flakes in the cat's bowl, she grabbed a package of Pepperidge Farm chocolate-chunk cookies from the cupboard and headed upstairs. She shed her clothes in the bedroom, then walked into the bathroom and turned on the shower.

While she waited for the water to get hot—it had a long way to come from the water heater in the basement to the second floor—she tore open the cookie package and lifted out the little plastic tub containing four cookies.

The nutrition information on the side of the bag claimed a serving size was one cookie. Where did these people come from, Planet of the Barbie Dolls? Obviously a real portion should be what the plastic basket held.

Once she had showered, blown her hair dry, and gotten dressed for the square dance, Skye went downstairs to see if any calls had come in. There were still no messages, so she phoned the police department.

After exchanging pleasantries with the afternoon-shift dispatcher, Skye asked for Wally. The woman informed her that he was still working and hadn't taken a break to answer his messages all day.

Skye tried his home number—no one answered, not even a machine—and his cell, which apparently was still broken, since it went immediately to voice mail. Frustrated, she wasn't sure what to do. Trixie needed to get back from her vacation soon because Skye needed a brainstorming partner badly.

It was six o'clock. She had an hour before she had to show up at the pork-chop supper. What should her next move be? Her gaze wandered to the little antique desk in the corner of the parlor, and an idea came to her almost as if someone had whispered in her ear.

She'd write it all down and drop her notes at the PD. Maybe while she was there she could find out what was going on with both the missing girl and the murder.

CHAPTER 16

Pour Batter into Prepared Pans

The police department parking lot was full, which, at nearly six thirty p.m., was surprising. The PD shared a building with the city hall and library, which meant that from nine to five cars prowled the tiny lot looking for an empty space, but in the evening there were usually only two automobiles occupying slots—the dispatcher's and that of the officer on duty.

Wally must have called everyone in, including the part-timers. What was up? Had there been a break in either one of the cases?

Skye felt a surge of triumph when a young man exited the building and approached a silver Camaro. Skye eased her Bel Air into position and waited for the guy to back out. Instead he rolled down his window and a smoke ring drifted into the night air.

Shoot! This whole not being able to find a parking spot was starting to make Skye feel like she lived in Chicago rather than Scumble River. Gritting her teeth, she exited the lot and drove down the block until she found a space.

On the walk back she noted that the town was hopping. A steady stream of traffic filled both the road the PD faced and the street it intersected, which was remarkable for a Sunday night, when most of the Scumble River population was usually at home watching *60 Minutes* and preparing for the workweek ahead.

The cooking challenge's change in schedule had probably thrown everyone off, especially with school being closed the next day. Skye had been shocked to get that message. Dante must have pulled a lot of strings and made a lot of promises to get the superintendent to cancel classes so that the contest could use the auditorium/gymnasium for the award ceremony.

Before the country's heightened security, Fine Foods could have used the auditorium and only gym classes would have had to be canceled, but now the school district policy didn't allow that many strangers in the building while students were present.

Maybe the fact that they hadn't taken any of the year's snow days helped. However, snow days were really only a technicality needed because of the way the teacher contracts were written. They still had to be made up, so now they'd have to go an extra day into the summer, a detail everyone conveniently forgot as they were celebrating their impromptu holiday.

When Skye pushed open the glass door of the PD, she immediately noticed the busy hum. She waved to the dispatcher behind the bulletproof glass window that enclosed the counter on her right, and the woman buzzed her through the door leading to the rest of the station. Cubicles that were normally empty were filled with officers who were on either the phone, the computer, or both.

One young man Skye didn't recognize was performing percussive maintenance on his PC. He didn't seem to realize that smacking the crap out of an electronic device rarely improved its working condition. But then, artificial intelligence had never been a match for natural stupidity.

Skye shook her head and moved on. From the snatches of conversation she heard, half the officers were looking for Ashley and half for the murderer. Had something happened to stir up the search for the missing girl?

She was tempted to stop and ask, but the men looked too busy. Not to mention she had only a short time to turn up at the supper before May sent the search-and-rescue dogs after her.

Dashing to the back of the building, she quickly climbed the steps. Wally's office and a couple of small storage areas were the only rooms in the truncated upstairs space. There was no egress between the PD and the portion of the second floor that was located over the city hall, which contained the three-room Scumble River library.

Skye's heart skipped a beat when she saw Wally leaning back in his chair with his eyes closed. He exuded an attraction that enticed her like a golden box of Godiva chocolates. As she got closer she saw that his features were etched with exhaustion and defeat, and a soft gasp of pained empathy escaped her.

He immediately straightened, his eyelids flying open. At first he scowled, but his expression brightened when he saw Skye. In one swift movement he rose to his feet and met her halfway across the office in a fierce embrace.

She buried her face against his throat, enjoying a moment of pure pleasure.

His breath hot against her ear, he whispered, "How did you know I needed to hold you?"

"Bingo told me." She wound her arms inside his jacket and around his back.

His chuckle shed years from his face. "In that case he must be the one hanging up the phone every time I try to call you."

"What?" Skye was distracted by the touch of his thumb stroking her jaw.

"I tried two or three times today and your machine hung up on me every time."

"Guess I need a new answering machine." She struggled to focus, but the tingle where his thigh brushed her hip was hard to ignore. Breathlessly she continued, "And while I'm at it, I might as well get a cell phone, too."

"It's about time," he growled as he nipped at the sensitive cord running from her ear down her neck.

"Did you find out what was wrong with your . . ." Skye tried to concentrate. There was a reason she had stopped by, and something else she had to do tonight, but darned if she could remember. " . . . cell?"

"No. Bingo must have thrown it down the stairs last time I was over." His lips hovered above hers as he spoke.

Suddenly impatient, she pressed her open mouth to his. He needed no further invitation, and his kiss devoured her.

A few seconds, or minutes, or hours later—she had no idea how much time had passed—an apologetic cough from the doorway made her lift her head.

Anthony, one of the part-time patrol officers, stood on the threshold, his face beet red. "Uh, I'm really sorry, Chief, but your phone must be off the hook, and I finally got Mr. Alexander on the line. I know you wanted to talk to him."

After a quick squeeze and kiss on the nose, Wally released Skye. "No problem. What line?"

"Four. He sounded drunk or high or something," Anthony added over his shoulder as he retreated down the hall.

"I'll put it on speakerphone so you can tell me what you think," Wally said to Skye as he turned to his desk. "This jerk has been avoiding me all day."

Skye sat down and took a pad of paper and a pen from her purse.

Wally pressed the button and said, "Mr. Alexander, thank you for calling. I'm sorry for your loss."

"Thanks, dude. It's so bogus. She was so young. Who'd want her dead?" The voice on the speaker broke. "Are you sure it wasn't an accident?"

Wally shot a look at Skye, making sure she heard that, then ignored the man's question. "I'd really like to talk to you in person, Mr. Alexander."

"Uh, actually, man, my last name's not Alexander; it's Hunter. Cherry used her maiden name—you know, professionally."

"I understand." Wally made a note. "Sorry for the confusion. So, Mr. Hunter, would it be possible for you to come into the station now and talk?"

"Sorry, no can do. My son's asleep and I don't have anyone to watch him."

Skye scribbled the words *housekeeper* and *nanny* on her legal pad and held it up for Wally to read.

He nodded and said, "How about your housekeeper or the nanny?"

"I gave Juanita the day off, and we fired the nanny Friday night when we got home from the dinner."

"I see." Wally made another note. "Well, maybe you can come in tomorrow, Mr. Hunter, when your housekeeper is back at work."

"Maybe. There's just so much to do," Kyle whined. "We'll see."

"Okay. Try to get some rest, Mr. Hunter."

After Wally hung up, Skye raised an eyebrow. "Why do I think that Kyle Hunter will have company tonight rather than take a nap?"

Wally gave her wolfish grin. "Hey, I've been trying to have a face-to-face with that guy since Saturday morning. At least now I know he's home and will be staying there for a while."

"Interesting that the nanny was fired right before Cherry's murder."

"If he's telling the truth."

"Good point." Skye got up from her chair. "Listen, I know you're in a hurry to go see Hunter, and I need to get to the pork-chop supper/square dance before Mom sends out the FBI's missing persons unit, but I wanted to share some info with you."

"How about you come over to my house when the supper and dance are over?" Wally put his hand on the small of her back and walked her out of his office.

Skye studied her watch. "That should be around ten. Is that okay?"

"Great." He locked the door. "If something comes up, leave a message with the dispatcher, and I'll do the same." He frowned. "Tomorrow after the cooking contest is over, we're both going to Joliet to buy us cell phones."

As they descended the stairs Skye said, "Oh, remember

that argument I told you about between Hunter and the nanny? I forgot to mention that he said Cherry had an air-tight prenup so he couldn't divorce her, but Bunny said he's been a frequent flier in the bar at the bowling alley and is a real hound dog."

"Thanks. I'll keep all that in mind when I question him."

"Also, ask him if Cherry ever hired private investigators to look into the people she wrote about. She seemed to have found out a lot of secrets about the judges and the other contestants. Oh, and ask him who was going to be the subject of her next book."

"Got it." Wally opened the door leading from the PD to the garage. "See you at ten."

It was exactly seven p.m. when Skye arrived at the Brown Bag banquet hall. People stood two deep all the way from the buffet tables to the entrance. Skye spotted her parents near the front and waved. May motioned for her to join them, but Skye shook her head. In Scumble River, cutting into a food line was a crime punishable by social death. May, one of the queen bees, might be able to get away with it, but Skye, a drone, knew she could not.

Instead she walked into the hall's attached bar and ordered a Diet Coke with a slice of lime. The place was empty except for the owner, Jess Larson, who was sitting on a stool reading a book.

As he slid the glass in front of her, he said, "I hear you all had some excitement at the cooking contest. I told Dante I didn't have a good vibe about having it here."

"Yeah." Skye took a long drink and sighed. "Why doesn't anything ever go smoothly in Scumble River?"

"What would be the fun in that?" Jess was a relative newcomer to town, having bought the Brown Bag a couple of years ago from his cousin when she retired.

"You sound like some of my ADHD kids."

"I probably was, but we moved around a lot, so the school never had a chance to stick a label on me."

"Hey," Skye said sharply. "I do not stick labels on kids. I identify them so they can get the help they need."

"Whoa. Sorry." He held up his hand. "See, it's that poor impulse control coming out."

"Right." Sarcasm dripped from the word. "So, you hear much about the murder?"

"The usual." Jess pushed a dish of snack mix toward Skye, who helped herself to a handful. "Since the victim's from out of town, no one seems to know much."

"Yeah." Skye's voice retained its sarcastic tone. "Laurel is a whole forty-five minutes from here. Might as well be a foreign country."

Jess chuckled. "You sure you don't want some rum in that Diet Coke? You sound less perky than usual."

"Perky!" Skye glared at him. "I am never perky. Perky is for cheerleaders and Miss America."

This time Jess raised both hands in surrender. "I meant . . . uh . . . not in good spirits."

"Well, okay." Skye examined the bar owner. He was only an inch or so taller than she was, with black eyes and brown hair. She didn't know his age, but guessed he was nearing thirty. He seemed friendly enough, but didn't socialize and rarely mentioned his past. She grinned. He needed a girl-friend. Who could she fix him up with?

"I don't like that smile," he said, his gaze wary.

"I don't know what you mean." Skye waited for a beat, then asked, "Do you ever take a night off?"

"I think you're real cute and I like talking to you, but . . ." Jess backed away. "One thing I've learned is never to mess with a cop's girlfriend."

"Not me, silly." Skye giggled. "But I have some single friends."

"No. I do not do blind dates or fix-ups." Then, as if to dis-tract her, he said, "Speaking of cops, the chief's father has been in here a couple of times—though I almost didn't rec-ognize him this time, what with him having shaved his head and all."

"Yeah, that was a surprise," Skye bluffed.

"Is he moving to Scumble River or something?"

"I don't think so." Skye's thoughts started to race. Or was he? Maybe that was why he was visiting. No, that was silly.

The head of a multinational company would not live in Scumble River. "Do you remember the last time he was here?"

"He left just a few minutes ago."

Damn! "He have anything interesting to say?"

"Nothing special." Jess shrugged. "Mostly we talked about the stock market and baseball—I was trying to explain to him why the fans stick by the Cubs even though they continue to lose year after year. He had a hard time with that concept. Seemed to think winning is the only thing that matters."

That was certainly consistent with the picture Wally had painted of his father. "Anything else?"

"I mentioned the murder, and he said it was a shame, because the bad publicity would hurt Grandma Sal's business."

Jess and Skye chatted for a few minutes more; then Skye paid for her drink and walked back to the banquet hall. The line had disappeared, and Skye stepped across the room to the buffet. She made her selections, then looked over the sea of faces, trying to find a place to sit.

She spotted an arm waving. Not surprisingly it was her mother. She waved back and made her way to the table. When she got near enough to see who else was sitting with May, a sense of déjà vu washed over her once again. This whole weekend seemed to keep repeating itself.

Just like at Friday's dinner, her parents had somehow managed to sit with the people Skye most wanted to avoid.

How in the world had both Simon and Kathryn Steele, the owner of the *Scumble River Star*, ended up at the same table as May and Jed? Simon was clearly escorting his mother, whom May loathed, which should have guaranteed they wouldn't choose to sit together.

And Kathy really had no connection with Skye's family, unless . . . Could Vince have asked her out? He was supposed to be dating Loretta Steiner, Skye's sorority sister. If he was cheating on her, Skye would have to kill him, but if she never found out, she wouldn't have to do anything. Thus it would be better to sit at another table. But she hesitated a second too long before attempting her escape.

Her mother shot her a stern look and said, "Where did

you go? We've been saving you a seat, but we're almost ready for dessert."

Skye gave in and sank into the empty chair between her brother and Uncle Charlie. No matter what she did, this conversation would not be pretty.

May pursued an answer to her question. "We saw you come in and then you disappeared. What's going on?"

"I bought a soda at the bar while I waited for the line to go down."

"Iced tea and coffee are free." Skye's father spoke between bites.

Before Skye could respond, Bunny, seated on Uncle Charlie's opposite side, said, "But, Jed, when you were fixing up my car you said you get what you pay for. So, if something's free, wouldn't that mean you get nothing?"

May glared at Bunny, then turned her laser stare on her husband. She hated any reference to the time Jed had spent in the redhead's company, still believing in her heart of hearts that the two had had an affair.

Next to Bunny her son, clearly wanting to stop his mother from continuing on the sore subject, said, "So, Skye, did your contest entry turn out well?"

Skye was grateful for the chance to divert her mother's attention. "Better than any of my practice ones. I doubt I'll win, but at least I didn't embarrass myself." She remembered Bunny's wish that Simon know she had been a help, and added, "Your mom saved my last dish."

"That's great." Simon smiled at his mother, then beamed approval at Skye. "That's really nice of you to share the credit. I know cooking has never been your forte, so you must have worked extremely hard. But then, I know you can do anything you set your mind to."

Skye basked in his admiration. There was something different about him tonight. Except for Friday night's dinner, she hadn't talked to him since the fight they'd had at a diner Thanksgiving weekend, and at that time his harsh words had caused her to finalize their breakup. Now he seemed changed, but how?

Before she could analyze Simon's transformation, Vince

said, "You are way too nice, Simon. Skye at a cooking contest is like the pope at a bar mitzvah. Both have heard of the concept, but neither really wants to be involved in the ceremony."

Kathy Steele leaned around Vince and added, "Didn't I hear that Skye set off the sprinklers over her cooking area?"

Skye worried briefly that that would be the headline on this week's *Star*, but Kathy's next words replaced that concern with a worse one. "Of course, a little water is nothing compared to Earl Doozier trying to bribe people for their voting points, then claiming Skye gave him the idea."

Shit! She should have realized the media would pick up on that—at least the local paper. Too bad she couldn't tell Kathy anything about the murder investigation or the missing teen. That might at least move the Doozier story from the front page to the inside, and with any luck the article about the sprinklers would get cut completely to make room for the school cafeteria menu.

May must have been thinking along the same lines, but had no compunction about trading info about the murder or the kidnapping to get what she wanted. "Kathy, I'm surprised you're interested in the fantasies of a fool like Earl when there's been a murder committed and a teenager is still missing."

Kathy laughed. "Don't worry, May; those two crimes are my headline for tomorrow's special edition. But there will be plenty of room in Wednesday's regular newspaper for Skye's sprinklers and the Doozier debacle."

Skye hissed in her brother's ear, "Stop her from running that story."

Vince whispered back, "Me? How?"

"Since you're dating her, figure out a way."

"What are you talking about?" Vince looked confused. "I'm not dating Kathy. You know I'm going with Loretta."

"Then why is she sitting at our table?"

"How should I know?" He shrugged. "She came in with Simon, Bunny, and Charlie. Maybe she's Charlie's date, or Simon's."

Skye flinched. Simon was an attractive, intelligent man.

May had warned her that he wouldn't have any trouble finding a new girlfriend.

She swallowed hard. It really wasn't any of her business.
She certainly wasn't jealous. She was happy with Wally. She
just wanted Simon to find someone wonderful. True, Kathy
Steele was beautiful and smart, but she was too cold, too
aloof. Simon needed a woman who would love him with all
her heart, not just be with him for his money and position.
Just as Skye had once tried to explain to him, he needed a
soul mate.

Before Skye could continue fretting about Kathy's presence, Charlie said, "I'm surprised you're going to the expense of a special edition tomorrow. Everyone already
knows about the murder and the kidnapping. They aren't exactly a scoop."

"Maybe." Kathy's eyes glowed. "But I have an exclusive
interview with the girl who supposedly abducted the missing teenager. Her story is definitely breaking news, and not
even the *Chicago Tribune* has that."

Xenia! Skye's heart skipped a beat. Why hadn't she
thought to talk to Xenia herself? The only reason Skye could
come up with was that the girl frustrated her. She did not
respond to any of Skye's clinical training, and Xenia's supe-
rior IQ put the adults around her at a disadvantage.

Skye hated being made to feel stupid by a sixteen-year-
old, which was why she avoided the teen. Had Skye's ego
made her miss a chance to rescue Ashley? If Ashley had
been harmed because Skye had been protecting her own
self-esteem, she would never forgive herself.

CHAPTER 17

Bake for
Twenty-five Minutes

"And then Kathy Steele said she had an exclusive interview with Xenia, and I realized how stupid I'd been in not talking to the girl myself."

Skye sat with her back against the armrest of the sofa. She and Wally were in his living room, and she had been giving him a rundown of her day.

Wally lifted her feet onto his lap and began to massage her toes. "Quirk talked to Xenia, but she denied everything. He said she was a tough nut, and it would take more than a visit from a police officer to crack her."

"Yeah, she's had too much experience with cops to be intimidated by them." Skye closed her eyes and enjoyed the sensation that Wally's fingers were producing. She'd been on her feet for nearly eleven hours and his massage was heavenly. "But I could take a different tack, try to convince her I'm on her side."

"Would Xenia go for that?" He moved on to Skye's arch and she sighed in pleasure. "Didn't you say she doesn't trust you, and you haven't been able to establish a good relationship with her?"

"True. But I could try again. Maybe approach it as being

good for the student newspaper." Skye opened her eyelids a crack. "For some reason she's really fierce in defending the *Scoop*."

"I don't think you ever told me what Xenia wrote that made Ashley's parents so upset that they decided to sue."

"I can't believe she hacked into our files and inserted her story just before we sent it to the printers. Of course, it wasn't too difficult; all she needed was our password, which we foolishly kept in the desk drawer. We're not used to the kids doing stuff like that." Skye added, half to herself, "Or maybe we just never caught on before."

"But what did she write?"

"Oh, she claimed that Ashley was having sex with the basketball team in their locker room the night they won the championship."

"Yep. That would stir up her parents, all right." Wally switched feet and started rubbing her left one. "I'm guessing the school is threatening to have the boys testify if the parents don't drop the suit."

"Right. Unfortunately, the parents don't believe the boys. They say that they're being coerced by the school to lie about Ashley."

"So, they're going ahead with the lawsuit?"

"Uh-huh. I think the only way they'd ever be convinced is if there were pictures." Skye paused. A memory nibbled at the edge of her consciousness. What was it? She concentrated. No. It was gone, but another recollection popped into her head. "Oh, I just remembered something that happened the morning the contest started. When we were finally dismissed from the stage, everyone had to go to the bathroom, so I headed for the teachers' restroom, figuring no one else would think of using that one. I had just gotten down to business when I heard two people talking in the lounge next door. Someone was berating someone else about not getting complete info on one of the finalists."

"Could you tell who they were?" Wally finished with her feet and moved on to her calves.

"No, not even their gender, although I'm pretty sure one was a woman. Oh, wait, the second voice said the woman had paid him to get her into the finals, so I guess that person would have to be on the Grandma Sal's staff. If I had known there would be a murder, I would have tried harder to find out." Skye's expression was sober. "Anyway, I've told you everything I learned today. What about you?"

"I never did find my dad. From what you said, I guess I should have checked the bars, but he's not usually a big drinker." Wally's brow wrinkled. "Other than that, I spent the whole time interviewing the contest people. I've got the entire force either doing background checks or looking for Ashley."

"Anything on either front?"

"Not a thing."

Skye *tsk*ed, then asked, "What did Cherry's husband have to say? I bet he was surprised to see you."

"He wanted to slam the door in my face, but he knew that was the wrong thing to do, so he let me in and tried to make me believe that he didn't know a thing."

"Don't they all?"

"Yeah." Wally leaned forward and picked up his can of beer. "He claims he has no idea who would want to kill Cherry—she had no enemies, and he stayed home when she went to the factory that morning. She went early to check and make sure everything was perfect."

"Did he claim the housekeeper could alibi him?"

"He said she was there, but they weren't in the same part of the house."

"What about the prenup?" Skye took a sip of her wine.

"He says there is no prenup. Told me to check with his lawyer if I didn't believe him."

"Hmm. Why would he lie to his girlfriend about having one?"

"Because he really didn't want a divorce." Wally's grin was devilish.

"What makes you think that?"

"Because he told me. Hunter enjoyed his life as Mr. Cherry Alexander. He didn't have to work; she made enough money for both of them. And she bought him anything he wanted—a motorcycle, a boat, trips to Hawaii to surf."

Skye nodded thoughtfully. "And he really does love his son."

"Right. The prenup line is something he brings out when the current girlfriend gets too serious."

"He used it to get rid of them." Skye finally understood.

"He liked them to break up with him, but if that didn't work he pretended to be noble and said he couldn't keep seeing them, knowing he'd never be able to get free of his marriage." Wally finished his beer and got up to throw away the can. "This time, though, the nanny endangered his child, so the breakup wasn't amicable."

"Did Cherry ever hire a PI?"

"Yes. Hunter gave me the name, and I was able to get hold of the investigator just before you got here. The PI said that Cherry did have him investigate the judges. He found something on all of them. The food editor is being treated for bulimia, the cookbook author was once accused of plagiarizing a recipe, and the radio restaurant critic is under suspicion for taking kickbacks to write good reviews. I'll be talking to each of them again tomorrow, but none of what Cherry had on them seems enough to kill for."

"Especially since it would all be public knowledge if anyone really wanted to dig around for it." Skye tilted her head, thinking. "Did you ask who Cherry's next book was going to be about?"

"Hunter said she never told anyone except her investigator, and he said she hadn't selected a new subject yet."

"Shoot." Skye frowned. "I bet Kyle isn't left-handed either."

"Nope." Wally's voice was flat. "But we found out a lot of people are. Heck, even my father is a lefty."

"So Kyle's no longer a good suspect, is he?"

"Not if what he said checks out with his attorney. There was no life insurance or savings, and everything was mortgaged to the hilt. They lived beyond Cherry's real means. Her royalties go to the kid's trust, so Hunter will have to go to work to survive. He'll learn real soon that it's not so easy to play the clown when you have to run the circus."

"I bet he finds himself another sugar mama." Skye got up

and joined Wally in the kitchen. "Who's our lead suspect now? The nanny? Maybe she thought if Cherry were dead and he didn't have the prenup to stop him, Hunter would marry her."

"I doubt it. According to Hunter, he fired her before Cherry was killed. If the nanny did it, it was revenge, not love." Wally leaned a hip against the counter. "I've got Quirk looking for her. Hunter claimed he has no idea where she would go."

"Which means we're back to square one." Skye rinsed out her wineglass and put it on the drainer. "What's the plan?"

"Tomorrow we reinterview all the contestants and contest people who don't have alibis." Wally stepped behind her and slipped his arms around her waist. "If the murder's not personal, maybe it's professional. Who had the most to gain with Cherry out of the picture?"

"Good question." Skye found it hard to think with his warm breath fanning the sensitive spot below her ear.

Wally's nuzzling was interrupted by his yawn. "Sorry," he murmured.

"I'll bet you're exhausted. Thea said you were at the PD by six this morning and never took a break." Skye turned to face him, tracing a fingertip across his lip. "I should go home and let you get some rest."

Slowly and seductively his gaze slid downward. "I think I'm getting my second wind."

Her heart jolted and her pulse pounded. His appeal was undeniable. His hands burrowed under her sweater and locked against her spine. Skye inhaled sharply at the contact, a shiver rippling through her.

He whispered into her neck, "You're driving me crazy. I can't concentrate. I think about you all the time."

She had thought that once they had made love the first time her craving for him would lessen, but it seemed to grow each time they were together. She buried her hands in his hair and lifted his head, staring into his dark eyes.

It had taken them years to get to this point, and somewhere in the back of her mind she was always afraid that she would lose him. His father's unexpected and unexplained presence intensified those fears and paralyzed her tongue. She wanted to tell him how much he meant to her, but the words refused to come.

Wally gazed at her, waiting for her to respond. After a moment his broad shoulders heaved as he sighed.

She knew she had hurt him, and gathered him close, trying to show him how she felt with her kiss.

His lips devoured her and the room spun.

Skye didn't notice that they had moved into his bedroom until she felt the mattress press against the back of her knees. Gently he eased her down on the comforter, sliding her sweater off over her head, then stood to discard his own clothes.

She watched as his powerful, well-muscled body emerged, and when he lay down and gathered her in his arms, all her doubts and fears drained away.

Skye pressed the accelerator to the floor, increasing the Bel Air's speed until it almost seemed to skim the ground. She had fallen asleep at Wally's and hadn't woken up until his alarm clicked on at seven thirty. Which would have allowed plenty of time to get home, shower, dress, and still be at the awards ceremony on time if he hadn't persuaded her to stay for an encore of the night before.

Now she had less than an hour to get herself together and arrive at the school auditorium by ten. Gravel flew from under her tires as she turned into her driveway, and her brakes squealed as she slammed her foot on the pedal to avoid rear-ending the Ford Escort parked in front of her house.

Who did she know who drove an Escort? Certainly no one in her family; they all drove either pickups or cars the size of parade floats.

As she ran down a mental list of names, a tall, good-looking man in his early sixties emerged from the driver's-side door. He wore crisp khakis and a black polo shirt with a little alligator embroidered on the pocket. His head was shaved and his eyes were hidden behind mirrored sunglasses.

Shoot. What was Wally's father doing at her house at nine o'clock on a Monday morning? No possible answer she could come up with suggested he was the bearer of good news.

Skye considered throwing her car into reverse and getting the heck out of Dodge, but she had a feeling he would follow her—possibly to the ends of the earth. He had that look, like a pit bull that had chomped down on a hand and wasn't letting go until he had reached the bone.

Dang. She did not want to meet Wally's dad for the first time dressed in yesterday's clothes, with no makeup on, her hair skinned back into a ponytail, and smelling of . . . well, a lot of things, none of them a morning shower. Could this be any more awkward?

She glanced in the rearview mirror. Nope, nothing she could do about her appearance. She had approximately five seconds before he reached her car. She clawed through her purse, closing her hand on a small glass vial—a bottle of Chanel. She whipped it out and sprayed. The spicy scent gave her the self-confidence to face what was coming; even if she looked like the Bride of Frankenstein, at least she smelled like Miss America.

Opening her door a second before he reached the Bel Air's front fender, Skye stepped out of the car and said, "Mr. Boyd, I presume?"

"Carson Boyd, at your service, ma'am." He held out his hand. "And you must be Skye."

She nodded, but narrowed her eyes. He had called her *ma'am*. How old did he think she was? She couldn't say what she wanted to, and couldn't think of anything else to say, so for once she kept her mouth shut.

"I'd like to have a word with you, if you have a moment." His request sounded more like an order.

Skye bristled. "I'm sorry, Mr. Boyd; as a matter of fact I don't. Perhaps we could schedule something later in the day, or tomorrow."

"Would that we could, but I'm leaving Scumble River this afternoon, and I know you'll be tied up with the cooking contest all morning."

How did he know that? Probably Uncle Charlie or Jesse had mentioned that she was a finalist. "Unfortunately, that's the reason I don't have time right now. I need to freshen up and get back to town for the awards ceremony." Skye bit her lip to stop from smirking. Freshen up—that was a good one. What she really needed was to be run through a car wash, complete with the wax option.

"If you could just give me fifteen minutes," he persisted, following her as she walked up the steps. "It's about my son. I need your help to do what's best for him."

Holy crap. How could she say no to that? "Okay. But I really have a limited amount of time."

Skye unlocked her front door and led him into the parlor. At least this room was freshly painted and contained some beautiful antiques. If he would just not notice the worn and stained carpet, she might be able to pull off a good first impression.

She sat on the settee, offering the delicate Queen Anne chair to her guest. She hoped its uncomfortable seat would make him leave that much sooner.

After a few minutes of silence, she prodded, "What can I do for you, Mr. Boyd?"

"Call me Carson."

"Okay, Carson, what is it you wanted to say?"

He took off his sunglasses, and she was struck by his resemblance to Wally.

He cleared his throat. "I understand you and Walter are seeing each other."

"Yes. It's not exactly a secret."

"How serious are you?"

Skye tilted her head. "Are you asking me what my intentions are?"

"Yes, in a way I am."

"Shouldn't my dad be having this conversation with your son, instead of the other way around?"

Carson gave her a serious look. "I'm sixty-four years old. I own a multinational corporation, and instead of preparing to take my place in the business, my only son is off playing

Sheriff Andy Taylor in some Northern Mayberry. I'm not playing around here."

"So you've suddenly traveled to Scumble River to persuade Wally to return to Texas with you and run your company." Skye's stomach cramped. It was just as she had feared.

"In part, yes."

"What does Wally's choice of occupation and hometown have to do with me?"

"My dear, don't be so modest." Carson ran his fingers over his head as if he'd forgotten he had no hair. "From what I hear, my son has been infatuated with you since you were a teenager, and now that you two are finally together, I doubt a Texas twister could tear him from your side."

"Interesting." Skye forced herself not to beam. After the last couple of days of self-doubt, it felt wonderful to have Wally's father verbalize his son's devotion. Even if it turned out not to be true, she would bask in the moment. "But I still don't know what you want from me."

"Before I answer that, let me ask you something." Carson stared into her eyes. "Would you be willing to pack up, move to Texas, and live there for the rest of your life?"

His question caught her unprepared. If he had asked it of her when she first graduated from high school or college, or even just a few years ago, she would have jumped at the chance to leave Scumble River, but now . . . she had friends, family, a house. She wanted to know how things would turn out for the kids she was working with at school. She just didn't know if she could leave all that.

"Your silence is enough of an answer." Carson shook his head. "What in the world does this little nowhere town have that makes you and my son want to stay here?"

"It's home." Skye shrugged. That really wasn't a good answer, but it was the only one she could put into words. "Now that we've settled that, I repeat—what do you want from me?"

"I want you to break up with Wally. Tell him you don't love him. You've changed your mind. You really love that funeral director you were going with before dating my son."

Skye couldn't stop her gasp. "Why would I do that?"

"I had planned to offer you money, but I understand you gave away a painting that was worth hundreds of thousands of dollars, so maybe cash doesn't motivate you." He stared at his sunglasses, almost as if he had forgotten she was there. "Still, it's worth a try." He looked up at her. "I will help you set up an offshore account and transfer a million dollars into it, if you will agree never to speak to my son again."

"You were right. I'm not as motivated by money as I used to be." She smiled to herself. She'd come a long way since she'd been blinded by her ex-fiancé's wealth and position. "How Wally makes me feel is worth ten times that amount."

"Then I'll ask you to do it because it's the right thing for my son. The only way he'll fulfill his destiny and be the great man he was born to be."

"But that's not the life Wally wants." Skye tried to calm her emotions and think straight. "He moved here and became a police officer long before he ever met me."

"He did that as a young man's foolish act of rebellion. He's more mature now."

"So, now that he's older and wiser, what did he say when you asked him to quit his job, move back to Texas, and take over for you?" Skye held her breath.

"He turned me down." Carson continued before Skye could comment. "But not because of his love for this town or his job—because of his love for you. If you were willing to move with him, he would come home."

"Did he say that?"

"Not in so many words. But a father can tell what his son really means."

Skye briefly contemplated turning Wally's dad over to her mother—of course, first she would tell May that Carson was trying to get Skye to move to Texas. She smiled thinly before realizing that her mother would be thrilled with Carson's other suggestion—that she break up with Wally and get back with Simon. *Hmm*. No, her mother would be no use in this situation.

"I'm a firm believer in hearing something from the horse's mouth," Skye said, watching the older man's expression carefully. "If Wally tells me that he wants to move home and take over for you, but doesn't want to leave me, I'll either break up with him or agree to move with him."

"He'd never tell you that, but what if I arranged for you to overhear him say it to me?"

"Fine." Skye stood up.

Carson followed suit and she led him into the foyer.

"I'll let you know where and when."

"You do that."

"I'm not a monster, you know." He paused, one foot over the threshold. "All I want is what's best for my son."

"I know." Skye closed the door after him and leaned against the smooth wood, her emotions at war. "Me, too."

After several minutes, she sighed and started up the stairs to change. Her heart was focused on her feelings concerning Wally, but her brain was telling her she had missed something important in her conversation with his father. But what?

CHAPTER 18

Toothpick Inserted in Center Should Come Out Clean

Why am I always running late? Skye fumed as she hurriedly bathed, threw on clean clothes, and jumped into her car. *Just once I'd like to get dressed without feeling as if I'm a quick-change artist.*

Cursing Carson Boyd, she roared out of the driveway toward town. His visit was not only extremely upsetting; it had cut her primping time in half.

Skye's bad temper worsened when she arrived at the high school a little before ten and discovered the parking lot was full. By the time she drove around the block to the middle school, found a spot to park there, cut across the stretch of lawn that divided the two buildings, and walked into the auditorium, her irritation had blossomed into a full-fledged huff.

Her mother's glare did not improve her disposition. Skye glared back at May as she crossed the stage and took her position among the other One-Dish Meals contestants.

From what Skye could tell, the ceremony had just begun.

Grandma Sal wrapped up her welcome speech, then introduced Dante, who spoke for a few minutes about how pleased Scumble River was to be this year's host for the contest. He also managed to squeeze in a mention of his own self-sacrifice in being wounded for the good of the town before turning the stage back to Grandma Sal.

A serious expression on her face, she said, "As you all know, a terrible tragedy occurred during this year's challenge. We lost one of our wonderful finalists, Ms. Cherry Alexander."

Someone in the crowd yelled out, "She was murdered, not misplaced."

Skye cringed.

Grandma Sal ignored the outburst and went on. "To honor Cherry's valiant spirit, we have created a special award to be given to the finalist who showed the most stick-to-itiveness. And here with us today to present it is her husband, Kyle."

Dressed in a sober black suit, his hair gelled back from his face, he looked ten years older than the man who had been with Cherry backstage three days ago. He stepped up to the microphone and read from an index card, " 'Cherry would be honored to have this award named after her. She was a person who never gave up and demanded the best from everyone, especially herself.' "

A voice from the audience bellowed, "You should be taking Fine Foods to court, not giving out an award for them. Their negligence contributed to your wife's murder."

Skye squinted past the stage lights. The heckler sounded a bit too well educated to be one of the Scumble River regulars. Who was trying to make Grandma Sal's company look bad in front of all the press?

There was no way to tell, and Skye's focus returned to Kyle, who pulled at the neck of his white shirt and darted a glance toward Grandma Sal.

She murmured in his ear, and he straightened and said, "The winner of the Cherry Alexander Award for Perseverance is . . ."

He squinted at the card Grandma Sal handed him, and

Skye wondered just how much Fine Foods was paying him to do this, rather than file a lawsuit.

"Glenda Doozier." Kyle waited for the applause to end, then continued, "Not only did this plucky little lady come into the contest late and as an alternate, but she made it through some very difficult family issues, still managing to turn her dish in on time."

Skye would have swallowed her chewing gum if she'd had any. Glenda Doozier, plucky? Little lady? Family issues? Her husband had been trying to bribe people, and her brother-in-law had shot up the place. How did that constitute being worthy to win a prize?

The Red Ragger queen pranced up to the mike in four-inch spike-heeled black plastic sandals and a Dolly Parton wig. Her leather skirt was the size of a Post-it note, and her lipstick-red tube top was no bigger than a rubber band. Every man in the place held his breath and prayed for a wardrobe malfunction.

Kyle seemed to be having trouble forming words. Finally managing to gasp, "Here," he thrust the silver spoon-shaped trophy at Glenda's 38DD chest. When it caught in the elastic of her top, several men in the audience growled like hyenas about to tear into their dinner.

Clearly Grandma Sal had dealt with testosterone-induced stupidity before. She casually reached over, disengaged the utensil's handle from the stretchy material, and gently moved Kyle backward, taking his place. She then grasped Glenda's arm, and as she walked her to the stairs said, "Mrs. Doozier, thank you so much for participating in our little contest. You'll be contacted to come and pick up your check at the factory."

Skye overheard Grandma Sal mutter to herself as she walked back to center stage, "Why in the world would he pick *her* to win the special prize? Is he trying to ruin us?"

The older woman straightened as she approached the microphone, pasted a smile on her face, and addressed the audience again. "Now, for our regular awards. We'll be giving one in each of our four categories; Special-Occasion Baking, Healthy, Snacks, and One-Dish Meals. The grand prize will go to one of those winners."

Skye looked at the little table placed on Grandma Sal's right. Several plaques and one trophy—the size of a small child—were waiting to be passed out.

Jared stood between his mother and the table. He picked up the first plaque and handed it to her.

She peered at the name, then announced, "The winner of the Healthy category is Monika Bradley, our CPA from Brooklyn, for her Gluten-Free, Dairy-Free Sponge Cake and Frosting."

It took several minutes for the attractive blonde to hobble up to the front of the stage, her leg still immobilized by a brace, but when she got there she kept her speech short. "What characterizes a dish as healthy is different for each person. If you have diabetes, it's sugar-free. If you have high cholesterol, it's excluding trans fats. And if you have high blood pressure, it's low sodium.

"While most people are aware of these dietary needs, many are uninformed about life-threatening food allergies. I entered this contest to bring the issue of celiac disease and other life-threatening food allergies to the public's attention. My winning entry has no gluten or dairy and is still delicious. Thank you all for the opportunity."

Next Grandma Sal awarded the Snacks winner. Skye had half believed Charlie would win, but a woman from Laurel took the prize for her Fiesta Italiano Dip.

The Special-Occasion-Baking category was next. Skye looked down the row at her mother. May was holding the hands of the contestants on either side of her as if she were in the Miss America Pageant.

Grandma Sal took the plaque from Jared, checked the nameplate, and said, "The winner of Special-Occasion Baking is . . . Diane White, our cookie blogger from Clay Center, for her Chocolate Brownie Tiramisu."

The blogger shrieked and ran over to Grandma Sal. Her hug nearly knocked the older woman off her feet. After releasing Grandma Sal, Diane whipped a piece of paper from her pocket. She unfolded it like an accordion, grabbed the microphone, and began to read, "I'm grateful to my wonderful husband, my three lovely children . . ."

The thank-you list was endless, and when Diane expressed her appreciation to the fish in her aquarium for being a calming influence, naming each individually, Skye tuned her out and looked back at May. Her mother's smile was shaky, and Skye could tell that it cost her a great deal not to burst into tears.

Her own throat closed; she knew how much it had meant to May to win. Skye wished she had done a better job on the casserole, so she could have won for her mother. *Darn.* She should have practiced more and kept her mind on the cooking rather than on sleuthing.

Diane showed no sign of coming to an end of her roll call, but Grandma Sal wrestled the mike away from the excited woman by tempting her with the plaque. The blogger was still thanking people as she returned to her place clutching her prize.

Grandma Sal took the fourth award from her son, squinted at the engraving, and frowned. She whispered something to Jared, who answered her. She shrugged and said, "Last but not least, the winner of our One-Dish Meal is . . ."

Skye glanced to her left and smiled at Butch King, the firefighter whose mother had tried to obedience-train Earl Doozier. She hoped Butch would win. He'd been so nice that first day when they'd had lunch together.

" . . . Syke Denison."

Had her name—at least, a version of her name—really been called? Skye was rooted to the spot. Even after she heard her mother screaming and saw her jumping up and down, she didn't believe it was possible she had won.

Skye shot Grandma Sal a questioning look, and the older woman nodded. Finally Skye managed to move her feet, and she walked carefully to the front of the stage. She was still more than half afraid that she'd misheard and was about to make a huge fool of herself.

Grandma Sal handed her the plaque and said, "Syke is a school psychologist from right here in Scumble River, and she wins for her Chicken Supreme Casserole." Skye whispered in the older woman's ear and Grandma Sal said, "Sorry, her name is Skye. I thought the other was wrong, but my son insisted. You know these youngsters; they think they know everything."

The crowd laughed politely, and Grandma Sal handed Skye the mike.

Skye took a deep breath and tried to think of something to say. "Uh, well, I just want to thank my mother for teaching me to cook, and Wally Boyd for eating all of my practice attempts, even the burned ones."

As Skye stumbled back to her spot, May met her halfway, hugging and kissing her. "You did it! You really did it! I knew you could."

Grandma Sal waited for May to calm down, then turned to the audience. "Now for what you've all been waiting for. The grand prize of ten thousand dollars goes to . . ."

May's nails dug into Skye's hand.

". . . Diane White for her Chocolate Brownie Tiramisu."

Skye's shoulders sagged. She had no right to be disappointed. It had been a miracle she had won her category, and there was no way she'd had a chance to win the grand prize. Still, for just a second she was let down.

Then May hugged her and whispered, "She was probably sleeping with the judges."

Skye shook her head. "Two of the judges are women."

May raised an eyebrow. "So?"

Skye giggled and May hugged her again. "We did great. Next year we'll get the grand prize."

"There won't be any next year." Skye hugged her mother back and stepped out of her embrace.

"We'll see."

"No next year," Skye insisted.

"Sure. Whatever you say." May nodded toward the front of the stage. "Now be quiet. I want to hear what our winner has to say."

This time the cookie blogger's speech was even longer, and not even being handed the huge trophy shut her up. Twenty minutes later she wound down, after thanking her

Kindergarten teacher, her minister, and the manufacturers of the Easy-Bake oven, in which she first learned to cook.

Grandma Sal asked the winners to stay so the media could ask questions, then dismissed the audience and the rest of the contestants. The Grandma Sal's Soup-to-Nuts Cooking Challenge was officially over.

Most of the media wanted them to talk about Cherry's death, but they all professed to have nothing to say. After several "No comments," "I have no ideas," and "What are you talking abouts?" the press gave up, and the winners were free to go.

Before they dispersed, Jared told them all they would be notified when their checks were ready. They would need to pick them up at the factory so they could fill out the paperwork for the IRS.

Waiting for Skye when she was finally released were the four huge guys who had been rooting for Janelle to win the contest. Skye's heart skipped a beat as the largest man, the one she had dubbed Mr. Elephant, stepped forward.

He stared at her without speaking, then turned his head slightly. Skye followed his gaze and saw the prison cook standing a few feet away making a "go on" motion with her hands.

"My posse and me jus' wanted to give you props on your win. Your recipe was killer."

"Thanks." Skye was pretty sure he had given her a compliment. "Your friend Janelle's recipe was, uh, phat, too."

Mr. Elephant smiled at her use of slang. "We hears that you got juice in this 'hood."

That was a little easier to translate. "Maybe some."

"Little Boy Blue listens to you, and word is you represent for your peeps."

"I try to help when I can."

Janelle cleared her throat loudly, and Mr. Elephant took a deep breath before saying, "I know the poe-leece ain't goin' listen to a dude like me, but I heard that dead chassis say to that biddie that jus' won the contest that she be a bammer. That she be cheating by bringing in brownies from the bakery—not making her own."

"Oh, my." If Skye understood him correctly, he had accused Diane White of cheating and said that Cherry confronted her about it. The cookie blogger now had a motive for murder.

"You tell your man what I heard." Mr. Elephant turned to leave.

"No, you have to tell Chief Boyd yourself." Skye looked the man in the eye. "I promise, he'll listen to you and not disrespect you."

"That be whack."

"No. Chief Boyd is straight-up."

Janelle had moved closer and spoke up. "Jus' do it and get it over with. You gonna go straight, you gotta learn to live with the man. That chief of police be cool." She gave Skye a level look. "Right?"

"Right." Skye looked around and saw Anthony talking to Diane and Monika.

He had each of them by the arm and was leading them down the hallway saying, "I need you to come this way, please. We have a few more questions for you both about Ms. Alexander's death."

Wally had mentioned that he planned to reinterview the contestants and staff who didn't have alibis for the time of Cherry's murder. Skye hadn't realized he would do it right at the school, but it made sense. They were already assembled, and there were plenty of rooms for the interrogations.

As Anthony led Diane and Monika past her, Skye said to him, "Anthony, this gentleman has some information he needs to tell Chief Boyd. Where is he?"

"In the principal's office."

Skye nodded and escorted Mr. Elephant, his herd, and Janelle toward the front of the building. As Skye walked, she tried to decide whether she should tell Wally about his father's visit, or give Carson the chance he had asked for and see if she really was standing in the way of Wally's desire to go back to Texas.

Part of her said that tricking Wally like that would damage their relationship forever. But another part wondered if she would ever know the truth if she didn't go along with Carson's plan.

She still hadn't decided what to do when she reached the main office. She'd just have to wing it and see what popped out of her mouth. Perhaps not the best plan, but the only one she had.

The outer office was empty, and Skye asked the group to wait there. Once they complied, she proceeded down the narrow hall and knocked on the door at the end.

"Yes?" Wally's voice held a slightly annoyed tone.

She inched open the door, poking her head inside. "Could you step out here for a minute?"

"Now?"

"Now."

When he was outside the office with the door closed she explained about Mr. Elephant and what he had heard. Wally immediately went to talk to them, saying to Skye over his shoulder, "After we get done with this guy, do you have time to help me reinterview Jared's wife?"

"Sure."

Mr. Elephant repeated to Wally what he had reported to Skye. Friday night at the dinner he had overheard Cherry tell Diane White that if she didn't drop out of the competition, Cherry would inform Grandma Sal that Diane had used brownies from a bakery during the practice session that afternoon, and that she had an order for three more pans of brownies from that same bakery the next morning.

Wally asked a few questions, but it was clear Mr. Elephant didn't have any other information, and since he and his crew had alibis for the time of the murder, there was no reason to suspect he was lying. Wally took his address and phone number, then let them go.

When Wally and Skye returned to the principal's office, he said to the woman sitting in one of the visitor's chairs, "Mrs. Fine, this is our psychological consultant, Ms. Denison."

Tammy appeared impatient, and as Skye took a seat next to her, she demanded, "Are you nearly finished? We have a dinner party in Chicago tonight and we need to get on the road. My husband and mother-in-law may have to come back here, but this is the last time I ever have to pretend to want to be in Scumble River."

Wally leaned forward and rested his elbows on the desk. "Sorry, Mrs. Fine; I still need to talk to your husband and mother-in-law. I was able to catch your sons while the awards ceremony was going on, but Mr. and Mrs. Fine were onstage. Where were you, by the way? I'm told you only arrived at the school fifteen minutes ago."

"I was packing and having the car loaded. I can't wait to get out of this town."

"And yet your factory here provides a good living for your family," Wally reminded the woman.

"Things change." The slim brunette stared at Wally.

Skye caught Wally's eye and silently asked if she could jump in. He nodded, and she said, "Rumor has it your family may be selling Fine Foods. Is that what you're referring to?"

"Well, I can't confirm or deny." Tammy's smile was predatorlike. "All I can say is, read tomorrow's newspaper."

Wally took the conversation back. "So, Mrs. Fine, you were alone in your motel cabin sleeping the morning of Ms. Alexander's death?"

"Yes. How many times do I have to tell you?"

"Have you thought of anyone who might be able to corroborate your story?"

"No, Jared left early to go to the factory. I took the phone off the hook and put the 'Do not disturb' sign on the door."

"Did you know Ms. Alexander before the contest?" Wally steepled his fingers.

"No."

"Have you read any of her books?"

"Certainly not. They're all lies. It's clear she has a grudge against anyone rich or famous."

Wally was silent for a few minutes, then said, "Okay, Mrs. Fine, that's all for now. We have your number." He paused, letting the double meaning of what he had said sink in, then continued, "And your address in Chicago. Don't leave the state."

Tammy rose from her chair in one fluid movement and marched out the door, slamming it behind her.

"That was interesting," Skye commented. "Did she have anything of value to say before I got here?"

"No."

"Who all are you talking to today?"

"I've already interviewed Tammy, JJ, and Brandon. Neither Mrs. Fine nor her two sons seems to have any connection to Cherry. There's no evidence that they ever met her before this weekend, and since they aren't contest judges, she wouldn't have had any reason to blackmail or bribe them."

"Do any of them have alibis?" Skye asked, making sure she understood. "Are any of them left-handed?"

"No alibis. Tammy and Brandon are both lefties, as is the male judge, and two contestants—Monika Bradley and Diane White."

"But they aren't your top suspects," Skye guessed.

"No. Tammy says Jared is ambidextrous, and he's the one who was at the factory, which places him near the scene of the crime. Also, he could probably change the results of the contest if he wanted to, so he's number one on my list. I'm planning on seeing him next. Then I need to talk to his mother again."

"I should get out of your way then." Skye got up. "Is there anything you need me to do?"

Wally peered down at the legal pad on the desktop. "Anthony and Quirk are interviewing Monika Bradley and all three judges, but considering Mrs. Bradley's leg injury, I don't think she would physically be able to get Cherry into the chocolate fountain."

"No," Skye agreed. "Unless she's faking her injury."

"That would mean she came into the contest knowing she was going to kill Cherry." Wally made a note. "I'll have someone look a little deeper into her background, see if she and the vic ever met before."

"Anything else?"

"Quirk located the nanny. Turns out Larissa went home to her parents after she was fired. They live in St. Louis, and she claims to have driven there that night and arrived about five on Saturday morning. A neighbor walking a dog saw her pull into the driveway, which gives her a pretty good alibi."

"How about the others?"

"The others involved in the contest have alibis, too, except Diane White, and now that we know she had a motive, I want *you* to talk to her."

"Sure, but why me?" Skye asked.

"She's my other top suspect, but she resorts to hysteria anytime I've tried to question her. Which means she's a prime candidate for Scumble River PD's finest psychological consultant."

"You mean Scumble River PD's *only* psychological consultant."

"That, too." Wally got up and escorted Skye to the door. "You ready to rock and roll?"

"Always." Skye put her hand on the knob. "Where is she?"

"Waiting for you next door." He kissed her on the cheek. "Go get 'em, tiger."

"Grr." Skye made a clawing motion with her hands, then walked out of the principal's office and into the nurse's.

While she was explaining her role as psychological consultant to Diane, Skye realized she hadn't told Wally about his father's visit. Did that mean she wouldn't, or had it just slipped her mind?

CHAPTER 19

Cool Fifteen Minutes

"I'm through with Mrs. White." Skye had finished with the cookie blogger and gone to report to Wally, who was ushering Grandma Sal into the principal's office.

He seated the older woman and said he'd be right back. Closing the door behind him, he asked Skye, "Anything?"

"She's a much cooler customer than I'd expected. That slightly daffy cookie-blogger persona of hers is as fake as Bunny's boobs, although not as uplifting. At first she tried the hysterical routine with me, but once she saw that I wasn't buying it, she shifted to her real self."

"What did she say then?"

"I told her we knew about Cherry threatening her and about her cheating. She denied cheating. Said that Cherry had been mistaken; she only used the bakery brownies in her practice recipe to save time, but never intended to use them in the contest. The bakery must have made a mistake if they thought she had ordered three pans for Saturday." Skye leaned against the wall. "Diane also insisted that she told Cherry that, and thus had nothing to fear from her."

"A logical explanation."

"Right, and, really, she had nothing to fear from Cherry unless she used the bakery brownies during the contest. Nothing in the rules says you even have to participate in the practice session, let alone how you have to prepare your recipe."

Wally crossed his arms. "Not to mention she'd have to be pretty stupid to use the bakery brownies, even if she had originally intended to, once Cherry had discovered her plan."

"True. Diane did admit that she arrived at the warehouse before the official practice time, found the front door locked, and went around back to see if she could get in through the factory, which she did. At that point she spotted Cherry in the chocolate fountain and started to scream."

"Did she say anything else?"

"Nope. Just told me that the police should talk to her attorney if they have any more questions."

"What do you think about her explanation for being at the crime scene?"

"The timing's plausible." Skye drew her brows together. "I wonder how many other people entered the warehouse through the factory entrance."

"Good question. Mr. Fine claims that door should have been locked, too."

"Did Jared have anything else helpful to say?" Skye asked. "I passed him on his way out and he seemed pretty preoccupied."

"He claimed he was doing paperwork in his office in the factory and had no idea what had happened until we called his mother and then she buzzed him on the intercom. Her office is a few doors down from his, so they can't alibi each other." Wally shook his head. "So far we have nothing. After I talk to Mrs. Fine, that's it. We're out of leads. We'll have to wait and hope forensics tells us something. But it could be weeks before we get those results."

Skye made a sympathetic sound and patted his arm, then asked, "Do you need me for anything else?"

"No. Why?"

"Because I'm going to go talk to Xenia about Ashley's disappearance." Skye drew a deep breath. "Which I should have done several days ago."

"Don't be so hard on yourself. I doubt she would have talked to you."

"You're probably right, but I should have tried. Ashley's life may be at stake."

"Or she could have just run away." Wally ran his fingers through his hair. "Listen, we both need a break. Why don't I pick you up around five and we'll go into Joliet for dinner and a movie? And while we're there we can buy a pair of cell phones."

"That sounds wonderful." Skye smiled, thinking that maybe Wally's father would give up if they weren't available, which would mean she wouldn't have to choose between finding out the truth and sticking to the moral high road.

Xenia lived with her mother, Raette, in a newly remodeled house near the river. When Skye pulled into the driveway, she saw that Raette's Sebring convertible was in the garage. Skye felt a small ray of hope. Maybe she'd be lucky and both of the Craughwells would be home.

Raette threw open the front door before Skye could even ring the bell. She was a tiny woman, less than five feet, with platinum hair that hung straight down to the middle of her back. She and Skye had a history, some good and some bad. Skye hoped the favor she had done Raette and her daughter in the fall would gain her access to Xenia.

Raette looked as if she would have liked to close the door, but instead she said, "Oh, what a surprise. You weren't who I was expecting."

"Is it okay if I come in?" Skye put her foot on the threshold.

"Uh, sure, but I'm leaving soon."

"Then I'll try to be quick." Skye stepped into the foyer, forcing Raette to back up. "Is Xenia home?"

"Yes. She's in her room."

"Could I talk to her?"

"Well, uh, I guess so. Is it about school?"

"In a way." Skye smiled noncommittally. "Do you want to get her for me, please?"

"Okay. Why don't you have a seat in the great room and I'll be right back."

Skye walked down the hall Raette had pointed to, and found herself in a large room with a sweep of windows that faced the water. It was a beautiful panorama, and whoever had decorated hadn't tried to compete with the natural beauty by putting any art on the other three walls.

Not wanting to be distracted, Skye chose a chair with her back to the view. As she settled in, she could hear Xenia protesting from the other end of the house.

The girl entered the room alone, a sullen expression on her face. "What do you want?"

"Hi, Xenia. Nice to see you, too." Skye kept her tone cool. The teen loved to cause adults to lose their tempers. "Have a seat."

"Why should I?"

"You're right. Just because my feet are tired doesn't mean yours are. Feel free to stand."

Xenia frowned and sat down in the chair facing Skye. "So, what do you want?"

"I understand that Ashley Yates is missing, and you may have been the last to see her." Skye figured enough people had accused the teen of the kidnapping, so she'd try a different approach.

"Yeah. So what? That doesn't mean I had anything to do with her disappearance."

"That's right. It doesn't. In fact, one of her friends told me that she thinks Ashley is holed up somewhere with a guy."

Xenia raised her chin. "Whatever."

"After all, Ashley is a beautiful girl; she could get any boy she wanted."

"If you like that type." Xenia studied her black Doc Martens. "Or maybe she knew she was a lying whore, and when she found out there was proof of her being a two-faced slut, she ran away."

"Why do you think that?" Skye made sure not to make eye contact. Xenia was like a wolf—she had to be the alpha in any situation.

Xenia shrugged. "Just a guess."

"You know, it's been more than three days now. At first I wasn't too worried, thinking maybe her friends were right. But now, even if she were with a guy or had run away because she didn't want to face some truth about herself, I'm starting to think she might be hurt or in trouble. Don't you think so?"

"How should I know?" Xenia toyed with a hole in her black T-shirt, making it larger.

"Maybe you could put yourself in her place, which is hard for me to do because I'm too old." Skye hoped she wasn't laying it on too thick. "Maybe we could figure out what happened that way."

"What if I do that and I'm right? Everyone will think I was involved, and I'll get into trouble."

Skye tried to keep the surprise off her face. This was the first time Xenia had ever admitted to caring if she got in trouble. Was the teen actually starting to develop a conscience? Could Skye use it to find out about Ashley?

"I'm here as your school psychologist, and I promise you anything you say to me is confidential, and I can't tell anyone what you told me, unless you say you're going to hurt yourself or someone else." Skye wanted to make it clear she was not here as the police consultant.

"What if I told you I already hurt someone else?"

Skye shook her head. "Unless you tell me you'll do it again or do something else in the future, I can't tell anyone."

Xenia tugged her short skirt down toward her knees. "Yeah, that's what my other shrink says, and she's been cool about stuff."

"So, if you had to guess, what happened with Ashley?" Skye held her breath.

"Maybe someone caught her by herself, with none of her posse around, you know, and sort of forced her into a car?"

Skye nodded.

"Then maybe this person drove her away from school and showed her proof of something that Ashley was claiming was a lie. Something that her parents were suing the school about. Something that would get Ashley in big trouble with her parents, who don't know what a slut their daughter is."

Skye nodded again, afraid anything she said would interrupt Xenia.

"And Ashley got out of the car and ran away crying and hasn't been seen since."

"So, this person who forced Ashley into the car has no idea where she is now?"

"Right." Xenia's attention was focused on peeling the black nail polish from her thumbnail.

"Where do you think this person drove Ashley to?"

"Well, the town's been sort of full of people, especially over by that factory where they're having that stupid cooking contest. So, if it were me, I'd go over there, because who would remember seeing any one car when there are lots and lots of them around?"

"Like in the parking lot?" Skye asked.

"Not the one in front, but there's one around back where the employees park, where people aren't coming and going that much."

"And I suppose once Ashley ran off, maybe whoever was with her might have spent some time looking for her. Then maybe been too scared to come home right away, but after a while figured it was better to be home, because if she was missing, that might make people think she was connected with Ashley being missing?"

"That sounds about right." For the first time that afternoon Xenia looked Skye in the eye. "You know, Ashley's a twit, but I bet whoever snatched her didn't mean for any of the rest of this to happen."

"I'll bet you're right." Skye got up to go. "Thank you for talking to me. If you ever want to talk at school, just put a note under my door and I'll send you a pass."

Skye drove back to the factory, parked in the employee lot, and made notes on what Xenia had said. By the time she was finished her legal pad was full of squiggles and arrows. Staring at the yellow paper, Skye chewed on the end of her pen. What had she learned?

1. *Xenia forces Ashley into her car Friday morning and drives her to the Fine Foods factory's back parking lot.*
2. *Xenia shows Ashley "proof" of what was written in the school newspaper. (Must be a picture—probably taken with one of those cell phones that take pictures.)*
3. *Ashley flees the car and no one has seen her since. Could she have hopped one of the trains that stop there to deliver supplies and pick up finished product?*
4. *Xenia searches for Ashley, but can't find her. Xenia hides out for a while, realizes that is suspicious behavior, comes home, erases her blog, and claims she has no involvement.*
5. *So where is Ashley?????*

Where hadn't they looked? Skye gazed out of the Bel Air's windshield. The factory sat on several acres of land bordered by a cornfield, which in early April was nothing but chunks of dirt and the occasional weed, certainly no place to hide.

The buildings were set about a quarter mile back on the property. The front was a large expanse of green lawn with a reflecting pool and a fountain. The water was too shallow to drown in, and besides, it was clearly visible from the road. Surely someone would have noticed a teenager lying in it for the past three days.

The back of the factory was taken up by the employee parking lot, where Skye was sitting, and truck bays that the semis used to load and unload the product. If Ashley were in trouble, inside the factory were guards and hundreds of workers she could go to, or there were phones she could use to call for help.

Which meant Skye still had no idea where to look for the missing girl. She might know what had happened, but that knowledge didn't help her find Ashley.

After a quick walk around the grounds, Skye checked her watch. It was already three thirty. The employees worked a seven-to-four shift. Should she wait around and look through the factory after they all left?

No, not unless she was willing to try to get permission for the search. During their tour of the factory the guide had explained that since September 11, because they manufactured food that could easily be poisoned, all of the factory entrances and exits were kept locked except for the employee entrance, which had a guard who checked identification.

During the day, if there was a crisis, workers could get out through doors with alarms wired directly to the fire department. But once the employees left for the day, the emergency exit doors were locked from the inside.

So, unless she had the Fines' consent, even if she were able to sneak in to look for Ashley, Skye wouldn't be able to get back out. She'd just have to wait until Wally came over at five; then she'd tell him what she had figured out from her chat with Xenia—not revealing how she had come to those conclusions—and see if he could get a search warrant.

A few minutes later she was pulling into her own driveway. It was a relief to be home for a little while, and after showering she decided to do some laundry. She gathered up the clothes she had worn over the last few days and took them downstairs. Before she stuffed them into the washing machine, she emptied out the pockets—she had a bad habit of sticking Post-its, used Kleenex, and change in them.

As she stuck her hand into the pocket of the jeans she had been wearing the day before, she pulled out the piece of paper May had found by the factory. Flattening it, Skye drew in a startled breath. It was a March schedule for Scumble River High cheerleading practice. Was this proof that Ashley had been around the factory in the past couple of days? Another thing to discuss with Wally.

After she started the machine, Skye checked her messages. The little light was blinking merrily, and she pushed the PLAY button.

The first voice was Trixie's. "Hi. Sorry I missed you. Owen and I got word that school was canceled, so we stayed another day. I should be home by midnight or so tonight. See you tomorrow morning before the first bell. Can't wait to hear what you've been up to."

The second message was from Carson Boyd. "Wally tells me he's picking you up at five at your house. I'll be there at quarter to, and we can get set up so you can hear the truth for yourself."

Holy shit! Not only was Carson still in town; he still wanted to set Wally up. What should she do?

CHAPTER 20

Remove from Pans

The doorbell rang at precisely four forty-five. Skye looked through her peephole, but almost didn't recognize the man standing on her front porch. Instead of the khakis and polo shirt he had worn earlier that day, Carson was dressed in a British tan Armani suit with a cream-colored Egyptian-cotton shirt and a chocolate brown Italian silk tie.

On his head was an ivory Stetson, and ostrich-skin cowboy boots had replaced his Wal-Mart tennis shoes. His sunglasses were no longer cheap rip-offs; instead they were expensive Ray-Bans. His current ensemble probably cost more than her annual salary.

For a moment Skye felt her throat tighten. This was what Wally would be giving up if he stayed in Scumble River, which was why it had to be completely his decision with no influence from anyone, including her. Taking a deep breath, she opened the door and let Carson Boyd inside.

He immediately took off his hat and said, "Miss Skye, I'm real grateful you're allowing me this chance to get my boy back."

"Well . . ." Skye noted that he now had a Texas accent. He hadn't had it that morning.

"I know that with your help, Walter will be home with me soon."

"Uh . . ." Skye's heart pounded. She hated this. Why? Why had she been forced into this position, and more important, had she made the right choice?

"Right?"

"Please." She swallowed with difficulty and found her voice. "This is between you and Wally."

"If that's what you want to believe. But you'll keep your word?" His stare drilled into her. "If you hear Wally say he wants to come back to Texas, you'll either agree to go with him or break up with him. And if you break up with him, you'll convince him you love that other fella."

Skye nodded. "If I hear him say he wants to live in Texas, I'll keep my word." She led him into the parlor and sat on the settee. "So, how are you going to do this?"

"When he arrives, I'll answer the door and say you had to run to town for something, but you'll be back in a few minutes. I'll tell him I'm leaving and I know he's only staying here because of you, and I understand and respect his decision, but I would like to hear the truth. Would he come home if you agreed to go with him or if you were no longer in his life?"

"So you'll lie, because you don't really respect his decision?"

"That's a minor detail. A means to an end." He glanced at his Rolex. "He'll be here soon. Where will you be so you can hear?"

"She can have my spot, Dad. You can hear really well what's said in the parlor if you stand in the hallway." Wally strolled through the archway and took a seat next to Skye.

"Walter." Carson's tanned face paled. "I can explain, son." He shot Skye a confused look.

"I'm sorry, Mr. Boyd, but I couldn't set Wally up that way. It just wasn't right," Skye stammered. "It's better all around if the three of us discuss this openly and together."

Carson slumped in the chair. "You've ruined everything."

"No." Skye leaned over and put a hand on his shoulder. "Really, I haven't. Not if what you want is a better relationship with your son. This is the way to get it. Not by deceiving him."

"But he'll never come back to Texas now. He'll never take over for me as CEO of CB International."

"That would never have happened anyway, Dad." Wally shook his head. "I told you more than twenty years ago when I was in college that I didn't want that kind of life. I'm happy here. Yes, a lot of that is due to Skye, but even if she dumped me or agreed to move to Texas with me, I don't want to be a CEO."

"I'm getting old. I want to retire." Carson tried to regain some ground. "Who'll take over for me?"

"I hear my cousin is doing a mighty fine job. He'd be the clear choice to take over."

"You have a nephew who works for you?" Skye demanded, outraged that Carson had let her believe that he was alone, with no one to turn to. "You never mentioned a nephew."

Carson nodded, not meeting her stare. It was clear he was beaten. He stood up and thrust his hand out at Wally. "I hope that we can at least stay in closer touch. I've enjoyed visiting with you the past few months."

Wally shook his dad's hand, then put his other arm around the older man's shoulder and hugged him. "Anytime, Dad. You're always welcome here. And maybe Skye and I can take a vacation to Texas this fall."

"I'd really like that." He put his hat on. "Well, I'd better go. I told my pilot to have the Cessna ready for takeoff by eight."

"Wait one minute." Skye struggled to put together the bits and pieces that had been bothering her. "You were here for another reason, besides to bring Wally back into the fold. What was it?"

"I guess it won't hurt to tell you now." Carson shrugged. "It'll be in the papers by tomorrow."

Where had she just heard that?

She glanced at Wally questioningly and he gave a slight nod and murmured, "Tammy Fine."

"That's right." Carson nodded. "For the past several

months CB International has been in talks with Fine Foods. I've been traveling here to negotiate the deal."

Skye wondered if Wally felt betrayed that his father hadn't been coming just to see him.

"Why the disguise this time?" Wally asked.

"Previously I was meeting with the Fines to look over profit-and-loss statements, check out the condition of the factory, and examine their distribution networks, but this time I was interested in their morals and values. I only acquire companies that have a good reputation, which is why I usually only go after businesses that are family-owned."

"That seems a little hypocritical, Dad, considering your own morals aren't exactly squeaky clean."

"Nothing personal." Carson shrugged. "It's just good business."

Skye and Wally exchanged a knowing glance. Evidently Carson's thinking was like that of a lot of the parents she dealt with, who wanted their kids to do as they said, not as they did.

"So, that's why you toned down your appearance and lost your accent—you wanted to fit in to Scumble River, be able to hang out and ask questions during the contest," Wally guessed.

"That, and I didn't want the Fines to recognize me, although I think a couple of them did."

"Quite a coincidence that you decided to buy a factory in Scumble River," Skye commented.

"Not really," Carson corrected her. "I was hoping that if all else failed, maybe Walter would at least agree to run that part of my company. He's the reason I got interested in Fine Foods. I had my people look for something for us to buy that was within thirty miles of Scumble River."

"So, why didn't you offer me that job, Dad?" Wally looked puzzled.

"Because he's decided not to buy the factory after all," Skye blurted out. "Right?"

"Right." Carson grinned at Skye. "Maybe I should offer *you* a job with the company."

"Thanks, but no thanks." Skye smiled back, then explained to Wally, "Fine Foods didn't pass the reputation test. There was dissention among the family—Jared and his mom arguing over the loudspeaker at the dinner, the contest practice being sabotaged, and, of course, the murder."

"There were a few other things, too, but those were the major issues," Carson agreed. "Someone in that company doesn't want it sold, and that's a sure sign that an acquisition is going to bomb."

"The Fines don't know you're backing out. Right?" Skye remembered what Tammy had said.

"No." Carson moved toward the door. "They'll get a notice delivered from my lawyer tonight at eight, and I want to be in the air headed back to Texas when they read it."

"Have a safe flight, Dad." Wally shook Carson's hand.

Skye kissed his cheek. "You be good now, you hear?"

As Carson made his way down the front steps to his rental car, Skye shut the door and asked Wally, "You okay with what just happened?"

"Yeah. I am." Wally took her hand in both of his. "I feel good about us. I'm glad you told me what my father had planned; otherwise it would have felt like you two had ganged up on me. And strange as it may seem, I think Dad and I are better now than we have been in years. I think he may finally understand me a little more, or at least accept who I am."

"I'd say trying to buy a factory for you proves his love, too."

"So you want me to buy you a factory?" Wally teased.

"You are so not funny." Skye stuck out her tongue. "Hey, speaking of factories, I need to tell you something about Ashley Yates."

"Did Xenia admit to kidnapping her?"

"Because I talked to Xenia as her school psychologist and not as the PD's psych consultant, all I can tell you is that Ashley was last seen alive and well Friday morning at the Fine Foods factory. She got out of a car at that location of her own free will, and hasn't been seen since."

"Let me see if I can extrapolate. Xenia and Ashley were together at the factory for whatever reason, and Ashley got out of Xenia's car." Wally scratched his chin. "At least it wasn't the day of the murder."

"Can we get a search warrant for the factory?"

"I doubt it. There's nothing to suggest she went inside. Is there?"

"Maybe." Skye reached into her pocket and handed him the March schedule for the high school's cheerleading practices. "Mom found this near the sidewalk in back of the factory."

"That's not enough to show she went inside, but tomorrow I will ask the Fines to let us look around." He tilted his head. "I'm surprised you didn't sneak in and take a peek this afternoon."

"I would never do that, now that I'm with the police force." Skye crossed her fingers and didn't mention the factory's elaborate security measures. Then she changed the subject. "Did you find out anything from your interviews after I left?"

"No, Quirk and the others couldn't break anyone's story. I'm still thinking it's Jared. He had opportunity and he's strong enough."

"That's means and opportunity, but what about motive?"

"Maybe Cherry was blackmailing him," Wally suggested. "Now that we know about my father's interest in buying Fine Foods, and his requirement that the company have a good moral character, that would make sense."

"Any idea how to prove it?"

"No. I'm hoping that when the forensics come through, there'll be something I can use."

"Shoot. Our first unsolved case." Skye frowned.

They were silent for a few minutes; then Wally asked, "Do you still want to go to Joliet for dinner?"

"No. It's too late. By the time we drive back and forth that's at least an hour and a half, say a couple hours for a movie and an hour for dinner and an hour to buy the phones—we wouldn't be home until midnight, and I have school tomorrow."

"Right. Let's do it this weekend instead."

Wally followed Skye into the kitchen.

She looked in the fridge, shook her head, and closed it. "I'm starving, but the cupboard's bare. Unless you want me to whip up my prizewinning casserole."

"Hey, congratulations, I heard you won. That's great, but . . ."

"But you never want to taste that dish again. That's okay; neither do I."

"Phew." Wally mimicked great relief. "I was afraid that since you had won, you'd want to make it all the time."

"Right." Skye snorted. "So, back to the age-old question— what shall we do for dinner?"

"How do Italian beef sandwiches sound?"

"Yummy. From where?"

"That place in Braidwood. Antonia's."

"Sounds good. Just let me put some lipstick on, and I'm ready."

Wally dropped her off back home at ten. They had talked some more about Wally and his dad's relationship. It seemed that Wally really was fine. Skye wished she could be that casual about the twisted branches of her family tree, but that would probably never happen.

She was exhausted, and for a second considered sleeping in the sunroom rather than climbing the stairs to bed, but the thought of trying to stretch out on the short love seat spurred her up the steps. Once she successfully made it to her bedroom, she fell across her mattress fully clothed. The next thing she knew her alarm was buzzing and Bingo was licking her nose. The workweek merry-go-round had begun, and she needed to move her butt, or her carousal horse would gallop away without her.

After more than a week off, school was crazy. She had only a few minutes to say hi to Trixie before Homer swept her into his office. He sat behind his desk and rubbed his beer belly as if he were about to give birth. The kids had several nicknames for him, including Nitpicker, Homie, Crapik, but Skye thought the most appropriate was Hairy.

Homer was the most hirsute man she had ever seen. Hair grew in tufts from his head, ears, and eyebrows, and covered

his body like a pelt. The principal's habit of petting himself
while he talked made it hard to concentrate during a conversation with him. Even after having worked with him for several years, Skye had to make a concerted effort not to stare
as he stroked his furry forearms.

At first Homer drilled Skye about Ashley's disappearance, the lawsuit, and other issues she had little or no control over, but finally he got to the real reason he had snatched
her from the hallway—Mrs. Cormorant, the oldest teacher
in the district and Homer's archnemesis. "You won't believe
what Corny has done this time."

"What?" At this point in her career Skye was ready to believe almost anything.

"She added a box in the comment section of the report
cards."

"Oh?" Skye was cautious in her reply. "I was under the
impression that teachers were encouraged to write in additional remarks."

"Not anymore. Last time she did it the parents sued us, so
we discontinued the policy of allowing teachers to insert un-
approved statements." Homer ran his fingers through the
clumps of hair sticking up from his scalp. "But that didn't
stop old Corny."

"What comment did she add?"

" 'Shallow gene pool.' "

Skye held back a snort of laughter and tried to look serious when she said, "But report cards came out nearly a week
ago. Why is this just coming up now?"

"Someone explained what the comment meant to the parents. Before some freaking Good Samaritan enlightened
them, they thought the teacher wanted them to have their son
swim in deeper water this summer."

Skye bit the inside of her cheek to stop herself from
laughing. "I take it once the parents received this little
nugget of wisdom, they were not amused."

"They're demanding an apology from the school and the
teacher."

"And my guess is Cormorant refuses to say she's sorry."

Homer nodded, and Skye went on, "And my second guess is that you want me to convince her."

Homer nodded again.

"We've been through this before; Pru Cormorant does not like me. I am the wrong person to get her to do anything."

"Hey, we all know her receiver is off the hook, but everyone else is afraid of her."

"What makes you think I'm not?" Skye demanded.

"Anyone who has faced down as many murderers as you have should be able to handle one little old lady."

"Except that she isn't little, and she isn't a lady."

Homer took up another hour of her time whining about various other situations, then glanced at his watch and verbally shoved her out the door with the admonishment, "Remember, talk to Corny and make her see the light."

As Skye walked away, she muttered, "I'd rather make the harridan go into the light than try to make her see it."

Despite her grumbling, Skye had long since realized that it was easier to do what the principal told her to and get it over with, rather than argue. With this in mind she checked the master schedule and saw that Mrs. Cormorant was free for the next seventeen minutes. Perfect. By the time the next bell rang, the distasteful task would be done.

Pru Cormorant had one of the best classrooms in the building. It had actual walls—instead of folding curtains—windows, and even a door to the outside. Because of this it was a well-known fact that if the weather was nice she usually spent her planning periods on a lawn chair on the grass.

Skye found Pru there reading a spicy romance, which she quickly hid under a copy of *Moby-Dick*. Skye pretended not to notice, not that she cared what the other woman read, and said, "Hi, are you enjoying the sunshine?"

"Yes, it's so nice to be able to pop out here during the day." Pru's watery blue eyes were malicious. "Your office doesn't have a door to the outside, does it, dear?"

"No, but then, I'm usually too busy to notice."

"Yes, I suppose you are." Pru raised an overplucked

eyebrow. "The students nowadays aren't like they were when I started at Scumble River High School."

Skye bit her tongue to stop herself from asking what it was like to teach in the Stone Age, and instead said, "Actually, that's what I wanted to talk to you about. Homer asked me to see if you might have changed your mind about apologizing to those parents who were insulted by your comment on their son's report card."

"No."

"No?"

"No, I haven't changed my mind and I won't." Pru patted her stringy, dun-colored hair. "We need to stop coddling these parents. No Child Left Behind, my eye. Anyone with the slightest knowledge of the bell curve knows the largest portion of students are going to be average; then there's going to be a certain number who are gifted, and, sadly, there are going to be an equal number who are dim-witted. The sooner the parents accept that not every child is going to Harvard or even to a community college, the better. Look at the poor Fines."

"The Fines?" Skye had been letting Pru ramble, having heard her opinion on the subject before, but suddenly she tuned in. "You mean the family that owns Fine Foods? What about them?"

"They spent a fortune on tutors and donations getting those two boys through college." Pru licked her thin lips. "At least they were satisfied when JJ got a BA in business, but they poured even more money into getting Brandon through law school."

"But he got his degree, right?" Skye frowned. "Money is never wasted on an education."

"He got his degree, all right, but it's useless."

"Why?"

"He can't pass the bar exam." Pru smiled meanly. "He's tried and tried, even other states' bar exams, but there's only so much being rich can do for you. And buying you a license to practice law isn't one of them."

*   *   *

After leaving Pru, Skye checked with Frannie and Justin, as well as Ashley's fellow cheerleaders. No one had heard from Ashley, and no one seemed particularly worried. They all claimed the girl was behind her own disappearance, and that she'd show up when she got bored, but Skye suspected the students knew more than they were saying—maybe not about where Ashley was, but about why she had disappeared.

The rest of the day whizzed by as Skye prepared for and attended both the junior high and the high school's bimonthly Pupil Personal Services meetings. She was kept busy pulling and reading files, taking notes, and getting paperwork ready to start several reevaluations.

Students in special education had to be evaluated by the psychologist triennially, so every three years a third of the kids receiving services had to be tested. These assessments often took up the majority of a school psychologist's time, and Skye was no exception.

When the final bell rang at three, Trixie Frayne burst through Skye's door. Skye hurriedly finished filling in a consent form, tucked it into its folder, and filed it away. She was anxious to talk to her friend, hoping Trixie would provide a fresh take on both the murder and the disappearance.

Trixie was the school librarian, cheerleading coach, and cosponsor of the student newspaper. She reminded Skye of a brownie—not the Girl Scout, the forest imp. She had short nut brown hair and cocoa-colored eyes, a size-four body, and high spirits.

Her first words were, "Why does everything exciting happen when I'm gone?"

Skye ignored Trixie's question—Trixie had been involved in lots of Skye's past adventures—and asked, "Did you have a romantic getaway?"

"Yes." Trixie's grin was lascivious. "Times like this weekend remind me why I married Owen. Woo, that man has stamina."

"My number one criteria for a good husband," Skye said dryly.

"Yeah, right." Trixie sneered. "That's why you dumped Mr. Nice for Mr. Hot."

"We are so not going there."

"You brought it up." Trixie snatched a piece of Easter candy from the jar on Skye's desk.

"Can we talk about something else, like our missing student and the murder?" Skye filled Trixie in on what she could about what Xenia had told her about Ashley, avoiding breaking confidentiality by a hair.

"Boy." Trixie crossed her legs and dangled her pink high-heeled sandal from her toe. "That girl is a pepperoni short of a pizza."

"True," Skye agreed, then gave Trixie the lowdown on the murder and Wally's dad, concluding with, "It all seems to coalesce around the Fine Foods factory."

"It does, doesn't it?"

Skye got up and went over to a portable blackboard someone had stored in her office. She'd asked the custodian to remove it, but hadn't bugged him enough yet to stir him to action. For now she'd put it to good use.

She picked up a piece of chalk and began to outline. "The first thing that happened is that Wally's dad decides to look into acquiring Fine Foods. He'll buy it only if the company has a good reputation, so he comes to town in disguise during the cooking contest—their biggest PR event—to check that out."

Trixie nodded. "Number one: The sale of the factory hinges on its good name."

"Second, the Friday morning before the contestants get to the factory, Ashley runs away from her abductor in the Fine Foods parking lot and has not been seen again."

Trixie grabbed a foil-wrapped candy egg. "Number two: Does Ashley get inside despite the security measures you mentioned, and if so, is she still there?"

"Third, the contest has an unusual number of problems this year. The practice round is sabotaged. Jared and Grandma Sal's private argument is broadcast on the PA, doors that were supposed to be locked aren't, and to top it off, a woman is murdered." Skye paused, thinking. "Not to mention, who in his or her right mind would think Glenda Doozier's cooking is worthy of finaling?"

"Number three: Someone knew Carson Boyd was here watching the contest. Knew he wouldn't go through with the deal if Fine Foods ended up looking bad, and so this person made sure that it did."

"That's it!" Skye jerked as if she'd been zapped by a cattle prod. "Wally and I have been thinking that Cherry was murdered because she had something on the company that would ruin its reputation, but it's the opposite. I'll bet she caught someone sabotaging the contest, and that person killed her to keep her quiet."

Trixie licked the chocolate from her fingers. "So who wouldn't want the company sold?"

Skye wrote a list of names on the board. "Jared and Tammy can't wait for it to sell. If I remember my brief conversation with Brandon and JJ, both of them don't like it here at Scumble River either, so that only leaves Grandma Sal and maybe all the factory workers, if they're afraid for their jobs."

"Isn't Grandma Sal a little old to be lifting bodies into chocolate fountains?"

"She may be in her late seventies, but she's a big, strong woman who could probably outrun me in a race, maybe even you if it was an endurance event." Skye bit her lip. "The big question is, would she be willing to make her own company look bad in order to keep it? And since she owns the majority percentage, why would she have to?"

"Yeah. As Nancy Reagan used to urge, she could just say no." Trixie pursed her mouth. "On the other hand, would anyone outside the family know about the terms of the sale? The employees might know CB International is interested in buying Fine Foods, but would they know the one thing that would stop the sale?"

"Good question."

Trixie and Skye sat in silence as they tried to think of another suspect.

Finally, when neither of them could come up with anything new, Trixie jumped up from her seat. "I'd better get home. There's a pile of laundry with my name on it. And I need to stop at the grocery store. Owen will be looking for his supper at five on the dot, and I don't have a thing to cook."

Skye waved good-bye to her friend, then closed her eyes and thought about what she and Trixie had discovered. *Hmm.* If Grandma Sal was not a suspect—and since she could stop the deal simply by refusing to sign the papers, she didn't look likely—that meant maybe she'd agree to answer a few questions. It was only three thirty, and she might still be at the factory.

A quick phone call verified that Skye was in luck. Mrs. Fine wasn't officially there, but she had stopped by to sign some papers. However, she was leaving in an hour, and although she was willing to talk to Skye, Skye needed to arrive within fifteen minutes.

While dialing the police station, Skye hurriedly packed up her tote bag. The dispatcher said that Wally was out, but had left a message that he hadn't been able to secure permission to search the factory and would stop by her house when he got off work at five. Skye left him a message saying she was going to talk to Grandma Sal, and would try to change the older woman's mind about giving them permission to look for Ashley.

Wishing she and Wally had stuck to their plan and gone to buy cell phones yesterday, Skye got into her car and headed toward the factory. As she drove, she fingered the container of pepper spray in her blazer pocket, wondering if she was making a bad move. If she was wrong, and Grandma Sal was the killer, Skye could end up looking very stupid . . . and possibly very dead.

CHAPTER 21

Cool Completely

Entering Grandma Sal's office, Skye was taken aback at both the decor and Grandma Sal herself. Instead of the sweet old lady she had met at the cooking contest, whose image was on all the products, a well-dressed, attractive woman sat behind a sleek chrome-and-glass desk.

Gone were the gray curls, the wire-rimmed glasses, the flowered dress, and the old-fashioned hat. Instead Grandma Sal's hair was now ash blond and styled in a smooth French twist. She wore a stylish pink Chanel suit with matching high-heeled pumps.

Skye stood staring while the secretary announced her.

Even after Grandma Sal looked up and said, "What can I do for you, dear?" Skye was speechless.

The older woman prodded, "A lot of people are surprised when they see the real Sally Fine, after meeting 'Grandma Sal.' I only dress like a little old lady for public appearances."

"Oh, of course." Skye's cheeks flamed. "I understand completely."

"I'm so sorry we had your name wrong throughout the contest. I assure you we'll get the spelling fixed on your plaque, and it will be correct on your check."

"Thank you. It's an unusual name. I completely understand the mix-up."

"Then I take it you're here for another reason. Have a seat."

"Thanks." Skye sat in one of the leather-and-chrome visitor's chairs, put her tote bag by her feet, and craned her neck to look around a huge rolling pin–shaped trophy that was directly in front of her.

"Go ahead and move that thing over." Mrs. Fine blew out an exasperated breath. "I can't quite figure out what to do with it. Fine Foods won it for having the most homemade-tasting packaged foods."

Skye reached out her right hand to shove the prize to the side, and was surprised by the weight of the marble award. Grunting a little as she pushed, she said, "I'm here as the police department's psychological consultant."

"Is there news about Ms. Alexander's unfortunate death?"

"Well, we have put some pieces of the puzzle together, but still haven't quite found that final part—the name of the murderer. Which is why I wanted to talk to you."

"You think there's something I can do to help?"

"I hope so." Skye wrinkled her brow, choosing her words carefully. "Once we learned about CB International's interest in Fine Foods, and the fact that they would buy the company only if it had an exemplary reputation, we figured that whoever killed Cherry did so to stop the sale of the business."

"No." Mrs. Fine toyed with her Montblanc pen. "I don't believe that for one minute."

As Skye tried to decide the best way to respond to the older woman's denial, she was startled by a loud whistle. "What was that?"

Mrs. Fine put down the pen and smiled, seemingly relieved at the interruption. "It's just quitting time."

"Right." Skye nodded to herself. "You don't run an evening shift anymore."

"Not for quite some time. That's one of the reasons it would have been good for us to sell to CB International.

They would have expanded our sales by three or four times, and we could have gone back to running around the clock."

Skye filed that piece of info away, then asked, "Who was familiar with the conditions of the transaction with CB?"

"The only ones who knew about their stipulations were the family." Mrs. Fine paled under her artfully applied makeup. "The only ones with anything to gain or lose are Fines."

"Would any of the workers not want the factory sold?"

"They were all assured that no one would lose their jobs, and, in fact, it was highly likely that more positions would be created."

"In that case, *who* didn't want the transaction to be completed?"

"No one." Mrs. Fine's voice cracked. "I was the only one who was the least bit against the sale, and Jared and JJ convinced me it was for the best."

"What about Brandon and Tammy?"

"They don't have a say in the matter. Tammy has nothing to do with the company, and Brandon is only Jared's stepson. Although we allow him to use the Fine name, Tammy had Brandon before she married Jared. He was already six months old at the time of their wedding."

"Jared never adopted Brandon?"

"No, not officially. Brandon and Tammy aren't really Fines. My husband left fifty-five percent of the company to me, thirty percent to Jared, and fifteen percent to JJ. He felt strongly that only blood relations should own Fine Foods." Mrs. Fine closed her eyes, lines of pain etched in her forehead. "Which is why I didn't want to sell it to CB International."

Skye refrained from pointing out that Mrs. Fine wasn't a Fine by blood either, and instead asked, "If the company is sold, would Tammy and Brandon get a share then?"

"Well, Tammy would have access to Jared's money, but I doubt Jared or JJ would give any significant amount to Brandon. They just aren't that close. And I'm leaving all my money to the Fine Foundation for the Arts."

Interesting family dynamics, not that Skye was surprised.

After several years as a school psychologist, she'd seen a lot worse. "So, you can't think of anyone who had anything to gain or lose if the company was sold?" She knew she was on the right track and was frustrated that she couldn't figure out what she was missing.

"No, but I'll think about it and give you a call if something comes to me."

"Thank you." Skye pushed back her chair and grabbed her tote bag; then as she got up she remembered Ashley, and asked, "I know you've already said no, but is there anything I can say that will convince you to reconsider, and allow us to search the factory for the missing girl?"

"What missing girl?"

Skye explained, ending with, "So the last time she was seen was outside your factory."

"No one told me about this. Of course you can search for her." Mrs. Fine rubbed her temples as if she had a headache. "I can't imagine how she'd get in here or why she'd stay, but feel free to look around."

"That's wonderful. Can I do it right now?"

"Certainly." Mrs. Fine reached into a black lacquer box on the desk and took out a key. "I have to leave for an appointment in the city, so you'll need this master to look around and to get out—the guards lock up when everyone goes home for the night."

"Everyone's already gone?" Skye looked at her watch. It was only four thirty.

"The building empties out fast once the whistle blows. Even the guards are gone by this time."

"You don't have twenty-four-hour security?"

"Not inside the building. They have a booth near the gate and patrol the perimeter of the property."

"Oh." Skye nodded. "What should I do with the key once I let myself out?"

"You can drop it off tomorrow."

Mrs. Fine walked with Skye as far as the lobby. "If you need to use the phone, the only one that works after hours is the one in my office. Help yourself." She waved, unlocked the front door, and left.

Skye paused to figure out what to do next, then decided the best course of action was to return to Mrs. Fine's office and call the PD for help with the search. The factory was just too big, with too many nooks and crannies to look through all by herself.

As she walked back, she read the nameplates on the doors she passed. Jared's office was closest to the front, then the business office, then the legal department, then . . .

She stopped and stared at the door. Suddenly the memory of what Pru Cormorant had said, added to what Mrs. Fine had just revealed, and what she and Trixie had figured out about the killer coalesced and she blurted out, "That's it! Brandon killed Cherry because—"

Before she could finish her thought, someone grabbed her arm and she shrieked. Brandon Fine loomed at her side, a scowl on his face. Had he heard her? She had to quit talking out loud to herself—a habit she had picked up since adopting Bingo.

She quickly ran through various mental scenarios and decided that if he hadn't heard her, maybe she could distract him. "Uh, hi, Brandon. I, um, was just getting permission from your grandmother to search for a missing teenager."

"Shut up!" His fingers dug into the flesh of her upper arm, and her tote bag thumped against her hip. "I thought you were supposed to be so smart. Who do you think turned down the cops in the first place?"

"Oh." Great, he wasn't just the murderer; he had something to do with Ashley's disappearance as well. "Anyway, your grandma said yes, and the cops will be here any minute, so I'd better get to the door to let them in before they break it down." Skye's laugh was forced.

"Drop the act. I was standing at my grandmother's secretary's desk when you called earlier this afternoon. I'd heard how nosy you are and that you 'help' the police, so I hung around and found out you were coming here to talk to Grandma. I've been following you and eavesdropping on you since you got here."

Skye fought to keep her face expressionless. If she played dumb, maybe she could convince him she thought his brother was the killer. "But why would you do that? Are you protecting JJ?" She slipped her free hand into her jacket pocket and grasped the small can of pepper spray.

She read the hesitation in his dark eyes as he considered what she had said, and whether he could put the blame on his half brother. Taking advantage of his momentary distraction, she jerked her left arm free and used her right hand to empty the pepper spray directly into his eyes.

He howled, clawing at his face.

Now what should she do? He stood between her and the exit, and she was afraid he would recover before she could get around him and unlock the dead bolt. She had only one choice: She dashed into the factory and was frantically looking for a door when she heard Brandon's footsteps thundering toward her. She quickly hid behind the giant mixer—ironically the same one he had demonstrated during last Friday's tour.

A second later Brandon came into sight. He paused, looked around, then approached the huge machine. As he leaned over the rim and peered down into the enormous bowl, Skye darted from behind the control panel and shoved him with all her strength. At first he teetered, then nearly regained his balance, but one more thrust from her and he fell inside. She whirled around, flipped the switch to the ON position, and ran.

Skye came to a dead end in the area Brandon had called the Boneyard. Here ancient machinery was piled against the rear wall, and there was a feeling of longtime disuse and abandonment. She anxiously scanned the equipment for a hiding place. Draping the straps of her tote bag across her chest, she wiggled behind an apparatus bristling with rusting steel hooks. As she stood holding her breath, she examined the spot she had wedged herself into.

The walls were puke green, and there were no windows or doors. Her gaze dropped to the wooden floor and stuttered to a stop on a section to her right where the seams didn't seem to meet evenly. It probably didn't mean anything, but just as she always had to check the coin tray when she passed a vending machine, knowing it would be empty, she scooted over and nudged the wood with her toe. Had it wobbled just a tad?

It was a tight squeeze, but Skye managed to get down on her hands and knees. She found a nail file in her tote bag and slipped it into the irregular area. She could feel a definite wiggle this time as she used the file as a lever.

For a heart-stopping moment nothing happened; then a square of the wooden floor swung upward . . . and stuck halfway open. It had caught on a piece of equipment shoved against it. Skye braced herself against the hook machine and pushed.

The door moved only a few inches, but Skye thought she could fit—maybe. She peered over the edge and saw a ladder nailed to the wall. Slithering into the small space like a dancer going under a limbo bar backward, she managed to get her foot on the first rung.

She was still half in and half out when she heard the mixer stop. Had Brandon escaped or had the motor burned out?

Ignoring the painful scraping of the skin on her back, Skye jerked herself through the opening, blindly stepping down until she could shut the door. She'd been prepared for total darkness, but once her eyes adjusted she could see a light coming from somewhere beneath her.

As she descended, she prayed for help. She was afraid to take her eyes from the ladder, so she was surprised when her foot encountered solid ground. Stepping away from the wall, she saw that she was in some sort of storage basement.

Now what? Her only hope was that if Brandon had escaped from the mixer he wouldn't find the trapdoor, which he wouldn't see unless he stood in the exact place Skye had been standing. If he only gave the area behind the old machinery a cursory look, he wouldn't notice it.

At first all she could see were old file cabinets, desks, some boxes, and bookcases, but as she took a few steps farther into the area, she swallowed a scream. Lying on a worn leather sofa, eyes closed, perfectly still, was Ashley Yates.

A tear slipped down Skye's cheek. Ashley was dead. She was too late to save her.

But a husky voice penetrated her grief. "Is that you, Ms. Denison? How'd you find me?"

Skye's head jerked up, and she ran to the sofa. "It's me, all right." She knelt beside Ashley. "Are you okay?"

"No." The teen started sobbing. "I think my leg's broken, and I'm hungry and thirsty."

Skye lifted the strap of her tote bag over her head and plunged her hand inside. Grabbing the bottle of water she always kept there, she opened it and handed it to Ashley, cautioning, "Drink this slowly, or it will make you sick."

In between sips, Ashley said, "I ran out of water and food yesterday."

Skye found her emergency candy bar and handed over the Kit Kat. Ashley tore off the wrapper and stuffed a piece of chocolate into her mouth.

Skye had met the girl's basic needs for food and liquid, but there was nothing she could do for Ashley's leg.

After giving the teen a few seconds to compose herself, and remembering to keep her voice low, Skye asked, "What happened? How did you get here? I mean in this basement. I know how you got to the factory."

"Xenia told you?" Ashley followed Skye's lead, keeping her voice barely above a whisper. "When Xenia showed me the pictures Friday morning, I knew my parents would kill me, so I decided to run away. I thought I could hide in the factory while I figured out where to go, but all the doors were locked. I was about to give up when a semi pulled away and I noticed that the big door it had been backed up to was still open. I climbed up onto this kind of wooden deck thing and suddenly I was inside. I spent most of the rest of the day hiding in a storage closet, and then I spent the night in the employee lounge."

Skye examined the area they were in as Ashley talked. She was listening to the teen, but also searching for a way out. So far there was no sign of Brandon. Had she killed him by shoving him in the mixer and turning it on?

When Ashley paused, Skye asked, "Then what happened?"

"I figured I'd have the place to myself on Saturday, since

the factory would be closed, but way early I started hearing noises. First an old lady came in with a middle-aged guy. They went to the front part of the plant and into separate offices. Then I saw this younger guy unlock the back door where the workers come in and put on one of those white jumpsuits they wear. He went into the warehouse, and I could hear all kinds of rattling and clunking."

Skye nodded to herself. That must have been when Brandon sabotaged the cooking contest. No doubt he arrived early on Friday, too, and substituted ingredients, messed with timers, and switched the dials on the ovens.

Ashley had paused to lick chocolate from her fingers, but continued, "Next this redheaded woman slips in and it's quiet for a while, but suddenly it sounds like a battle of the bands. So I sneak in and that's when I saw it."

"Saw what?" Skye glanced nervously upward. Had she heard footsteps?

"The guy in the jumpsuit hit the redheaded lady over the head with this hammerlike thing my mom uses to flatten meat. After he hits her, he dumps her in this fountain and holds her under."

"What did you do?"

"I ducked into one of the little kitchens." Ashley took a swig of water. "I could still see what was happening through the gap where the partitions went together."

"What happened next?"

"I heard a noise in one of the other little kitchens; then Mayor Leofanti came around the corner. When he spotted the woman in the fountain he ran up and bent down to help her; then Jumpsuit Guy threw a tablecloth over his head, spun him around, and stabbed him in the stomach with this little knife he had in his pocket. Blood gushed out like a geyser." Ashley took another drink. "That's when I screamed."

"And?"

"And Jumpsuit Guy must have followed the sound, because he found me and tried to kill me." Tears welled up in her eyes. "He really tried to kill me."

Skye patted the girl's hand. Most teenagers had no

concept of their own mortality, but Ashley had looked the Grim Reaper in the face and seen her own death in his expression. "Is that how you broke your leg?"

"No." Ashley took a deep breath and went on. "He came after me with that hammer thingy, and just as he swung downward with it to hit me I fainted, and it must have just grazed my forehead. He obviously thought I was dead, because when I came to I was wrapped in a sheet and lying in the back of one of the Fine Food vans. As I was getting out I spotted Jumpsuit Guy coming toward me, so I ran the other way around the van and circled over to the side of the factory."

Skye patted her again and made an encouraging sound.

"My head hurt and I was dizzy, but I knew he'd kill me if he found me. I was looking for someplace to hide when I saw these windows." Ashley pointed up.

Skye looked at the row of windows near the ceiling of the basement. Weren't basements supposed to have low ceilings? This one had to be twelve or fourteen feet high.

"The locks were all old and rusted, and I was able to push one open. Just as I was climbing inside I heard the guy coming, and I miscalculated, so instead of stepping in and hopping down, I crashed to the floor. Luckily the window must have snapped closed behind me, because Jumpsuit Guy walked right by and never found me. I think I passed out again, because when I came to it was dark and I couldn't move my leg."

Skye sucked in her breath, feeling the pain and terror that Ashley must have experienced. "And you've been trapped here ever since?"

"Yes. I was able to drag myself around using that." She pointed to a wheeled stenographer's chair. "But I couldn't climb the ladder you came down, and I couldn't get back up to the windows, and my cell battery died before I could get a signal in here." She took a teary breath before going on. "At first I tried screaming. Then I realized: What if Jumpsuit Guy was the one who heard me yelling? There's a bathroom over in the back there, but after the second day the faucet stopped working. I had a bottle of water and some energy bars in my backpack, but I ran out yesterday. I thought I was going to die here."

Skye opened her mouth to reassure Ashley, but before she could come up with any comforting words, the teen asked, "So, how did you get here, and how do we get out?"

CHAPTER 22

Frost the Cake

After Skye explained to Ashley how she had found her, Skye tried to come up with an answer to the girl's second question. How could they get out?

Pacing the length of the basement, Skye searched for an exit. She found evidence of a door that had long since been bricked over, but there was no way to remove the concrete blocks.

Her next objective was a weapon, but there was nothing except abandoned office furniture and box after box of tightly packed paper files dating back to the first year the company was in business. Clearly Fine Foods' philosophy was the same as the school system's: Never keep just one copy of a document when you can keep twelve instead.

After several circuits Skye was forced to accept that the only way out was via the windows that Ashley had entered through. Unfortunately there were a couple of problems with that solution. First and foremost, with her broken leg, there was no way the teen could climb up that far, and second, even if Skye could make the climb—which was iffy—that would mean leaving Ashley behind.

Skye went over to the girl, knelt back down, and took her hand. "It looks like I'll have to go out the window you came through."

"No." Ashley's fingers clutched Skye's. "Please don't leave me. I'm sorry for everything. For having sex with all those boys, for lying about it, for getting the paper in trouble. I'll be good if you get me out of here; I promise."

"Ashley." Skye put her other arm around the girl. "I'm not leaving you because I'm mad at you or because you were bad. I'm going because it's the only way out, and I need to get help. We can't wait to be rescued. The guy chasing us is Brandon Fine, and eventually he's going to find us."

"But what if he finds me before you get back?"

"Once I'm out the window, I promise I'll have help back here in ten minutes, fifteen at the most."

"Don't go," Ashley sobbed. "I just know he'll get me while you're gone."

Skye hesitated. What if the girl was right? No. She had to play the odds. If Brandon hadn't found Ashley before now, that meant he didn't know about this basement. Judging from the dates on the files, the room hadn't been used since before he was born.

"I'm sorry, honey, but I have to. I just can't figure out any other way to save us both."

Before starting to build her ladder to freedom, Skye climbed back up the wooden one and listened at the trap-door. She couldn't hear anything. Either the floor was extremely thick, which would explain why no one had heard Ashley's screams for help, or Skye had killed Brandon when she pushed him in the mixer. Better yet, he might have simply given up—but she kind of doubted that. He was probably lying in wait like a shark at a shipwreck, poised to pounce once Skye jumped overboard.

Skye pushed a double filing cabinet under the window bank. Next to it she shoved a desk and a chair; then she went to work piling boxes full of paper on the desktop. Once she figured she had enough, she got onto the desk and transferred the cartons onto the file cabinet. She followed this system until she had steps that reached nearly to the sill.

She took her car keys and the factory key from her tote and stuffed them both down her bra, then stripped off her blazer. When she was down to slacks and a cami, she considered her shoes. They were loafers with an inch-and-a-half heel; was she better off with or without them?

Deciding to try the ascent with the shoes and discard them if they got in the way, she started up the shaky box staircase. With each step she felt as if the whole structure were about to come tumbling down, but she reached the top unscathed.

Taking a deep breath, she grasped the handle of the window and pulled. Cool, fresh air poured into the dank basement. Skye took a greedy breath before placing her foot on the ledge and heaving herself upward.

She teetered—caught halfway between the top box and the windowsill. *Crap.* If she made it out of here alive, she really had to work on her upper-body strength. Steeling her arms and praying to the gym gods, Skye pulled.

Suddenly she was on the sill, then through the window. Stunned, she stood there for a moment. A few seconds later she was running toward the parking lot, keys in hand. She skidded to a stop by the Bel Air and suppressed a scream of frustration. Someone had slashed all four tires— probably Brandon.

Okay, plan B. The guards Mrs. Fine had mentioned earlier that afternoon. She had said they had a booth near the road. Skye jogged the quarter mile down the lane, gasping for breath. She really needed to get more exercise if she was going to keep running away from killers. Now she knew why Charlie's Angels were so skinny.

Skye arrived at the security booth, only to find it empty. Now what? Plan C was to wave down a car, but who would drive by on a road that dead-ended at the gate? That left plan D, otherwise known as Dumb Move—go back to the building and try to use Grandma Sal's phone. But she couldn't think of a plan E—it would take her at least half an hour to walk into town, which was just too long to leave Ashley alone with Brandon on the prowl. If only she knew whether she had incapacitated him in the mixer.

Maybe she could find a guard patrolling the factory's perimeter. Summoning up the last of her energy, Skye ran back down the lane and around the building, but there was nothing stirring, not even a mouse. Where were the fricking guards? If she got out of this alive, she would make Mrs. Fine fire them all.

Finally she faced the fact that there was no one to help her; if she wanted to save Ashley, she would have to do it herself. Having come to that conclusion, Skye knew she had to go back inside and get to the telephone. Too bad Ashley had used up her cell phone's battery trying to get a signal.

With no other choice, hoping she wasn't being as stupid as she felt, Skye used the key Mrs. Fine had given her and slipped back inside. She stopped briefly to wedge the door open with a flattened soda can she had found in the parking lot.

She kept to the wall, edging around the lobby and down the hall to the offices. She eased into Mrs. Fine's office, closed and locked the door, then grabbed the phone and dialed.

The dispatcher answered on the first ring. "Scumble River police, fire, and emergency. How may I help you?"

"Thea, this is Skye. I'm in the Fine Foods factory and need backup right away. I've found Ashley Yates, who is injured. Cherry Alexander's killer is in the building trying to find and kill both of us."

Thea gasped and dropped the receiver. Before she came back on the line, Skye heard the sound of splintering wood. The office door crashed down and Brandon rushed in. His maniacal grin reminded her of Jack Nicholson in *The Shining*, except that instead of brandishing an ax, he was wielding a wooden mixing paddle, and instead of his being covered in blood, batter dripped off him like alien sweat.

Skye grabbed one of the chrome-and-leather chairs and backed toward the window, wondering if she could break the glass and escape before Brandon reached her.

He advanced, yanking the phone cord from the wall, then swung the paddle at Skye. She leapt to the side and he missed, cracking the windowpane.

Backing away, she kept poking the chair at him as if he were a lion and she his tamer. Her goal the door, she moved around the desk, trying to keep it between her and her attacker.

Unfortunately Brandon had not read the same self-defense book that Skye had, because instead of chasing her around the desk, as he was supposed to, he employed a flying tackle that would earn him a place on the Chicago Bears football team, if they ever decided to recruit homicidal maniacs. Landing on top of her, he wrapped his hands around her neck and squeezed.

Skye tried to pry his fingers from her throat, but he tightened his grip. She knew she had only a few minutes before she lost consciousness, and she groped blindly behind her in search of a weapon.

Just as she was starting to black out, her hand encountered the rolling pin trophy. With her last bit of strength she grasped the handle, dragged it off the desktop, and brought it down on Brandon's skull.

His hands relaxed a fraction, but he didn't remove them from around her neck. She didn't have the strength to lift the heavy trophy and hit him again. This was it. She would die. She would die at the hands of a wannabe lawyer who couldn't even pass the bar exam, and was willing to kill in order to ensure the huge salary he couldn't earn anywhere but in his family-owned business.

Suddenly he stiffened, then collapsed on top of her. When his fingers fell away from her throat and she was able to draw in desperate breaths, she shoved him off of her and got unsteadily to her feet.

He lay limp, unmoving. Had her blow killed him? Skye wasn't taking any chances. She had to get away from him. She limped toward the exit, and had just put a foot on the downed door when the thunder of pounding footsteps was followed by a blur of navy blue uniforms rushing through.

Wally was in the lead, and he swept her up in his arms and out of the way of the column of officers swarming the room. He helped her out into the hallway

"Are you okay?" His dark gaze searched her face.

She nodded, gulped in more air, and managed to get out, "Now I am."

Wally's arms tightened around her. "Forget about me buying you a cell phone. I'm having a GPS chip implanted in your butt."

Makes Twelve Servings

As per tradition, May and Jed entertained his side of the family for Easter. Also, as per tradition, May invited anyone she thought might be alone for the holiday. Which meant that in addition to the Denison clan, Frannie, Xavier, and Uncle Charlie were also present. Mr. and Mrs. Boward had declined, but allowed Justin to attend without them.

Vince was absent, as well. He and Loretta had opted for her family's celebration. It was clear to Skye that her mother was torn regarding that situation. On the one hand, this was a first for Vince and showed that he was serious about his relationship with Loretta. On the other hand, Vince was not at May's table—nor under her control.

Knowing her mother as she did, Skye had wondered briefly if May would invite Simon and Bunny. After all, she had included them in the past. But thank goodness, there was no sign of either Skye's ex or his mother.

Dinner was over, and the men who had followed Jed to the living room were sprawled in various stages of digestive stupor, watching—or at least snoozing in front of—the television set, which was tuned to a baseball game.

Skye had stayed in the kitchen with her mother and most of the other women, having long since given up on the notion of ever achieving equality between the sexes in her family. As she helped clear the table, she thought of the hope and renewal she'd felt while attending Easter Sunday Mass.

After she'd spent the past week enmeshed in the greed and despair that had ultimately resulted in the murder of Cherry Alexander and the attacks on Ashley Yates and Dante Leofanti, the service had been exactly what she needed.

As usual, Father Burns had ended with a bit of gentle wisdom. "If you're having trouble sleeping at night, don't count the sheep; talk to the shepherd."

Skye smiled, thinking of the priest's advice. May asked, "What are you so happy about?"

"I was just thinking about Father Burns's comment at the end of Mass."

"Yeah, that was one of his better ones." May nodded. "At least he didn't try to be funny." She took a breath and changed the subject. "I'm glad I took this week off from work. Thea tells me it's been crazy around the station."

"That's for sure. Even though Brandon is still in the hospital under guard, his lawyers have been all over us." Skye delivered another pile of dirty dishes to the sink. "Thank goodness that at least Ashley is okay, her parents have dropped their lawsuit, and the school newspaper is up and running."

"Why are Brandon's lawyers all over you?" Uncle Charlie marched in and pulled out a kitchen chair. "They caught the little bastard red-handed."

"Not exactly." Skye wiped the table with a dishrag. "I had already hit him over the head with the trophy by the time the police arrived—though, luckily, I had the bruises around my throat to prove he had tried to strangle me."

"Yeah." May snorted. "That was real fortunate."

"Ms. D." Frannie walked into the kitchen and sat next to Charlie. "I know at first you said you didn't want to talk about it, but can you tell us now how you figured out who the murderer was and why he did it?"

Justin had followed Frannie, and now sat on her other side. "Yeah. We're dying to hear what happened."

"Okay." Skye wasn't really ready to discuss the subject, but there was no escaping some things in life. "Since you and Justin have been so good about visiting Ashley while she recovered this week, and have promised to help her get around once she comes back to school, I'll tell you the whole story.

"Let's see, it all started when the Fines decided to sell their company to CB International. All the 'real' Fines would make a lot of money from the deal, but Brandon, being only a stepson and not owning any of Fine Foods, would get nothing. Worse than that, he would lose his position as head of the legal department. Where else could an attorney who couldn't pass the bar be put in charge and earn such a huge salary from the very start?"

"So, his motive was to stop the sale?" Uncle Charlie spooned sugar into the mug of coffee May had put in front of him.

"Right, and being family and head of the legal department, he was aware that the sale would go through only if Fine Foods' reputation was squeaky clean. So he set out to sabotage the contest." Skye took a seat on Charlie's other side. "Then, when Cherry caught him switching the temperature-control knob on the oven in my cubicle so I would burn my dish, he lashed out with a meat mallet and knocked her out, then held her down in the fountain."

"How do you know that?" Justin demanded.

"Before Brandon's mother stepped in and got him a team of criminal lawyers to defend him, he claimed he was going to defend himself, and he told Wally everything to 'explain' his actions. His attorneys are now claiming that he wasn't thinking straight due to his head injury and are trying to get the confession suppressed."

Charlie harrumphed. "You'd think a lawyer would know enough to keep his mouth shut."

"Yeah." Justin shook his head. "That guy has to be really stupid to think he could justify murder."

"Well, that would explain why he couldn't pass the bar exam," Frannie pointed out.

From the sink May said, "He could have just bribed Cherry with winning the contest."

"He didn't know she'd be receptive to that, and besides,

he wasn't thinking at that point, just reacting to what he per-ceived as a threat. The problem was, Brandon had counted on the warehouse being empty, not realizing that in Scumble River 'on time' is actually fifteen minutes early."

Frannie snickered.

"So, Dante was nosing around before the official start time and discovered Cherry's body in the fountain. Brandon saw him and threw a tablecloth over Dante's head so he couldn't identify him. Then Brandon stabbed Dante in order to distract him while Brandon made his getaway. Inciden-tally, they found the pocketknife on Brandon. He'd tried to clean it up, but it contained traces of Dante's blood type. A sample has gone for DNA analysis."

"That's got to be one for the good guys." Charlie sipped his coffee.

"Anyway, as he stabbed Dante, Brandon heard a scream and realized there was another witness—Ashley Yates, who had spent the night in the factory because she couldn't face her parents' knowing there was proof of her sexual es-capades. He hit Ashley with the meat mallet, stowed what he thought was her body in a company van, and went to get the keys to the vehicle. While he was gone, she came to and climbed out of the van. Unfortunately he returned at that precise moment. She ran away from him, and he chased her back toward the factory."

May waved her soapy hand in the air. "That must have been when I stopped him to help me carry my cooking sup-plies."

"Right. He was the person in the jumpsuit and hairnet." Skye shook her head. "Only you, Mom, could get someone in the middle of committing multiple murders to stop and do what you wanted."

May's smile was smug. "Why didn't he find Ashley? He ran away as soon as Dante came barreling out of the ware-house."

"First she got lucky in that the window closed behind her as she fell, so from the outside it still looked locked. Second, Brandon wasn't aware of the storage basement. The factory had stopped using it before he was born, and the only real door had been bricked over years ago. And third, he never had a lot of time to search."

"It is busy around there." May nodded.

"Yep, and just as he rounded the corner of the building, he caught a glimpse of his brother coming around the opposite side. He barely had time to take off the jumpsuit and hide it behind some boxes before JJ spotted him. Then, once his brother saw him, JJ grabbed Brandon and hustled him back inside the plant because Grandma Sal was looking for him."

"Didn't Brandon go back later to look for Ashley?" Frannie asked.

"He couldn't do much while people were working in the factory. Then he had to be available for the contest, and he was rooming with his brother, who would have wondered where he was if he left in the middle of the night."

"What I don't understand is why he didn't at least dispose of the jumpsuit." Uncle Charlie frowned. "It was one of the few pieces of physical evidence that tied him to the murder."

"Remember how windy it was that day?" Skye asked. "It had blown away by the time he was able to get back to pick it up. When I found it later, there were too many people around and he couldn't do anything about it, except hope it would never be linked to him. But the lab found traces of Dante's blood type and chocolate similar to the fountain. They're testing to see if the blood really is Dante's and if the other DNA on it is Brandon's, but we know it is."

May finished the dishes and opened the drain. "What else did he do to interfere with the contest?"

"Three things I know about." Skye got up and poured herself a glass of Diet Coke. "One, he arranged for Glenda Doozier to take Cherry's place. He'd heard stories about the Dooziers his whole life, so when he saw she had entered, he figured her family would stir things up during the contest. Second, he made sure she won the special Cherry Alexander Award, counting on her doing something during the ceremony to make the contest look bad."

"You said there was a third thing?" Justin reminded Skye.

"After the press conference the first day, I overheard two

people talking in the teachers' lounge, and I finally figured out Brandon might be one of those people, so I had Wally ask him about it. Turns out one of the contestants, Imogene Ingersoll, bribed Brandon to give her all the background info that Fine Foods had gathered on one of the other contestants. He was glad to do it, figuring that if she got caught it would be another black mark for the contest, and the company."

"Wasn't Brandon afraid Imogene would take him down with her?" asked Justin.

"I guess he didn't think his family would believe Imogene over him." Skye shrugged.

"Imogene Ingersoll was the woman I said looked so familiar." May wiped her hands on a dishtowel and came over to the table. "I wish I could place her."

"Hey, I almost forgot." Skye grabbed her tote from the utility room, where she had left it on top of the dryer. "Here's a picture of the finalists that was taken during the awards ceremony, and there's Imogene." She pointed to a woman standing next to Vince. "Does anyone know her?"

While everyone around the table examined the print, Wally came in from the living room and joined them. "Maybe I do, but I'm not sure."

"Who do you think it is?" Skye prodded.

"If you visualize her without the glasses and wig, and a little thinner, she's that woman who impersonated a state police officer when we were investigating the murder of that model last November." Wally leaned closer to the picture. "Only then she was going by the name Veronica Vale."

Skye reexamined the photo. "You could be right." She turned to him, frowning. "How come you recognized her when Mom and I didn't?"

"I spent a lot more time with her than either of you did," Wally explained. "You both saw her for at most thirty to forty-five minutes while you were stressed out, while I spent several hours with her."

"If you're right, and Imogene is Veronica, that's pretty creepy." May made a face. "Why would she turn up again, and with a new name?"

Skye suddenly felt a little light-headed and abruptly sat down. Wally turned to her in concern. "Are you all right?"

"Yes. It's just that Brandon said that the person whom Imogene/Veronica was asking him about was me. Why would she want to know about me and my family?"

Everyone was silent as they considered Skye's question. Finally Wally said, "Maybe she had you confused with May. Everyone thought she had the best odds to win, so maybe this woman was trying to get a leg up on the competition."

"But why pretend to be a police officer and change her name?" Skye shook her head. "I don't like it. She's after something. I just wish I knew what it was."

They all spent the rest of the afternoon and evening trying to figure out who the mysterious woman was and what she wanted. Everyone had a guess, but no one had an answer.

By the time she and Wally left, Skye had a headache and wanted nothing more than to go to bed, even if it was only eight o'clock at night. She said good-night to him without inviting him in, then fed Bingo and went upstairs.

After changing into her nightshirt, she crawled into the big four-poster and lay staring at the ceiling. Tired as she was, she couldn't shut off her whirling thoughts. Was Imogene Veronica? Why would she change identities? Why would she want to know about Skye and her family?

A half hour went by, and Skye still couldn't think of a reason. Another half hour went by and Skye stared at the clock. Something else was bugging her, but what?

Was it that Wally hadn't had her meet his father when Carson Boyd first came to town? He had explained his reasoning, but did she believe him? Not being introduced to the potential in-laws was a red flag that a guy wasn't that into you. Was that the case with Wally?

Skye pulled the blanket up over her head. She couldn't answer either question tonight. She needed to sleep. Everything would look better in the morning.

Winning Recipes from Grandma Sal's Soup-to-Nuts Cooking Challenge

Try these four "winning" recipes, personally created by Denise Swanson, her friends and family. Denise likes to cook a lot more than Skye does. . . .

Winner of the Healthy Category
Monika's Gluten-Free and Dairy-Free Sponge Cake

6 eggs
1 cup white sugar
5 tablespoons white rice flour
5 tablespoons cornstarch
2 teaspoon baking powder
½ teaspoon xanthan gum*
Optional: 1/2 cup Hershey's cocoa powder

Preheat oven to 350 degrees. Break eggs into a warm mixing bowl and beat with an electric mixer on medium-high speed until thick (several minutes). Gradually add half the sugar and continue beating until the mixture holds together. Sift together flour, cornstarch, remaining sugar, baking powder, xanthan gum, and cocoa, if using. Fold dry mixture into egg mixture. Beat on low speed for one minute.

Spray two 8-inch round cake pans with PAM, then pour in batter.

Bake in preheated oven for 15 minutes or until toothpick inserted into center comes out clean.

Immediately remove cakes from their pans. Cool on a cake rack. **Warning:** Be gentle—cakes break apart easily. When cakes are completely cooled, frost and assemble layers.

* Xanthan gum is used in gluten-free baking to give the dough or batter a "stickiness" that would otherwise be achieved with the gluten. It is available in health food stores and specialty grocery stores.

Gluten-Free and Dairy-Free Frosting

Blend together in a mixer on medium speed:
One stick Nucoa Margarine* and one stick Crisco until fluffy.

Gradually mix in one box (or 1 lb.) confectionary sugar—more as needed to make a fluffy frosting.

Beat in one teaspoon vanilla extract.

Add a few drops of soy milk until frosting is easy to spread.

* Nucoa is the brand name of a margarine that does not contain any milk solids and is thus dairy-free, as well as free of protein and phenylalanine. It is a lactose-free, cholesterol-free margarine that is distributed by GFA Brands, Inc., Cresskill, NJ, and is available at most large grocery stores.

Winner of the Snacks Category
Fiesta Italiano Dip

¼ cup sour cream
½ cup mayonnaise
10-oz. package frozen finely chopped spinach, thawed and
    drained
14-oz. can artichoke hearts, finely chopped
1 teaspoon garlic salt
¼ teaspoon basil
¼ teaspoon oregano
¼ teaspoon red pepper
4 oz. mozzarella, shredded
4 oz. provolone, shredded
8-oz. can of Italian-seasoned chopped tomatoes
Thinly sliced rounds of Italian bread

Preheat oven to 350 degrees.

Mix together the sour cream and mayonnaise. Add spinach, artichokes, and seasonings. Mix well. Stir in cheeses. Pour into a medium-sized casserole dish and bake at 350 degrees for thirty minutes, or until cheese is melted. Sprinkle with room-temperature tomatoes and serve on bread rounds.

Winner of the One-Dish Meals Category
May's Chicken Supreme Casserole

Note: You'll notice that for purposes of the plot, Skye's version of this recipe differs slightly from mine, which comes from Grandma Swanson.

2 cups cooked chicken, diced
7 oz. elbow macaroni, uncooked
2 cups milk
1 can cream of mushroom soup
1 can cream of celery soup
½ pound Velveeta cheese, cubed
1 4-oz. jar pimentos, drained
¼ cup chopped green pepper
1 small onion, chopped
1 teaspoon salt
½ teaspoon pepper
1 cup bread crumbs
¼ cup butter, melted

Preheat oven to 350 degrees.

Combine all ingredients except for the bread crumbs and butter in a large bowl. Pour into a greased casserole dish and refrigerate overnight. Bring back to room temperature before baking. Bake at 350 degrees for 50 minutes.

Combine 1 cup bread crumbs and ¼ cup melted butter. Sprinkle on top of hot casserole and return to oven for 5 to 10 minutes, until bread crumbs are browned.

Winner of the Special-Occasion Baking Category and the Grand Prize Chocolate Brownie Tiramisu

For the brownies:

1 cup shortening
4 1-oz. squares unsweetened chocolate
4 eggs
2 cups sugar
2 teaspoons vanilla
1½ cup flour
1 teaspoon baking powder
1 teaspoon salt

Preheat oven to 350 degrees.

Melt shortening and chocolate together in double boiler. Cool to room temperature. In a separate bowl, beat eggs with a mixer on high speed until light. Stir in sugar, then add chocolate mixture and vanilla. Sift together dry ingredients, then add to batter and mix well. Pour into a greased 9-by-13 pan and bake at 350 degrees for 30 minutes. Set aside to cool.

For the topping:

8 egg yolks
½ cup sugar
¼ cup milk
2 cups whipping cream
16 oz. mascarpone cheese
½ cup sugar
2 cups brewed and cooled Godiva raspberry-flavored coffee
¼ cup Godiva liqueur
2½ oz. semisweet chocolate, grated
Cocoa powder
Chocolate shavings

Whisk together egg yolks, sugar, and milk in a 2-quart saucepan until smooth and blended. Bring to a boil over medium heat, stirring constantly. As soon as mixture reaches a boil, remove from heat. Immediately refrigerate until cool.

With an electric mixer, beat whipping cream at high speed until it forms very stiff peaks. Set aside in the refrigerator.

Mix the mascarpone cheese and sugar. Stir in the yolk mixture. Fold in the whipped cream.

Combine the coffee and Godiva liqueur in a large mixing bowl.

To assemble:

Cut brownies into 2-by-½-inch strips. Quickly dip each strip in the coffee mixture and place on the bottom of a 9-by-13 baking dish. Sprinkle with half the semisweet chocolate. Cover with half of the cheese mixture. Add another layer of dipped brownies. Sprinkle with remaining semisweet chocolate and finish with the cheese mixture.

Sift cocoa powder over the top and garnish with chocolate shavings.

Refrigerate overnight for best flavor. Serve in chilled dessert bowls.

On Mondays, school psychologist Skye Denison liked to play a game called Name that Disaster as she made the ten-minute drive to work. It consisted of guessing what calamity, catastrophe, or cataclysm would be waiting for her when she arrived.

Skye's assignment included the elementary, middle, and high schools in Scumble River, Illinois. This meant the crises could vary from an eight-year-old girl scalping a fellow third grader in order to dance the lead in *Rapunzel*, to a thirteen-year-old methamphetamine user who thought he was Superman trying to fly from the roof of the junior high school, to a cheerleader holding her own private sex party for the winning basketball team, or any little mess in between.

Her job description was vague, allowing the principals to assign Skye any task they did not wish to perform, and, of course, any that even hinted of belonging in the realm of special education. One of the duties Homer Knapik, the high school principal, had recently handed over to Skye was faculty liaison to the Promfest committee—parents who were putting together an event designed to keep the junior and senior classes and their dates from getting high, crashing their cars, and making babies after the prom.

Homer had assured Skye that it was an easy assignment. All she would have to do was attend a few meetings and maybe help put up some crêpe paper. But as Skye approached the high school cafeteria where the first gathering of the 2004–2005 Promfest committee was being held, she knew he had lied to her. She could hear the raised voices five hundred yards away.

Skye crept into the cavernous room, willing herself to become invisible, which was a stretch considering her generous curves, long, curly chestnut hair, and emerald green eyes. From the back wall, she surveyed the crowd.

It was almost entirely women in their late thirties and early forties. An occasional male also occupied the picnic-style tables arranged in rows facing the stainless-steel serving counter, but they looked uncomfortable and ready to make a run for freedom at any moment.

Skye noticed one guy sitting by himself, and took a seat at his table. He was the only man in the room who didn't look as if he wished he were somewhere else. Instead, his expression was a cross between amusement and disbelief as he scribbled furiously in a small notebook.

Skye smiled at him, and asked, "Who are they?" gesturing to the front of the room where two attractive women were nose to nose, yelling at each other.

"The one with the black hair is Annette Paine and the blonde is Evie Harrington. They both think they're this year's Promfest chairwoman."

"And they want to be?" Skye couldn't imagine why anyone would actively seek that position. "Why?"

He nodded. "Lots of power and a good way to strengthen their daughters' chances of being elected prom queen. Both of them are prior queens themselves—Evie in 1984 and Annette in 1982."

"Oh." Skye cringed. "This is going to get ugly."

"Already has."

Suddenly the shouting increased in volume and Skye's attention was drawn back to the women.

"I don't know where you got the impression that you

were chairing this committee." Annette poked Evie in the shoulder with a perfectly manicured fingernail.

"I got the *impression* from the election last year." Evie bristled. "You remember the election, don't you?"

Annette smoothed a strand of hair back into her chignon. "That vote was not valid. We didn't have quorum. The legitimate election took place the next week." Her icy blue gaze lasered into the brown eyes of her rival. "I believe you were on vacation. If you call going to Branson, Missouri, a vacation."

"You deliberately held that meeting while I was gone." Evie stamped her Etienne Aigner–shod foot on the worn gray linoleum. "A meeting you had no right to call."

"As the assistant chair of the 2003–2004 committee, I was certainly within my rights to call a meeting." Annette flicked a piece of lint from her Yves Saint Laurent cashmere cardigan.

"The 2003–2004 committee had already been disbanded." A line appeared between Evie's eyebrows. "You had no authority whatsoever."

Skye was trying to guess how long it would be before the two women started with the "I did toos" and "You did nots," when a voice from one of the tables rang out, "Let's just have another vote and get on with it. Some of us have lives."

About a third of the women murmured their agreement, but the others protested. Clearly the group was divided into three factions—those who backed Annette's claim, those who supported Evie, and the rest, who didn't give a darn one way or the other.

Skye looked at her watch and blew out an impatient breath. Much as she hated to, she was going to have to become an active participant and hurry the committee along. If she didn't get out of there by the end of first hour, her whole morning's schedule would be messed up. She was supposed to be starting Brady Russell's three-year reevaluation—students who received special education services were required by law to be tested by the school psychologist triennially.

These reevaluations made up the bulk of her duties, and if she fell behind, she would have to cut her counseling and consultation hours—the part of her job she really enjoyed. She would need at least ninety minutes without interruption to give Brady the intelligence test. She would have to find another couple of hours to administer the academic and processing assessments on another day, not to mention time to do the classroom observation, teacher interviews, write the report, and attend the multidisciplinary meeting.

With the ten hours she would need to complete the entire reevaluation in mind, and the clock ticking away precious minutes, Skye stood up. She was ready to make an impassioned plea along the lines of "Can't we all just get along?" when Annette grabbed Evie by the arm, dragged her to the side, and whispered furiously in her ear.

Skye leaned over the man next to her and lowered her voice. "Prom queen for their daughters aside, I can't imagine why being in charge of putting a few streamers up, hiring a DJ, and getting some chips and punch out is such a big deal."

"Where have you been?" He smirked. "Maybe that was true when Promfest was originally conceived. Nowadays it resembles a Chuck E. Cheese party for teenagers, but on steroids."

Before Skye could grasp that image, her attention was drawn back to the front of the room by Evie's gasp.

As Skye watched, the blonde shot Annette a look of loathing, walked back to the center of the room, and announced, "For the good of the Promfest and the sake of our children's special night, I concede the chair to Annette Paine."

Skye sat back down and stared speculatively at the blonde, then raised an eyebrow at the man next to her. "What in the world could Annette have said to Evie to make her give up a position that was obviously important to her?"

"Got me." He tapped his pen on his notebook. "But I'm going to find out."

"Oh?" It wasn't often Skye met someone even more nosy than she was. "Why?"

"It's my job."

"Really?" Skye studied him for a moment. He was in his mid-thirties and devilishly handsome. "What do you do?"

"I'm the new reporter for the *Scumble River Star*." He held out a tanned hand to Skye. "My name's Kurt Michaels. I'm starting a column called Talk of the Town."

"Gossip?"

"I like to call it vital information." He shrugged. "After all, it's the lifeblood of any small town."

"True, but with you being an outsider, will people give you the real scoop?"

"I guess we'll see. My first column is in this week's paper. But ask yourself this—you're a native Scumble Riverite, right?"

Skye nodded.

"And which of us knew about the feud between Annette and Evie for Promfest chair?" He got up and headed for the door. "I'm out of here." Over his shoulder he added, "Nothing else interesting is going to happen."

Skye watched him as he left. His powerful, well-muscled body moved with an easy grace. On second thought, considering his sexy smile, hot body, and charm, the ladies of Scumble River would almost certainly be willing to tell him all their secrets, not to mention those of their neighbors and friends. Heck, if he took off his shirt, they'd probably be willing to make something up.

Kurt had been right; the rest of the meeting was a snooze.

It had started with Annette explaining that the main mission of the Promfest committee was to solicit donations and raise money, which eventually led to her announcement: "The first fundraiser of the year is our Witch's Ball haunted house. We need volunteers to sell tickets, construct the set, and act as the monsters. I'm sending around a sign-up sheet, and I expect to see not only your name, but your spouse's and teenager's, as well."

There was a murmur from the crowd and several hands shot into the air.

Annette ignored them and started the sheet of paper around. "Remember, in order for your student to fully enjoy Promfest, he or she will need a bank account full of Prom

Bucks to spend on food, games, and activities. And you can earn these PBs with every hour you volunteer, prize you solicit, and donation you make. Just for attending today's meeting you've earned your teen five thousand PBs."

Skye watched in amazement for a few minutes as the parents vied to sign away their free time; then she quietly got up and slipped out of the room before the volunteer list reached her table. Not that she would have volunteered for any activity, but she particularly hated haunted houses.

She hadn't been in one since she was six years old, when her brother, Vince, who was ten at the time, abandoned her to go play with his friends. She had wandered around lost and crying until some adult finally noticed her and led her to an exit.

Skye shuddered at the memory, quickened her steps, and nearly ran toward the safety of her office.

As she slid into her desk chair, panting, she noticed the phone's message light flashing. The bell would ring in five minutes. Three minutes after that, Brady Russell would show up at her door expecting to be tested. Did she have time to listen to her voice mail and get set up for him, as well?

She'd never be able to concentrate with that little red light blinking. Cradling the receiver between her neck and shoulder, Skye punched in her password. As she waited for her code to be approved, she grabbed Brady's file and started to fill out the identifying data on the IQ protocol.

She was figuring out his exact age—the current date minus his birthday—when the mechanical voice said, "You have three messages."

Darn. She'd been hoping for a hang-up, but nothing was ever quick and easy in this job. Skye shook her head and pushed the correct button to continue.

"Message number one, left Monday, September thirteenth at eight-fifteen."

There was a slight pause, then Homer's voice boomed from the receiver. "Where in blue blazes are you? Come to my office immediately."

The next one, left at eight-twenty-five, was also from the principal, but the volume of his voice had risen considerably. "Opal said you signed in at seven-thirty. Are you ignoring me?"

By the time Skye got to the last message, recorded at eight-thirty, his baritone blasted in her ear, "Get your butt down here ASAP. I don't have all day to babysit this woman."

Apparently, the first crisis of the day had materialized.